THE FAMILY
ACROSS
THE STREET

BOOKS BY NICOLE TROPE

THE FAMILY ACROSS THE STREET

NICOLE TROPE

bookouture

Published by Bookouture in 2021

An imprint of Storyfire Ltd.
Carmelite House
50 Victoria Embankment
London EC4Y 0DZ

www.bookouture.com

ISBN: 978-1-80019-827-2
eBook ISBN: 978-1-80019-826-5

For Mikhayla
As your wings grow stronger and the distances you fly grow further,
remember the nest is always here.

PROLOGUE
15 December, 2.30 p.m.

Margo lifts her son, Joseph, from his cot after his afternoon nap. His back is damp despite the air conditioning in the house. Outside the cicadas wail in the unrelenting heat. The temperature has reached the high of thirty-nine degrees predicted by the weatherman this morning, and Margo hopes that the cool change he also promised will be along soon.

'You're a hot baby, aren't you?' She smiles at her five-month-old son, and he gurgles in reply. 'Welcome to your first Australian heatwave – the first of many, I'm sure.' She smooths his damp brown curls with a soft brush and wipes his face with a cloth as she holds him.

As she lays Joseph down on his change table, she hears a crack outside, a burst of sound, and the loud noise startles him, his little mouth opening, blue eyes creasing as he gets ready to cry.

'Oh no, baby, it's nothing to worry about. It's just a car backfiring or a tree branch falling. Don't cry, little man.' She speaks in a low, soothing tone and his face relaxes. Scott thinks he's too sensitive to noise because Margo insists on the house being virtually silent while he sleeps, but Scott is at work all day and doesn't have to get up at night, and Margo knows that Joseph sleeps better when it's quiet.

The sound was close; she hopes it's not a branch from one of the big brush box trees on the street outside. A few months ago, during a storm, one fell onto a car parked outside a house down the street, shattering the windscreen and denting the bonnet. At least there was no one inside the car at the time. After the storm all the neighbours came out to watch the branch being removed and the car towed away. It was the most exciting thing to happen on the street all year.

Joseph smiles up at her.

'Now then,' she says, as she changes his nappy, 'what are we going to do this afternoon? Shall we go for a walk around the park? We can look at the ducks. "Quack, quack," says the duck.'

She lifts him up and lets him look in the mirror, something that he loves to do. 'Who's that little boy? Is it Joseph? Is that Joseph in the mirror?' She smiles at their matching pale blue eyes.

And then two more bursts of sharp sound fly through the air, startling Margo, who jumps a little.

Joseph starts to wail.

She carries him over to the window. Tall trees that line the road obscure the other houses, but Margo has a good view of the usually quiet street.

She wouldn't tell anyone this, but to her, the noises sounded like gunfire, a burst of thick sound that pierced the air. Not that she's heard gunfire anywhere except on television and in movies, but she cannot imagine what else it could be.

She experiences a moment of panic, suddenly aware of how isolated she is in her new house. She goes to find her mobile phone to call Scott at work.

Returning to the window, she waits for him to answer, clicking her tongue when she gets his message bank. Heat rises off the asphalt. A white van is parked outside Katherine's house across the street. Margo looks a little to the side and sees the old busybody Gladys standing on the pavement, staring at Katherine's house, her phone to her ear.

Margo watches as a police car pulls to a lazy stop outside the house. She and Scott have lived here for nine months now and she's never even seen a police car cruise past on the way to somewhere else. She stands frozen at the window, watching a drama unfold right across the street from her.

Gladys says something Margo can't hear, her hands gesturing frantically at Katherine's house as the police slowly climb out of the car, and then there is nothing slow about them. They start running, a policewoman talking into the radio attached to her shoulder.

'Oh my goodness,' Margo says, holding her son close, her hands trembling as she remembers the sound of a slammed car door this morning, a hoarse shout and then John's car screeching out of the neighbours' driveway at 6 a.m. She remembers thinking, *That must have been some argument.*

She was going to mention it to Scott, ask him what the couple might have argued about. John and Scott enjoy a beer on a Sunday afternoon sometimes, though she and Katherine have never really had much to say to each other. Margo thought that might have something to do with their different stages of life. Katherine's twins are five years old and the baby stage is far behind for her while Margo still feels like such an amateur.

But when Scott finished his shower this morning, Joseph needed a nappy change and she hadn't had the chance to speak to him. *I'll ask him tonight,* she remembers thinking.

And then she went about her day, thinking no more about it. Couples argue, husbands leave in a huff and everything is resolved that evening.

But the police don't get called for just an argument.

Margo bites her lip. She plants a soft kiss on her son's cheek and wonders exactly why the police have been called.

'Nosy old Gladys will know what's going on,' she says to her son. She goes to her front door and opens it, a blast of heat enveloping her cool body.

'What's happening, Gladys?' she calls, feeling like she's the nosy one now but dying to know.

'Oh, Margo,' says Gladys when she sees her, 'go back inside, go back. He has a gun. Go inside.'

'What?' Margo asks, believing she's misheard the older woman.

Gladys waves her arms. 'Get back inside, Margo,' she shouts. 'It's Katherine, it was... Didn't you hear? It was gunshots... Please go back, take the baby away.'

Margo opens her mouth to reply, but then Joseph moves in her arms and fear makes her clutch her son tight. Stepping back, she slams and locks the front door, and then she takes Joseph to her bedroom, locking that door behind her as well. She sits down in front of her bed, out of sight of the window, and holds her phone, dialling Scott again and again though she keeps getting his voicemail.

It doesn't seem long before the air is filled with sirens, drowning out the cicadas and every other sound. Margo waits on the floor with her son, her heartbeat drumming in her ear. Scott is not picking up but she keeps hitting his name on her screen, overwhelmed with the urge to tell him she loves him.

'It's fine, baby, it's fine,' she murmurs to Joseph, who is lying on his back beside her, trying to get his feet into his mouth. 'It's fine,' she repeats as she waits for her suburb to return to the peaceful place she has grown to love, though she knows, somehow, that it will never be the same again.

CHAPTER ONE

Seven hours ago

Logan

Logan pulls his van to a stop outside a large house with an emerald-green front lawn, cut short and neat. The hedging in front of the black metal fence is precisely square. An arch over the front gate has ivy curled around it, white flowers dotted here and there in the green foliage.

The van's temperature gauge reads twenty-four degrees and it's only seven thirty in the morning. It's going to be a scorcher of a summer's day and he's grateful that he only has to get in and out of the van to deliver his parcels, rather than actually working outside. He takes a deep breath and silently thanks his brother-in-law, Mack, for giving him this chance.

'I'm doing this for Debbie, mate,' Mack told him two months ago when he gave him the keys to one of his vans. 'I've always liked you, you know that, but I can't have anything out of order on your delivery runs. The first complaint I get and you're out on your ear – okay?' he said, pulling at the tufts of hair on his chin he insisted on calling a beard.

'I understand,' Logan answered, looking up at his tall, skinny brother-in-law and clenching his fists to control the anger he was feeling, knowing it was more humiliation than anger. He was too old to be begging for jobs. If Mack had spoken to him in such a condescending way five years ago, he would have felt the need to belt him one, brother-in-law or not. But that was then and this is now.

He gets out of his van and breathes in the morning heat, suffused with the scent of honeysuckle and something else that could be rotting fruit. The garbage bins line the street, waiting for collection, which explains it. He listens and can hear the hiss, whine and crash of a garbage truck doing its job a few streets away. Best if he gets this delivered and moves out of their way.

A text pings on his phone and he looks down.

Call me.

'Not likely,' he mutters and shoves the phone in his pocket, irritated that he can't seem to get through a day without his past tapping him on the shoulder. His past is why he's driving a van for Mack and nodding his head each time his brother-in-law tells him he needs to stay on the straight and narrow. His past and his hopes for the future with Debbie, who has the same high cheekbones, blonde hair and hazel eyes as her overprotective older brother but combined with full lips and a dimpled smile. Anna, Mack's wife, is also tall and thin and blonde. In group photos with Debbie's family, Logan – with his thick black hair, blue eyes and inked skin – looks like he must have wandered into the frame by mistake.

He slides open the side door of the van and locates the box containing what is clearly a new laptop. It needs to be signed for or he has to leave it at the local post office at the end of the day. He really hopes the owner is home. He hates driving around all day with expensive electronics in the back of the van. The fear of something being stolen and him getting the blame is always there.

Looking through the black metal gate at the front of the house, he admires the profusion of pink and purple in the summer garden and is relieved to see that there is no dog around. Two scooters lie on the grass, one blue and one neon-pink. They look about the same size; the kids who live here must be close in age.

He pushes open the gate and walks up the stone path to a timber front door with a large black handle and a small metal square that must be a peephole. He hits the button on an electronic pad next to the front door and listens as a bell chimes throughout the house – some tune he recognises but can't place.

He waits, expecting to hear footsteps or kids shouting. It's a bit early for them to have left for school already and he hopes they're still home. There's a school just one street away; he reminds himself to drive carefully through the area for the next couple of hours.

Logan looks around, admiring the large grey pots filled with marigolds by the front door. Their whole flat could fit into just the front garden of this house. The back garden must be even bigger, and he knows there will be a swimming pool and maybe even a tennis court. He feels no envy about this. Everyone has their life to live and their path to follow. He likes where he is right now, despite the boring job and his slightly condescending brother-in-law. He likes that he has a brother-in-law and a job.

He hears a scrape and realises that the peephole has been opened from the inside.

'Yes?' says a woman's voice, hesitant and wary.

'Yes, I have a delivery here for Katherine West.' He leans forward a little but he can't see anything except dark glass.

'Thanks… thanks… can you just leave it by the door?'

'Sorry, but it needs to be signed for.'

'I can't do that now,' says the woman.

Logan sighs. If he leaves the computer by the front door and she calls to complain it never got to her, it will mean the end of his job.

'I really can't leave it here, ma'am. It has to be signed for. If you need to… get dressed or something, I can wait.'

'No,' says the woman. 'I can't open the door.' Her voice is firm, as though she is explaining something to him that he should understand.

He feels his face flush. He is already sweating out here in the morning heat.

'I can't leave it here so I'll have to take it back to your local post office, okay? You can pick it up there any time after five.' He steps back, ready to go before he says anything stupid. He hates the way some of these people in their big houses look at him. He imagines her thought process as she peers at him through her peephole. She won't be able to see much except the small skull and crossbones tattoo on his cheekbone but that's enough for her to make a decision about who he is.

He gets it, but he's in a uniform and he's holding the box. He lifts it higher, almost covering his face. A trickle of sweat slides down his spine. The woman doesn't say anything else, although he can sense she hasn't moved away from the door. *This is not worth it.* He turns around.

'I can't open the door,' she repeats. 'Please just leave the box,' she says as he steps onto the path to leave. 'Please understand.'

'I'll leave it at the post office – you can collect it after five.'

'Please…' Her voice is strained, pleading.

'I'm sorry, ma'am,' he says firmly.

He turns again and walks to the front gate, cursing under his breath. Sometimes he feels like the first delivery sets the tone for how the whole day will go. Judging by this one, it's going to be a stinker.

Back in his van he cranks up the air conditioning and takes a few deep breaths. He mentally counts to twenty, feeling the anger settle and cool inside him. When Aaron first told him about the breathing and the counting, he thought it was crap. But the counsellor asked him to give it a try, and Logan has found that it does actually work. Logan was not the kind of person who took the advice of a psychologist. He wasn't the kind of person who even went to see a psychologist, unless it was mandated, and it *had* been mandated by the court. But once he started talking to Aaron, once he stopped sitting in every session with his arms folded, he actually got a lot out of it.

'Wouldn't you like someone to know what you've been through? Not what you've done, but what you've been through,' said Aaron after their third silent session.

'Maybe I haven't been through anything,' Logan said, feeling his jaw tighten.

'Really?' Aaron looked around the room, at the pale green walls and the bars on the window. 'Really?'

Logan scratched at his chin, where he was growing a beard, and said, 'My father used to slap me across the back of my head and laugh, telling me I was his drunken mistake.' As he said the words, he saw the look of disgust on his father's face, the same face he saw in the mirror now. Debbie says that all the ink is so that he looks different to the man who greeted his first tattoo with the words, 'Makes you even uglier than you were and that's saying a lot.'

'I imagine that was difficult to hear,' said Aaron. 'How old were you the first time he said it?'

'Four,' Logan said. And then he took a deep breath because a ball of pain had lodged itself in his throat. Not for himself but for the four-year-old kid he had been, who had only wanted to show his father his new Tonka truck but had unwittingly interrupted a football game. For the five-year-old boy who listened to his mates talk about fishing with their fathers, knowing that his father preferred mammoth Sunday drinking sessions followed by heavy Monday morning hangovers, preferred a hard slap over a conversation and made his disappointment clear every time he looked at his son. The pain was for all the other ages he had been as well, the list of disappointments piling up until he got to the age that landed him in prison.

'So perhaps you've been through a few things,' Aaron said mildly.

Logan cracked his knuckles, hot and angry that Aaron had made him think about it. He had never told anyone before, never. But once he started talking, it was hard to stop. He told the man things he thought he had buried for good, anguish that was never meant to see the light of day again. And it helped, as did the exercises Aaron gave him to control his 'understandable anger'. It made him a better big brother to Maddy as well, because he was able to help her process some of her feelings at being rejected by two people who should never have had children in the first place.

He obviously hasn't helped his little sister as much as he would have liked to or she wouldn't have found herself a boyfriend who seems to embody some of the worst aspects of their father. Patrick is a little younger, not as smart as she is and mostly a moocher. He has a nasty sense of humour, once telling Maddy she was the granny in her university class because of her age and was only doing well because the professors felt sorry for her, and then laughing when she looked hurt at the comment. 'Can't you take a joke?' he asked her, and Logan watched her force a smile the same way he and Maddy had been used to doing when they lived at home. 'Can't you take a joke?' their father said when he told Maddy she was turning into a little dumpling after she gained weight in her teen years. 'Can't you take a joke?' he asked Logan when he called Logan 'Captain Stupid' after he failed an exam. 'Can't you take a joke?' means the person being insulted is not allowed to get upset. The first time Logan heard a comment like that from Patrick, he looked at Maddy, holding back the need to shake some sense into her, baffled that she couldn't see the similarities.

Patrick also sulks if he doesn't get his way. Logan knows from the things Maddy has told him that if Patrick is unhappy, he makes sure she knows it by slamming doors and going quiet. Growing up, Maddy and Logan knew that when their father slammed doors and went silent, someone was going to get hit.

Bur Patrick doesn't hit Maddy because if he did… Logan drops the thought.

As he prepares to pull off, Katherine West's refusal to open the door bothers him and he realises that there was something in her voice, something like fear but also a kind of pleading in the last thing she said: 'Please understand.' Why would he need to understand it? She could either open the door or she couldn't because she wasn't dressed or she was busy with something. What did she need him to understand?

A shiver runs down his spine. In the time it took her to tell him she couldn't open the door, the whole delivery could have been done. All she had to do was stick her hand out, so why didn't she?

In the van with cold air blasting him, Logan experiences a prickling along his skin. He learned early to trust his instincts, to listen to what his body was telling him even if his brain didn't appear to know what it was.

Instinct tells him there is something wrong. That's what she was trying to make him understand. Something is going on in there. He looks back at the house, hidden by tall green hedging.

Usually when he delivers to a home with small kids inside, there are excited shrieks as the doorbell rings, and shouting from a mother or father: 'Don't open the door!'

But there was only silence from this house.

He meets his own blue eyes in the rear-view mirror and then he shifts the gearstick into drive, pushing his foot down on the brake while he checks his phone for his next delivery and programmes the address into his GPS.

Debbie believes he thinks too much about everything. She's not wrong. One thing that prison gives you is plenty of time to think. He might be reading way, way too much into this.

'It's not your problem, babes,' he knows Debbie would say, and she'd be right.

'Not my problem,' he says aloud and then sets off, attempting to dismiss the woman as the words 'please understand' repeat in his head and unease dances inside him.

CHAPTER TWO

Gladys

Gladys pulls the cord to open the curtains in the spare room, letting in the glaring sunshine. She pushes at the window a little, cursing at how it sticks, as she does every morning. 'Ha,' she says when it finally slides up. The air is warm and fragrant, already slightly sticky with humidity.

'You should keep all the windows closed today,' shouts her husband Lou from their bedroom. 'Keep the windows closed and the air conditioning on and pets inside. That's what they said on the news last night. It's going to get to thirty-nine degrees today, Gladys, you're only letting in the heat.'

'I'm letting out the stale air from last night. I'll only open them for a few hours. I can't abide not having fresh air,' Gladys shouts back, irritation rising. He knows she likes to open the windows every morning.

'I'm only telling you what they said on the news,' says Lou. 'You don't have to listen to the experts, you never do anyway.'

Gladys ignores this last remark. She cannot get into an argument with Lou this early in the morning.

She looks across at the house next door to the two sets of windows that face her. It seems that Katherine is running a little late this morning because the blinds and windows are closed in both bedrooms. Gladys knows that the one on the left belongs to George and the one on the right belongs to Sophie. George has deep blue blinds and Sophie has iridescent pink. According to Katherine it was Sophie's decision when the old animal-print curtains were removed last year. Gladys is not entirely sure that children should be given the choice on everything but she knows better than to voice her opinions. She's dealt with more than enough people saying, 'But you don't have children so you can't understand,' in her lifetime. A woman whose mothering is being questioned can turn quite nasty and Gladys has learned to let her face do the talking. She can feel her lips thin and her eyes scrunch up a little when she sees what she considers to be poor parenting but she doesn't say anything.

It's odd that the blinds haven't been opened yet. The children are usually up early and Gladys has become familiar with their routine of excited shouting as they run down the hall to wake their parents. There is a point in life at which a new day ceases to be a thing of joy and instead becomes something to be faced and dealt with. Gladys wishes she could pinpoint the age at which she stopped being delighted by the rising sun.

Now that she thinks about it, she didn't hear them this morning. They are very noisy children, and she wouldn't be able to hear them shouting in the morning if they were able to lower their voices a single decibel, but she has mentioned this to Katherine, breaking her own rule on not commenting on children's behaviour to their parents, to no avail.

'It's Lou who needs his rest,' she told Katherine. 'Our bedroom is on that side of the house and we can hear everything.' Gladys knows that she is guilty of using Lou's condition a little too much. 'My husband is ill,' she hears herself tell someone at least twice a day. She knows he wouldn't like her sharing his condition with everyone from her hairdresser to the young woman at the bakery, but it affects her life as much as it does his. Both their lives were irrevocably changed ten years ago.

'I'll ask them, Gladys, I will,' Katherine said at the time. Her hands were full of parcels and she looked a little flustered, so Gladys had to concede that she hadn't picked the best time to raise the subject, but needs must. When George and Sophie were babies, there wasn't as much noise as there is now. Although she used to sleep with earplugs then, finding Lou's snoring too much to bear. Now she needs to hear him. She is terrified that he will stop breathing in his sleep and she will simply sleep on, oblivious.

'No wonder we slept late,' she calls to Lou. 'I don't think those children are up yet.' Sleep is a goal Gladys fights to reach every night. She is always exhausted to her bones when she gets into bed but the moment that Lou's snores start, her brain cranks up and she goes through what she's come to call her 'wheel of worries'.

Have I paid the car insurance? When is Lou's next doctor's appointment? Did I make sure the electricity bill was on direct debit? Is there enough money in the account to pay for everything? Why is the car making that strange clicking noise? How much longer will Lou live? How will I live without Lou?

Round and round it goes, her brain a frantic hamster pedalling on a wheel. Last night was particularly bad and she knows that the last set of red numbers she saw on the alarm clock next to her bed was 03:00. Exhaustion made everything seem worse and Lou's snoring became a jackhammer in her head. Bitter tears arrived and she placed a pillow over her head so the noise of her crying wouldn't wake Lou. Finally everything was muffled and she slept. She was surprised to open her eyes at seven this morning instead of five thirty. She immediately felt the fright of oversleeping, realising the pillow had blocked out any sound, and sat up quickly to check on Lou, waking him. 'Sorry,' she said, as he groaned that he 'needed a bit of rest, woman', but she wasn't sorry really. At least he was still alive.

'They have to be at school soon,' calls Lou now. Every weekday morning, Katherine walks the children to school unless it's raining or too cold, in which case she drives. Gladys and Lou are usually sitting in their front room by then, by the lovely bay window that looks out onto the street, having their breakfast. Toast and egg for Lou and muesli for her. As the children pass their house, they peer through the grey metal front gate and wave at Lou and Gladys. 'There go those kids,' Lou always says, as though Gladys hasn't seen them. 'Yes,' she always replies, waving madly to make sure the children have seen her acknowledgement of their greeting.

'It's only seven thirty, Lou,' says Gladys.

She returns to their bedroom, wrinkling her nose a little at the stuffy heat that has already formed in the dark room since she turned off the air conditioner, knowing she was going to open the windows for a short while. As she opens the curtains and windows in there as well, Lou watches her, his lips thinned with the effort of not repeating his opinion. He is sitting up in bed, his grey hair sticking up and his face made older by the grey-white stubble of his morning beard. She notices that his blue pyjama shirt is misbuttoned and restrains herself from fixing it for him. He doesn't like to be fussed over in the morning as he prepares himself to get out of bed. She can see his feet moving under the duvet cover, stretching out the night's stiffness in his muscles.

'They should all be up already, after the way John left this morning,' he says irritably. 'I can't believe you didn't hear it. At least I managed to fall asleep again. There's no need for that amount of screeching – and I can tell you, I used to sell cars and it's not good for the tyres, not good at all.'

'I know you used to sell cars, Lou. We've been married for forty-five years. It's not something I'm likely to forget, is it?' Gladys hears her impatient tone and feels guilty, but she's already feeling peevish in the early-morning heat, made worse by the knowledge that she will be stuck inside today because Peter, Lou's carer, can't be here today. If not for that, she would have driven herself down to the beach for a swim. Or she could have called Penny, who is always up for a spot of lunch.

She takes a deep breath as she folds her nightdress and sticks it under her pillow, imagining she is down at the ocean with the salt tang ripening in the heat and the cool water eddying around her toes.

I'll go tomorrow. But today I will practise patience. Lord, please give me the strength to be patient.

Both she and Lou understood that Parkinson's is a progressive disease when he was diagnosed at the age of sixty-five. 'You're very lucky to have got this far without it really affecting your life,' their doctor told them.

'Well, I'm buggered if I'll let it affect me now!' Lou replied. He was unused to anything standing in his way. He was a barrel-shaped man, only slightly taller than Gladys but with a loud voice and a large presence. When he walked into a room, you knew about it. He had a deep tone that people instantly trusted, which was why he'd been so successful in the car game. Gladys had watched him once, many years ago, when she'd gone to have lunch with him. She'd had the day off and they were going to drive to a little restaurant on the harbour that served the most divine prawns. She'd been early so she had sat quietly in the BMW showroom, surrounded by the bright metallic cars, beaming their luxury, and watched Lou talk to a customer. He had taken the man's hand, essentially to shake it, but then he had closed his other hand over the top and whispered something, as though imparting a secret. Lou had nodded as he spoke and soon the man was nodding along with him and the sale was secured.

Parkinson's had affected him slowly but surely. He had moved through the stages and was now, at seventy-five, in stage three. He could get around after a fashion with his walker but he needed the wheelchair most days. Peter usually came for at least five hours every day, despite Lou's constant complaining that a carer was a waste of money. Gladys said, 'We don't have children, Lou, and we're old already. What else is the money for?'

'You might live on for a good decade or two without me, old girl. I don't want you to go without.'

'Don't fuss, there's enough for me to be very comfortable,' she told him, and then she had to hide in the bathroom so she could shed a few quiet tears. She had made her peace with not having children a long time ago, but in her mind, she had somehow assumed that one day she and Lou would just die together.

They've shared a whole life together, seen the world, experienced everything it has to offer from long holidays on sunlit beaches to a cruise to Antarctica. They spent Christmas in a different country every year for at least three decades, and they have so many lovely memories to look back on. When they are both in the mood, they compare opinions on the best hotels they've ever stayed in. Gladys thinks it was the Langham in New York, where they watched a snowstorm rage outside their window as they sipped champagne in the understated, elegant room, but Lou favours the InterContinental in Tahiti, where they enjoyed a room right over the sapphire-blue ocean. Both agree that the best meal they ever had was in a little restaurant down a side lane in Portugal, where only the locals seemed to be enjoying the chicken dish. Sometimes a memory will catch Gladys and she will say to Lou, 'I thought I would never stop laughing…' and Lou will finish for her, 'When the waiter in France scolded you for trying to speak French,' and they will laugh together again even years after it happened. They never ran out of things to talk about; only lately, as things have got worse, have their lives shrunk to this house and conversations around Lou's deteriorating health.

She wouldn't trade her life for anything, but the loss of her best friend looms large now and she sometimes thinks that her shortness with him, her need to be away from him as much as possible, is self-preservation. She has no idea how she will go on. She has friends in her life but no one she feels she could call every day. Penny is as close as she's got to a best friend but Penny only ever has an hour or so to grab lunch. She's busy with her grandchildren and her art.

Having Peter in their lives became a necessity only in the last year. Gladys knows herself and she knows that if she's trapped at home all day, her temper gets short and then she lashes out at Lou and then is eaten alive with guilt. He's never been an easy man but his failing body frustrates him and makes him fractious and cranky. She understands that but she doesn't always deal with it as graciously as she would like.

'Do you think I should call Katherine?' Gladys says as she smooths the duvet, along with her tone, and plumps her pillow. 'Maybe one of the children is sick and I could walk the other one to school.'

'You leave her alone, Gladys,' says Lou. 'She doesn't need your interfering.'

'She's a mother of five-year-old twins. I imagine she's glad of any help she gets. Anyway, she asked me to walk George to school when Sophie had tonsilitis last month, didn't she?'

'Then you know she'll ask you if she needs you,' huffs Lou. 'Now do you have any idea when you might get around to a cup of tea? I'm completely parched and you know I have to take my medication early in the morning.'

'Right now, Lou,' says Gladys, and she leaves their room and walks slowly down the stairs to the kitchen. She feels her knees protest but at least she can still walk; she feels terrible for Lou that it's such a difficult process. Last year they had a stair lift installed for Lou but she wants to avoid using it herself. Using it would feel like giving in to the aging process when she is supposed to be the strong one.

She fills the kettle and watches the lorikeets in the tree outside the window, waddling up and down the branches, their green wings flashing in the sun. Usually, the children would be out in the garden by now. 'They seem to be powered by an inexhaustible supply of energy,' Katherine has said. But Gladys can't hear the creaking of the swing set or the children chattering to each other as she usually does. She decides that she might go over later, just to see, just to check. It's the neighbourly thing to do. There is no reason for her to feel worried for the family except for that little incident yesterday that has somehow thrown her off a little. When she thinks about it, she experiences a tickle of concern, as though there is something she needs to remember or something she needs to do about it.

Maybe she should have mentioned it to Lou, or maybe even Katherine, but she's sure that it was nothing.

The first time she met Katherine and John she noticed Katherine's striking deep brown eyes and her beautiful thick hair hanging in lovely honey-brown waves down her back. A small bump was only obvious as she turned and the wind pushed her top against her stomach. Gladys didn't say anything, knowing that it was never a good idea to comment on a woman's body. She'd been asked once or twice if she was pregnant when she was younger, and having to answer that she was not always broke her heart. But Katherine placed her hand protectively on her stomach when she saw Gladys notice. 'Twins,' she said, smiling. 'As soon as we started trying, it just happened.'

Gladys smiled widely, the 'welcome to the neighbourhood' chocolate cake growing heavy in her hands. 'How lovely,' she said.

If there was something wrong, Katherine would tell her. She would, wouldn't she? They've been neighbours for long enough. They're not quite friends but Gladys hopes Katherine knows she can count on her if she needs her.

As she makes Lou's tea for him and takes it upstairs, she decides she will definitely go over there later and see if everything is all right. There's no harm in checking up on a neighbour, no harm at all.

CHAPTER THREE

Monsters are made, not born. I'm sure that I was an ordinary baby. I'm sure I was an okay toddler. I hit all my milestones; I talked and laughed and said cute things. I'm sure I would have grown up to be a pretty good man, if I had been given the chance.

I remember being seven and playing marbles at school, winning game after game and clapping with glee. I remember telling my mother and the way she smiled as she listened to me. I remember sharing the story with my father that night. He listened intently, nodding his head and smiling when I told him how well I'd done. I felt seen, loved. I try to remind myself of how he was then, for at least the first ten years of my life, but it doesn't always work. How he was then has been submerged by how he was in the years I remember more clearly, because those are the years filled with pain and confusion. They left their scars.

I can't say exactly when things changed because it was quite gradual. Simply pointing to their divorce and saying, 'That's when it happened,' doesn't feel right. It happened over time, one incident after another. And at some point, I realised that I didn't matter anymore. My mother would deny that. When she thought I was still listening she would shake her head and say, 'That's not what happened. You're remembering it wrong.'

But I know the truth. Caught up in their own fascinating drama, my parents stopped seeing me.

People get divorced and lives go on. It is possible for there to be an amicable split, an understanding between two people, and a resolution to look after any children involved. There doesn't have to be anger, betrayal, hate and death. It's not necessary to blow up everything around you just to prove you've been hurt.

But sometimes, that's exactly what happens, and when it does, those involved can hardly be expected to survive without being affected.

Whatever happened in my childhood, I thought I had left it all behind me. But I didn't, I haven't. It's still here.

My father hated the idea of the love of his life no longer being in love with him. That was what he couldn't handle. 'She told me she could never imagine loving anyone else and then she asks for a divorce? How is that possible? What about our wedding vows, what about honouring each other through the good and the bad times, what about that?' His confusion was obvious, his despair something I could feel.

I am my father's son.

I did not fall in love easily. I did not expect it to happen to me, but once it did, I wanted it to be for life. She had other ideas.

Now, three sets of eyes stare at me, naked fear on their faces. If someone had asked me last week if I was capable of this, I would have said no. But that's only because I've been hiding the monster for such a long time. Perhaps I haven't been hiding him as well as I thought. He's crept out bit by bit over the years and now there's more monster than me. That's what it feels like right now as I stare down at the three of them.

They are looking at me as though my teeth are pointed, my fingernails razor-sharp. The monster is here now and I know myself to be capable of anything. I looked in a mirror this morning, noting my red-rimmed eyes and the scratches on my face. I liked the way I looked. It's fitting to look this way when I'm going to do what I'm going to do.

'What…?' she begins. Her voice catches in her throat, her face pale, only fear in her brown eyes. She is afraid of me. I don't mind the feeling. Her hands are wound tightly in theirs, knuckles white as they squeeze, and she squeezes back, trying for reassurance but failing. She would like them to believe that everything will be okay because *that's what all mothers want their children to believe. My mother certainly wanted me to believe it. But it's not always the truth and it's certainly not the truth today.*

'Why?' she wants to ask me. But I know if she thought about it at all, she would know why, she would understand why.

'Shh, shh, shh,' I caution her. 'No talking. I'm in charge now.'

I think I tried to be a nice man, to be the kind of man who could be loved, but that didn't work. Nice men don't get to be in charge. Monsters, on the other hand…

'Shh,' I tell her again, just because I can, because now she has no choice but to listen.

'Shh.'

CHAPTER FOUR

Katherine

If she could unlock her hands from theirs, she would like to grab the skin on her arm and twist it hard enough to leave a mark just so she could be sure she is actually here. That she is actually looking at someone she loves and who supposedly loves her, standing in front of her and these two small children, casually holding a way to end all their lives. But as their little hands grow sweaty in hers, she understands that she cannot let go because they are desperate for the reassurance she is trying to communicate through her fingers. *Mama's here. It's okay. Mama's here.* But it's not okay because how can it be? How on earth has the day become this nightmare from which she cannot wake? *He loves me. I thought he loved me despite everything. How can he be doing this?*

This is not someone she knows or understands anymore. Before today she would have described him one way and she might even have admitted to the tension between the two of them, but right now she wouldn't know where to begin. *Who are you? Who have you become?* she wants to ask. She watches him rubbing his T-shirt over the barrel of the black metal gun and wonders when he became this kind of a person and how she managed to miss such a colossal change. How long has he been planning it? Days? Weeks? Months? How long?

'Please,' she says, 'don't do this.'

'Give me your phone,' he says.

'No,' she utters, 'I need it. People will be calling me and if I don't answer…'

He walks over to where they are sitting and rests the gun on George's temple, pushing slightly so the little boy's head angles. She feels her son freeze, his body against her body. She releases her tight hold of his hand and wraps her arms around his shoulders and Sophie's shoulders, pulling them closer, feeling them mould into her body.

'I said, give me your phone,' he says, and she reluctantly pulls her arms from around her children's shoulders to dig it out of her pocket and hand it to him. Her hands are trembling and he sees this and smiles. *Where did all that love between us go?* She has thousands of images stored in her brain of him laughing, smiling at her, of sunshine-filled days and star-filled nights – and yet here they are. And he looks nothing like those images anymore. She wonders if she's ever really seen him at all or just the version of him that she wanted to see. Wrapped up with her terror is a twinge of humiliation at how foolish she has been. *I thought I was smarter than this and now my children will have to pay for my mistake.*

He looks at her phone, at the screen saver of her and George and Sophie at their last birthday party. In front of each child is a cake with five candles, the glow lighting up their faces. She is between them, crouched down to get into the picture. 'Big smiles, everyone,' said her husband, their father. Big smiles.

Anyone looking at the picture would see the resemblance in their faces, heart-shaped with slightly too pointed chins. Her eyes are brown and theirs are green, but they get that from their father. When they were babies, their hair was blonde but now it's light brown, and Katherine knows that one day Sophie will colour it and change it, lamenting that it gets curly in the humidity like it has today. She hasn't had time to brush it for her yet. There was no time.

She remembers the hours it took to make the cakes, cutting and shaping so that she could produce the number five for each of them. She had made her own icing, some in pink and some in blue, messing up the first batch because she added too much water. She's not a good baker. She wants to be but it's not a skill she has. Her mother used to produce cakes easily, light and fluffy, perfectly decorated. If she had lived until their fifth birthday, she would have made them each a birthday cake as she did when they turned one and two and three and four.

Katherine swallows hard and tightens her hold on her children. What would her mother say now if she could see this? How broken would her heart be?

'Are you sure, my darling?' she asked Katherine on the eve of her wedding to John. 'Are you sure?' she asked, as she had done before every life decision Katherine made, giving her daughter time to take a step back. But there was no time for that this morning.

The children are both pushing against her side, trying to get even closer, and she can feel George shaking. His hands are clenched into fists and she knows that he believes that he has to be braver and stronger than Sophie because he is her older brother, even though he is only older by three minutes. Five-year-old children should not have to think about being brave.

Today should have been an ordinary day. She had prepared for the heatwave by freezing the children's water bottles so that they would melt over the day into ice-cold water to drink at lunchtime and playtime. They should be getting ready to go to school now. She was looking forward to walking them before the heat took hold, and then she had planned to get some exercise at the indoor pool at her gym before doing some shopping. She was going to stock up on ice cream.

'Is that a real gun?' her son whispers.

'Shh,' she says.

He smiles and nods. 'It's as real as it gets, Georgie boy.'

Yesterday George brought home a new marble from school, blue and filled with stars inside, which could be seen only if you put your eye right up against the glass surface.

'It's the best marble I've ever seen,' she told him because it was, and he smiled, a wide generous smile that filled his whole face and lit up his green eyes. Sophie isn't interested in marbles but is obsessed with Polly Pocket dolls, taking them everywhere and getting told off at school for having them.

Last night she stared at the ceiling for a few hours, unable to close her eyes, worrying about her daughter getting into trouble at five years old. She decided that she would make star charts for the twins, rewarding good behaviour. What concerned her was that her children, especially Sophie, were starting to sense the tension in the house. She'd thought, she'd hoped, they were managing to conceal things from the children, but she feared they were not.

Her mind turns to last night's argument – although calling it an argument is probably an understatement.

It led to John sleeping downstairs on the sofa before rushing out this morning, still wrapped in his anger, screeching out of the driveway. She had felt glad he was gone for the day – but then she hadn't known what was coming.

'Where's Daddy?' Sophie asked when she crept into her bed as the sun rose. She's been trying to get them to be quieter in the mornings. Gladys complains about too much noise and she feels bad for Lou, who needs his sleep. Mostly they forget, but this morning her children had both been so quiet, she hadn't noticed them until they were already in the room.

'He slept downstairs because his back was sore.'

'His back is sore a lot,' said George. 'Maybe he should see a back doctor.'

'Maybe,' Katherine agreed, her heart breaking over the lie she was telling her children, over the need for the lie, but she couldn't tell them the truth. Their world would be shattered and she wasn't sure yet that they couldn't find their way back.

But now… now it is too late. It is so much worse than too late. The knowledge that today can only end one way has settled around her, suffocating and thick. It is much worse than just too late.

Yesterday there was a new marble and worries over school and spaghetti for dinner and today there is a gun and the smell of fear beginning to fill up the room.

Last night there was an argument that felt like one argument too far and now they are here.

Nothing she can say will change the situation. The only hope she has is to save the children. She needs to keep them safe.

The words she spat float back to her. 'I'll leave you and take these children.'

'You won't be going anywhere, Katherine. Don't be ridiculous.'

He was right about that, terrifyingly right.

'Guns kill people,' says George.

She nods her head without thinking and then regrets it. They don't need to be any more frightened than they already are. She and John had agreed they wouldn't let the children play with toy guns, not wanting them to think of weapons as something to pretend with, not wanting to encourage any violent ideas. Now there is a real gun in her house, in her home, pointed at her and her children. Even when she was single and working in the city as an administrative assistant to a gruff old man who called her Katie, living in a one-bedroom apartment in a dubious neighbourhood, she had never seen a gun. Until now.

'It's going to be okay,' she says softly to them.

'It's going to be okay,' he repeats, pointing the gun directly at her head, his voice high and whiny.

Is it a real gun? Could he be doing this with something that is not real? But she can see it has weight to it. It's real.

'Actually,' he says, dropping to his knees in front of the sofa they are sitting on, 'it's not going to be okay at all. Not for you anyway.' He laughs, small droplets of spit coming out of his mouth, and Katherine feels a streak of burning hatred rise up from her toes. What's happened to him? How can he be doing this to them?

He looks at her phone again and then turns it off, slides it into his pocket. She feels a surge of panic as he traps her and the children in here with him, with no way to communicate with the outside world. She already tried this morning, when she answered the door.

The bell chiming had startled him, and for a moment he'd looked unsure. 'You expecting someone?' he asked quietly.

'No.'

'Then get rid of them, get rid of them quickly. Just talk through the peephole. Do not, under any circumstances, open the door.'

'Can I take the kids with me?'

He gave his head a long, slow shake, a parent disappointed with a child, his gaze holding her as he allowed the corners of his mouth to raise just a little at her ridiculous request.

'Apparently you think I'm stupid, Katherine? Do you think I'm stupid?' He tapped his own head gently with the barrel of the gun.

'No, no, I'll go, I'll get rid of them.'

'I will be listening to everything you say. Every. Single. Word.' As he said this, he moved the gun back and forth between her children's heads. Katherine swallowed so she would not throw up.

She sensed that the delivery man was irritated with her. She couldn't make him understand and he had left, taking her new computer with him. That had been part of her plan for the day. A swim, some shopping and setting up her new computer. A very ordinary day.

'What do you want?' she asks him now, her voice raspy with terror. How will she get the children out of here and away from him?

'I want… I want you to listen to me. Not to talk over me, not to explain, not to justify. I just want you to listen to me.'

'I'll listen,' she says, 'and then what? What's going to happen?' She wishes she could keep the desperation from her voice, that she could control her body as a tear escapes and rolls down her cheek.

'You'll have to wait to see,' he says and he sits down on the leather recliner, pushes the seat back and raises his feet, relaxed and calm. He has all the time in the world. Katherine knows that she and her children don't. He doesn't have a plan. What he has is rage and a weapon and she can sense, in the prickling of her skin, that this makes him more dangerous than if he did know what he was going to do. A lot more dangerous.

CHAPTER FIVE

Six hours ago

Logan

Logan climbs back into the van, setting off and turning the air conditioning vents to face him. He feels like he's been up forever but it's only 8.30 a.m. This last delivery was heavy – two boxes of books for what looked like a university student, living in a building with three floors and no lift. The boy had been so eager to open the packages he had started tearing at the tape before he even closed the door. Logan wonders what it must be like to be that passionate about something, to want to read everything and know everything about a subject. He struggles now to remember what he was like when he was that kid's age, eighteen or maybe nineteen.

Angry is a feeling that comes to mind when he thinks of himself at that stage of life, pissed off with everyone except Maddy, who was eleven years old at the time and had an infectious laugh that never failed to cheer him up.

His phone pings again and even though he knows he shouldn't look at it while he's driving, he risks a quick glance down.

Call me NOW.

'Oh, it's a command now, is it?' sneers Logan.

At a traffic light, he taps the screen on the dashboard of the van and calls his sister instead. 'Hi, it's Maddy, leave me a message.'

'Hi Maddy, just checking in. Wanted to see how things are going. Give me a call when you can.'

Maddy is probably already at university. She's getting a teaching degree as a mature student although he would hardly think twenty-five qualifies as mature. She's perpetually worried about falling behind so she works harder than most of the other students. That's another reason why the idea of her still being with Patrick irritates him so much. He doesn't like the fact that she works so hard because it takes her attention from him.

'Tell him to get himself a job then,' Logan told her. 'He should work so you don't have to waitress at night and study during the day.'

'He's trying, Logan, but he doesn't have any qualifications. He thinks he may be interested in architecture. He draws really well.'

'Does he?' Logan scoffed.

Logan wishes she still lived in Sydney so they could see each other regularly, but he supposes he should be grateful that she is only two hours away by plane and they can speak all the time. Maddy had felt like she needed to get even further away from their family than Logan did. 'I can't be in the same state as them. They keep trying to get me to come over and I don't want to be sucked back in.' He couldn't blame her for wanting to be away from them. He left when he was eighteen, having little choice but to leave. 'Take me with you,' Maddy begged but he knew he didn't have the ability to take care of a kid, even if it broke his heart to say no to her. 'I can't, Maddy, I don't have any money and I need to find a place to live, but I'll call you all the time.'

'Promise?' she asked on his last day at home, as his father sneered and his mother ignored him. Only Maddy had tears on her cheeks and he grabbed her and held her tightly to him. 'Promise,' he whispered. No matter what happened in his life, he would never neglect his sister.

She struggled for a couple of years once she got down to Melbourne, but now she seems to have found her way.

It took a lot longer for Logan. He couldn't see a way forward for himself in the world and so for years he knows he moved through his life letting things happen to him, getting involved in things that he never planned on being involved in. Until it all stopped, the night he met Debbie.

It's only since they got together that he's understood what a real family should be like. Debbie is forever on the phone to her mother and her sister-in-law and her various cousins. If someone is sick, everyone calls and worries. If there's a birthday, presents are discussed. Triumphs are celebrated and tragedies fretted over.

He touches the screen on his dashboard as he drives, tapping Debbie's number. She's home today instead of at the hospital. She's a nurse on the maternity ward, helping bring new life into the world every day. But it's tiring work and she seems to catch whatever is going around. This morning he made her a very early morning cup of tea and left it on her bedside table so she could have something to drink when she woke up, even though it would probably be lukewarm then.

She'll be up by now, he's sure.

'Hey babes,' she answers, 'is it hot enough for you?'

He laughs. 'Are you going to ask me that every time I call today?'

'Yep, I've just finished my book so until I download another one, you're my only avenue for amusement.'

'How are you feeling?'

'Yeah, slightly nauseous, slightly shitty. At least my nose has stopped running, but then I've taken enough stuff to help that.'

'You poor thing. Hey, I had a weird delivery this morning.'

'Ooo, do tell – a naked lady?'

'Nah,' laughs Logan. He had one of those once. Too bad she was at least eighty. He had felt really sorry for her, understanding that she wasn't even aware she was naked. He had averted his eyes and pretended she was dressed.

'I had to deliver a computer and that needs to be signed for but the woman wouldn't open the door.'

Debbie is quiet for a moment. 'Are you wearing long sleeves?' She asks the question softly because she knows this is the worst aspect of his job right now. It's fine in winter but he hates to be hot. It makes him feel trapped and claustrophobic and he hates feeling trapped.

'You know I am, Debs. I promised Mack, didn't I?'

It wasn't that his arms were covered in tattoos; it was more the *kind* of tattoos. The knife dripping blood; the gun firing a bullet with the words 'everyone dies' written underneath. The skull and crossbones with a woman's face screaming behind one of the eye sockets; the writhing, fanged snake creeping up his neck. Choices made when he was drunk or seething with rage. They are the choices he regrets every day. Removal would cost a fortune and leave him with scarring. He's thought about covering them up with different tattoos but just walking into a tattoo studio made him uncomfortable, brought back memories he had no interest in revisiting. A different man got his tattoos and he never wanted to meet him again.

'Course you did, sorry, babes. I know it must be really uncomfortable,' says Debbie.

'Don't worry about it. Anyway, so the woman wouldn't open the door and when I told her I would wait for her to get dressed or something she said that I needed to understand that she couldn't open the door, like she made sure to emphasise the word understand.'

'People are weird,' says Debbie.

Logan shakes his head. 'I think that something is wrong in that house. There wasn't even any noise from the kids and I know there must have been little kids because there were scooters in the garden.'

'It sounds like you're reading too much into what she said. Maybe the kids were at school early, or with their dad, or staying at friends, and she was having fun with her husband or her lover. You never know what's going on behind closed doors as they say.'

'Maybe, but I think something's wrong,' he says, frowning.

'Don't overthink, babes, just get on with the rest of your day and there will be a cold beer waiting for you when you get home. Maybe if I feel a bit better, we can drive down to the beach for a walk.'

Logan bites down on his lip. He knew Debbie would tell him not to dwell on the delivery. He is probably making things up, letting his imagination run away with him, but he can't help the unease he feels. It's almost a physical thing, a churning in his gut as though his body is telling him to pay attention.

'A cold beer sounds good,' he says, knowing that there's no point in saying anything else. He can't make Debbie understand because even he doesn't get why he's worried about some woman he's never met in a house he's never been to before.

'It will be. Love you, babes. Enjoy the rest of your day.'

'Love you too – rest and get better.'

Debbie ends the call with a kiss and Logan smiles. He rubs at his chin as he remembers the first time he met Debbie. It was at three in the morning in a hospital emergency room.

He was covered in blood from putting his fist through a window, woozy from the taser and shaking from the effects of his first try of the drug ice wearing off. The police had brought him in to have his hand seen to. Logan knows there were two of them and that one was a man and one was a woman, but when he thinks about it now, he can't remember their faces at all. It had been a beautiful high to begin with, as his body flooded with dopamine and adrenalin rushed through his veins. He can remember feeling invincible, believing that he could simply put his fist through the glass door at the side of a house where he had found himself standing, with no idea of how he'd got there. He didn't think it would hurt at all; he wouldn't even feel the pain.

He now knows that he had run five kilometres from Nick's place. Nick was his partner in crime, literally. A mate from the gym. Gym was the only place Logan felt at home – where he'd found people who understood him. Nick was small and thin, with an innocent baby face. He talked more than he worked out. He had a drug habit but he told Logan he kept it well under control. His parents had tried to help, his school had tried, therapists had tried – it seemed to Logan that the whole world had tried to help Nick get his life back on track – but Nick had no desire to actually be helped.

Together they had amassed a small fortune picking the right houses to break into. Together they had hit houses where cannabis was being grown in the basement, and those where meth was being made in the back. There was always money there, lots and lots of cash, and no one ever reported it to the police. It was dangerous work because there were also always guns and junkies and those who meant to protect what they were doing. But he and Nick were smart about things. They would hit a couple of places and then lie low for months, living off what they'd made. They'd been doing it for years, ever since they'd met when Logan was twenty-three and looking for a way out of the menial jobs he kept getting fired from because he'd mouthed off or hit someone. He didn't do well with authority and he took all criticism personally.

He and Nick didn't start off with drug houses.

'I know this house, near where my parents live,' Nick said one night over a beer. 'They've just moved in but they're not actually living there because they've just painted. The house is filled with stuff and no people.'

Logan frowned. 'So what?'

'So maybe we go in and help ourselves to some stuff. I know a guy who can get rid of it all. No mess, no fuss and they have insurance – they won't even care.'

'I'm not a thief, Nick.'

'Yeah, what are you, Logan? Just looking to finish your medical degree?' Nick raised an eyebrow at him, a smirk on his face.

'Don't be a dick.'

'I'm not being a dick. I'm saying this is easy money. We get in, we get out and we enjoy the cash.'

And it had been easy money. Logan remembers the feeling of control as he counted the notes in the pile that was his share. It had taken them an hour and they had the money for the stuff two days later. He put fifty dollars in an envelope and posted it to Maddy, telling her to hide it well and use it to buy what she needed for school, knowing that cash in his parents' house disappeared on cigarettes and alcohol pretty quickly. He felt like he was good at something for the first time in his life.

It wasn't always easy. There were houses with alarms and barking dogs and enraged owners. They would leave if there was any noise, and by the time the police arrived, they were long gone.

It was Nick who suggested targeting places where the thin blue line was crossed every day.

'No one calls the cops when you steal money they've collected from selling their product – no one.' He was so sure of himself, and he always believed that he would get away with it. And he did – mostly.

Nick's cocaine habit was still under control, or so he said, but he was starting to experiment with other things.

Logan has no idea why, on this particular night, they took some of the drugs as well as the money. Usually they left the drugs alone – that was part of their strategy. And that meant that they managed to get away with it for years.

Now, as Logan drives the van, he understands that whatever you do for a job, it's better than not having one. At the end of the day, he can sit next to his wife and know that he has done something – if not worthwhile, then at least acceptable and helpful.

Logan dismisses thoughts of Nick, who is still in prison because his self-belief could not keep the police away forever, and who is still raging at the world. Still intending to go back to his old life.

He pulls to a stop in front of another house and gets out of his van, noting the large German shepherd standing rigid at the gate.

He searches the wall of the house, relieved to see a keypad with a bell. He pushes the bell and steps back as the dog stares at him. 'You're a protective bugger, aren't you?' he says to the German shepherd. The dog growls softly.

The door opens and a young girl dressed in shorts and a tiny tank top comes running down the path. 'Sorry, sorry,' she smiles. 'James, you be a good boy. I'm going to open the gate and you're not to move.'

'His name is James?' asks Logan as she opens the gate and he hands her the box.

'It is. Thanks so much.' The young girl looks a little like Debbie, with the same tiny frame and big hazel eyes.

He returns to the van and thinks back to that night that landed him in the emergency room. He has no idea why he decided to take a hit at Nick's urging. He was a beer man, sometimes a good Scotch, but he never, ever touched drugs. He'd grown up in a neighbourhood where he'd watched what happened to those who succumbed to the promise of some time out from their misery. He'd watched Nick get all jittery and sweaty when he needed his next fix.

But that night he had agreed, had smoked what Nick had rolled for him, mistakenly assuming that smoking ice instead of injecting it would lessen its effects. He was tired of what he did with his time, tired of his lonely life and of Nick. Tired of himself. *Why not?* he had thought. He remembers the rush now, the feeling of being so powerful he could lift a car if he chose to.

He knows he stood up and left Nick's house and he knows that he started running. He felt like he could fly. When he found himself in some garden, in a suburb that he had never been to before, he looked at a pair of glass French doors and thought, *Those'll be easy to open.* And then he put his fist through the glass, smashing it, cutting his hand, causing the alarm to scream and the owner to come running. He smiled when he saw it was a woman – a tall woman, but a woman he could deal with. He would grab what he could and fly away again. But she swung out at him, furious and strong, and caught him on the nose. Blood gushed from his face and his own anger rose up and he swung back. He broke her cheekbone and fractured her eye socket and she went down.

He remembers the woman from his trial. He hadn't recognised her, hadn't even remembered what she looked like, but her victim impact statement bruised him with its fear and pain. He wrote to her in prison, asking for forgiveness. He wrote three times and then he stopped. He reasoned she had a right to move on with her life and hopefully think of him less with each passing year.

He checks for his next delivery. It's close by and in a street he's been down before so he doesn't need his GPS. As he drives, he wonders what would happen if he turned up to a house he had broken into. Would he recognise it, or have they all blended into one? He doesn't even know the address of the one where the woman he hurt lived. What if one day a front door is opened and she's standing there? The thought makes him push his shoulders back, suddenly uncomfortable. The image of her body sprawled on her stone-coloured kitchen floor comes back to him. He stared down at her, and then the police were there, appearing out of thin air. Now he knows she made the call before she confronted him. She had heard the glass break. He had thought he was moving quickly but in reality, he'd stood there for a few minutes watching the blue whirling light of the alarm glint off the shards of broken glass from the French door, mesmerised by the shiny flashes.

The police told him to stop, to get down on the ground, but Logan was still flying high and he advanced towards them. They told him once, twice and then the taser struck him in the chest, paralysing him and forcing him down. Tingling pain seared through his body and the high wore off.

The police got him up after a few minutes and he was given a towel for his hand. Only one ambulance arrived and Logan remembers hearing the words, 'We'll just take him in ourselves,' and then he was in the back of a police car, his body shaking as shock replaced every other emotion.

He knows that the hands of the male police officer were large and strong and that they wrapped around his arm tightly, pushing into the muscle so Logan understood exactly who was in charge. Once they'd got him onto a bed in a small curtained-off bay in the emergency room, he dropped his head as he felt tears pricking at his eyes. He was twenty-six and he had wasted his whole life without meaning to, without thinking anything through. He'd never had a plan or a dream and now he was going to prison. And no one would care, except Maddy – she would be bereft and disappointed in him. That is what made the tears burn in his eyes.

He knew he was screwed, knew it without a shadow of a doubt. He also understood that there was a small feeling of relief. He was never going to stop unless something stopped him, and now it had.

'Can you lie back please?' He heard a soft voice. He shuffled backwards and dropped his head onto the pillow. He felt his uninjured hand get handcuffed to the bed rail. 'I think he's calm now, officer,' said the voice. 'Perhaps you could just give me some space.'

Logan looked at the nurse, who was delicately probing his hand, wiping and touching softly to see if there was any glass stuck in his flesh. Her skin was pale in the harsh hospital light, but smooth and perfect. Her hazel eyes were fringed with long black lashes and a curl had escaped her neat bun.

'This looks clean and I don't think any of the cuts are deep enough for stitches. I'll clean it up and bandage it and then the doctor will be along shortly.'

Logan nodded, horrified to find that the way she was speaking to him, the kindness in her voice, was leading to more tears, slipping down the side of his face.

'Hey now,' she said gently and she reached up and wiped a tear away. 'This can be the worst day of your life if you want it to be. There can never be another day as bad as this. If that's what you want.'

Logan smiled. 'It's what I want,' he said and he looked at the nurse, her clean soap smell comforting, the hint of floral perfume a scent he would always remember. 'Debbie', her nametag said. She had a small mole above her full red lips and he wanted to touch her mouth, but he knew better and he was grateful that at least he had begun thinking straight.

'I bet all those tattoos hurt more than this anyway,' she said and he nodded. He couldn't explain then that there was pleasure in the pain of a tattoo, in the repeated sting of the needle, in being able to bear the ache that changed his skin, changed him. They were his pain and his anger detailed over his body, scars that could be seen.

He had never expected to see Debbie again. But in the months leading up to his guilty plea and being sent to prison, he'd thought about her. In prison he held on to her words. He needed to make sure that the day he was caught high and violent – the first time he had actually hurt someone who didn't deserve it – was the worst day of his life. He was a model prisoner, recommended for parole after three years. He worked out, took classes and wrote his final exams to complete his schooling. Most importantly, he stayed out of trouble. He was big enough to be left alone, quiet enough not to bother anyone, and on the day he got out, he took the biggest chance he'd ever taken in his life.

He went back to the hospital and asked for her, knowing that they probably wouldn't be able to identify her with just a name and a description, knowing that even if they could, he would probably get in trouble for behaving like a stalker. But the need to tell her that her words had meant something would not let go.

'I'm looking for a nurse,' he explained to the woman sitting at the front desk of the hospital, and then he stood quietly, trying not to let his six-foot-four, tattoo-covered frame look threatening. He hunched his shoulders and bowed his head, meek and mild. Nothing to worry about here. 'Her name is Debbie and she treated me a few years ago. She has blonde hair and hazel eyes and a mole just here,' he explained as the woman's lips thinned into a disapproving line.

'I don't know if she still works here,' he said, holding his hands up, 'but I just wanted to thank her for being kind to me. I'll sit down over there.' He indicated some fake leather sofas. 'I'll wait for a few minutes and if you want me to leave, I'll just go.' He moved away from the desk, the woman's eyes watching every step, and he sat down. He was being an idiot, but he couldn't seem to do anything else. He knew that he had to see her and thank her and then he could go out into the world and try to start rebuilding his life.

He watched as the woman lifted the telephone to her ear. He waited for the security guards to come over to him, waited for the police to walk through the front door. He stared down at his new phone, scrolled through news websites as his heart raced, noticing that his fingers were trembling a little. He took a deep breath, catching the smell of antiseptic in his throat.

'Excuse me,' he heard and he looked up and there she was. She looked exactly the same, except her hair was in a low ponytail and he could see that when it was loose, it would hang down her back. The floral scent was there as well, bringing the night they'd met back to him in a heady rush. He stood up, towering over her, then quickly sat down again when she took a step back.

'I don't know if you remember me, but you treated me three years ago and you said… You were so… I just wanted to…'

She smiled, a dimple appearing on one cheek, her teeth an even white line. 'Of course I remember you. It's hard to forget a six-foot-four, heavily tattooed man who cries. I was only on emergency duty that night because we were short-staffed. I usually take care of much smaller people, ones that cry all the time.'

'Can I take you for dinner? Or coffee? Or lunch? Or anything? You helped, you really helped, and I just wanted to thank you…' It took all his self-control not to reach out and touch her. He had not intended to ask her out, just to thank her – but that dimple, that smile. He prepared himself for a no. He couldn't remember half the women he had slept with before going to prison but he knew he had never cared if he saw them again or not. He knew she was going to say no.

'I get off at five and I'm very hungry because I missed lunch. How about then?'

'Tonight?'

'Yes, is that too soon?'

'No… it's… I'll be here. Thank you, Debbie – can I call you Debbie?'

'You can and I can call you… I'm afraid I have forgotten your name.'

'Logan.'

'I'll see you at five, Logan.'

She wasn't afraid of him, even though she must have known he was someone to be afraid of.

After they had been together for months, she told him, 'I saw something that night, the night I treated you. I figured you had gone to prison. I saw the boy you must have been once, and I knew you were mostly a threat to yourself. I mean, I wasn't stupid. I was shocked to see you again, but the way you held yourself told me something, and I was interested in who you were. I was a little scared, and I told about five people where we were going, and I didn't let you take me home. But I was just being safe. I knew you were a good bloke.'

And he has tried to be that 'good bloke' since he got out of prison. It hasn't been easy. Getting a job as an ex-convict is near impossible, which is why so many people end up back in prison. He has experienced moments of desperation since his release and when he thinks about the risk he almost took – a risk he prefers not to think about – he is grateful that he caught himself in time, that he didn't go through with it. He can only hope that nothing is ever going to come back on him.

His phone pings but he doesn't look at it as he pulls up outside the next delivery. He knows who it's from and he's not going to respond. Not today.

He looks at the clock on his dashboard. It's nearly ten and he could use a coffee and something to eat.

He thinks about the woman in the house again as he slides open his van door and grabs the right box. When he was breaking and entering, he developed a keen sense of danger. He would feel his heart rate speed up and his skin tingle, even when the house was silent, and he knew to be extra careful because it meant that something was off, that there was something he was missing, something that was a threat to him. That's what he felt speaking to that woman this morning, he now realises. He felt danger.

He stands at the front gate of this house for a moment, his skin tingling as he understands that this is what happened this morning. Old instincts returned, telling him to pay attention.

'Is that for me?' asks an old man who is standing in the front garden with a spade in his hand. Logan hadn't even noticed him. 'Oh yeah, sorry,' he says.

The man laughs. 'This kind of heat can make you lose your mind.' He opens the gate and takes the parcel from Logan.

'Thanks,' he says, and Logan nods and walks back to his van. His instincts are never wrong except for the one time when he was out of his mind on ice. Instinct kept him safe in dangerous situations for years.

And he knows it now, for sure. The woman is in danger.

CHAPTER SIX
Gladys

Gladys loads the dishwasher before going into the living room to check on Lou. He's fallen asleep again, something that happens more and more often these days. Just being awake seems to tire him out.

The children have still not walked past the house. She and Lou ate breakfast and watched carefully. She would like to sit and read, but she feels a little jumpy for no particular reason. She goes into the spare room again and looks at the house next door. The blinds are still down, the windows closed. Maybe Katherine is just taking the advice given on the news to keep windows and blinds closed, to keep the heat out. But this is not the first heatwave this year and she knows that Katherine has never before kept the blinds and windows closed during the day.

Gladys is aware that she is known as the neighbourhood busybody, and perhaps that's what she is, but when she was growing up, everyone knew everyone in their neighbourhood. Her mother regaled them all with tales of everyone's lives over dinner each night. It was not considered nosy to ask questions about your neighbours and to be involved in their lives. It seems that people now are open and honest about their lives all over the internet and then coy about exactly the same things in person. Perhaps because it's difficult to tell the truth about yourself when you're looking directly at someone.

When she and Lou first bought this house, the neighbourhood was filled with people who became their friends. Where Katherine lives now is where Roberta and Geoff lived with their three children. Gladys watched those children grow from babies to adults. Roberta would pop over for tea during the school holidays when Gladys was home and Lou still working. She had known when Roberta and Geoff had had an argument, when the children were sick and finally, she was one of the first to know when Roberta got her cancer diagnosis. Geoff sold the house after she died and then another family moved in – less friendly but still, Mira did like a chat over the fence every now and again. When she and her family moved to Melbourne, they sold the house to Katherine and her husband John. Even though Gladys welcomed them with a cake and tried popping over for tea once or twice, she got the feeling that Katherine needed her space. It's the same with Margo over the road, who always seems to be looking at her watch when they see each other, keen to keep her baby, Joseph, in a routine. She never seems to have time to talk.

She thinks about the first time she met Katherine. She and John were both so happy, a couple at the beginning of the big adventure of becoming a family. Even from a distance, they seem… less happy now. It's the stress of raising twins and of being the parents of young children, Gladys is sure. It isn't that she hears them argue, but then of course she wouldn't. She is sure that they are responsible enough to keep any arguments quiet. It's more that there is something odd between them when she's seen them together lately.

Last Sunday the whole family were in the front garden. John is a keen gardener and he was weeding, and Katherine was holding the hose so that the children could run in and out of the water, even though they have a pool at the back. Gladys had left Lou to have a stroll around the block, just to stretch her legs. It wasn't an overly warm day so it was pleasant to walk and admire the gardens filled with their summer flowers and magnificent colours.

'Hello,' she called, stopping at their front gate.

'Hello,' replied Katherine.

'Look what we're doing,' shouted George, running under the arc of water from the hose.

'I see,' said Gladys, 'it looks like fun.'

'Not so much for the one who has to hold the hose,' Katherine said.

'Then don't do it,' muttered John.

'I'm doing it for George and Sophie, not for you.'

'I never claimed you were doing anything for me.'

'Perhaps you don't want to be here gardening; perhaps you'd rather be somewhere else,' Katherine said, her voice tight with anger.

Gladys had the feeling she had stumbled into a conversation that had been going on for some time.

John stood up from the garden bed and walked towards Katherine, grabbing the hose out of her hands and using it to wash the dirt off his own.

'Hey!' shouted Sophie.

'Quiet,' he barked and then he stormed off away from them, back into the house.

'Bad morning?' Gladys asked in what she hoped was a jovial tone.

'Lots of bad mornings,' Katherine said, holding the hose over the children again.

It seemed to Gladys that Katherine's words were said more to herself than to Gladys. 'Oh, well,' she said, unable to think of any other reply, and Katherine gave herself a little shake. 'Sorry, Gladys… don't mind John. He's grumpy because he's tired. He's been working late a lot.'

'Of course, of course,' murmured Gladys and then she waved and went on her way.

It wasn't the silly argument that had bothered her but rather the tension between the two of them. It filled the summer air and darkened John's features.

He isn't a big man, only a little taller than Katherine, and Gladys doesn't think he's the type to become violent. He is an accountant in a large firm. Accountants are not a violent bunch – not usually at least. But in that moment, just then, it seemed as if he could have been, from the way he wrenched the hose out of Katherine's hand.

Gladys stares at the house, where the closed blinds look strangely ominous and secretive.

'Well, you need to just stop being ridiculous,' she says aloud. 'Just march over there and check on them.'

She nods her head and catches sight of herself in the guest bedroom mirror, makes a clicking sound with her tongue at her appearance. She hasn't put on any make-up this morning but she supposes there's no point. It will simply slide off her face in this terrible heat, and hardly anyone's going to see her anyway. She finds herself dressing up less and less these days, a feeling of defeat overtaking her as she applies base to cover wrinkles and age spots. It's not healthy, and she is trying to encourage herself not to think that way. She pushes her hair behind her ears and lifts her neck. She's not doing badly for seventy, and at least her body is still trim and fit. She likes the pants she's wearing today. The lovely flower-patterned design feels like she's wearing a garden around her legs. Clothes should be bright and cheerful, she's always thought.

As a young girl Gladys was conscious of her skinny arms and legs and her slightly hooked nose. She had nice eyes, wide and blue, but she knew that she didn't fit the description of pretty. Her brown hair is still cut in a short bob and she keeps the colour with regular visits to the hairdresser. She tried, throughout her teenage years, to make peace with the fact that she was not likely to find a husband. 'What nonsense,' her mother told her, 'beauty is in the eye of the beholder and you're a beautiful young woman,' and she was right.

She bumped into Lou at a pub on a night out with some of the teachers from the school where she was working at the time.

'We'll all move up a little – sit down,' said someone, Gladys can't remember who. And then she moved to create a space, assuming that the person sitting next to her would shuffle up as well, but Lou said, 'I'll take that seat, right next to the pretty one.' He sat down beside her and offered her his hand. 'I'm Lou and I sell cars. I'll get you the best deal on a new car if you let me buy you your next drink.' He had thick brown hair and grey-blue eyes. Gladys allows herself a small smile now as she remembers how she had flushed, heat rising up from her toes.

She leaves the guest bedroom and looks in on her husband downstairs. He is still asleep. She contemplates leaving him a note but then doesn't. She'll be back almost immediately, she's sure.

Outside the heat is starting to take hold, cicadas ramping up their song. She looks across the road and sees the dog who belongs to the Patel family lying in the front garden under a tree, panting. He's a golden retriever and even though he's had his summer cut, he looks very unhappy in the heat.

She ducks across the road quickly and looks down the side of the house where she knows they leave his water and food. She can see not just one bowl of water but three. She nods her head, satisfied, and crosses back over to her side of the street.

Pushing open the metal gate at the front of Katherine's house, Gladys walks purposefully up the front path.

Once she's rung the bell she waits, knowing that she will soon hear Katherine shout, 'George, do not answer the door until I'm there.' The little boy likes to answer the door. He is curious about everything and everyone and speaks to her as though they are the same age. Sometimes he calls her 'Glad', which sounds strange coming from the mouth of a five-year-old, but he is completely charming. Sophie is less interested in other people and more of a chatterbox, filled with information and ideas. 'Did you know that a worker bee lives for forty-two days,' she said to Gladys when they met in the street last week, as though handing over classified information, and Gladys nodded, making sure to register this fact with the gravitas it needed.

But the house is silent. There are no sounds of running children or Katherine shouting.

Gladys wonders if perhaps the family have left for an early holiday. School finishes up for the year on Friday. But then she remembers that John left for work this morning, with screeching tyres, according to Lou. And when they do go away, Katherine always comes over to tell Gladys so that she can keep an eye on the house.

She pushes the doorbell once more and waits. She could have just called Katherine because she has her mobile number. But phone calls are easily ignored and then Gladys would have been left still wondering if everything was all right. No, it's better to tackle this in person.

She hears the metal square that holds the peephole open and she smiles.

'Hey Gladys,' says Katherine through the door. 'Now isn't really a good time.'

'Oh,' says Gladys, a little flustered. Even in the early days, when she had rung the bell to find Katherine in the middle of changing a nappy, the door was always opened for her. Only Katherine's tight politeness would give Gladys any sense that she was not in the mood for coffee and a chat.

'Oh right,' she says, 'I just… well, I didn't see the children go to school and the blinds in their room are closed, and I just wondered if everything was okay, or if you needed anything, if the children are sick or something…'

She stops speaking, aware that she does sound like a very nosy person. She pats at her hair, making sure the clip is still holding in place.

'It's not a good time,' Katherine repeats. 'But thanks. It's just not a good time.' The peephole is closed.

Gladys folds her arms and feels the sun burning through the thin blue blouse she is wearing.

She thinks about ringing the doorbell again but decides against it. Katherine obviously wants to be left alone.

She sounded stressed, the poor woman. Perhaps the children are both ill with colds or something – but then why not just say that? Katherine knows that Gladys would sympathise and even offer to help.

She hears some movement inside – the sound of running footsteps – and she pulls her shoulders back a little, listening closely.

A voice comes through the door in a fierce whisper: 'This is a very strange house right now.'

She can't tell if it's George or Sophie speaking but she does know it's one of the children. She frowns and crouches down a little, hoping it will help her hear better. 'Why?' she asks.

'Sophie, get over here,' she hears George shout from further away, and then there are footsteps as Sophie moves away from the door.

Gladys stands up straight and once again thinks about ringing the bell.

Then she hears the peephole open again and waits in case it's Katherine, and in case she wants to say something. She stands still for a moment, a smile plastered on her face, but when nothing else is said she feels silly and turns around. She takes a couple of steps and waits again, but when there is only silence, she goes back down the stone path to the front gate. She walks slowly but is aware of feeling like she needs to move quickly. She feels like she's being watched. The hair on her arms stands up and even in the strong morning heat, she feels cold. Something is not right inside that house. She's sure of it.

Back in her own kitchen she puts on the kettle to make herself a cup of tea and then immediately switches it off again. She doesn't know what she should do or why she feels so strange about what just happened. It was probably just a joke, just Sophie being silly.

'Gladys,' calls Lou from the living room, 'Gladys, where are you?' He sounds frantic, as he does whenever he wakes up and can't find her.

'I'm here, Lou,' she calls. Before he retired, she used to call him at lunchtime every day and he would say, 'Now don't you worry, sweet pea, I'll be home at six on the dot and I won't smile at any woman except you.' It always made her laugh. He doesn't make jokes anymore.

In the living room, she fixes the pillow behind his back. He has slumped sideways a little in his sleep and she tries to right him, but he pushes at her to get her to step away from him.

'Stop fussing. Where were you?'

She steps back and folds her arms to stop herself from smoothing down his hair for him. 'Just in the kitchen, Lou, just making tea. Where else would I be?'

He gives her a look and she sits down in her chair. 'Truthfully, I went over to check on them.' She picks up her book from the small table next to her chair where she has left it and opens it, staring down at the pages.

'Ha, I knew you would, and I bet everything is fine and now they think you're an interfering old woman.'

Gladys closes the book, knowing that reading will not be possible. 'Don't be rude, Lou.' She debates with herself for a moment over whether to tell him anything or not but she needs to say something. 'Actually, everything is not fine. I don't think it is at all.' She shakes her head as Lou folds his hands in his lap and waits for her to go on. 'Katherine wouldn't open the door and then Sophie whispered to me that there was something strange going on in the house.'

'Probably just messing about.' Lou picks up the remote control for the television, pointing it at the screen.

'I don't think so. I think something may be a little bit wrong.'

'What could possibly be wrong?' he asks.

'I don't know, they seem unhappy sometimes – her and John, I mean.'

He shrugs his shoulders and then lifts his glasses onto his face. 'You can't judge someone else's marriage, Gladys. It's not your business.'

Lou switches on the TV, turning it to the news. The face of a pretty young woman flashes up on the screen.

'A young woman has been badly beaten and left for dead in her apartment,' drones the newsreader. 'It is believed that the victim knew her attacker although enquiries are still in the early stages. Police are interviewing neighbours and have established a crime scene.'

On the screen is a glaring shot of an ambulance surrounded by police holding up blankets to shield someone from the prying eyes of the media as they are being brought out on a stretcher.

'People are just terrible,' says Lou, shaking his head.

'Yes,' she agrees. 'Who would want to hurt such a pretty young girl? And in her own home too. Home should be a place where you're safe. It really should be.' She finds herself tearing up a little with no real idea why it's upset her so much.

'Weren't you making tea?' he asks, but he asks politely and she knows it's because she's scolded him for being abrupt with her.

'Of course,' she says and she smiles to let him know he's forgiven. He would make the tea if he could but his hands shake too much for him to perform this simple task now. Having to have a thick mug instead of the delicate cups he prefers is difficult enough for him to deal with. She stands up, grateful to have this task to perform as she mulls over her strange experience at Katherine's house.

In the kitchen she looks out at the garden, and she struggles to pinpoint her unease. Home should be a place you feel secure and her home has always felt that way. But after yesterday and Katherine's strange behaviour today, it feels as though something has changed in the neighbourhood, as though the safe place she has lived for decades is suddenly less secure. That's what this strange feeling inside her is. For the first time, she feels unsafe.

CHAPTER SEVEN

'You really should know how to discipline these kids better,' I say to her.

'Oh,' she says, reaching out to me where I have a hold of Sophie, my hands in her hair. Up close it smells like coconut.

She is hopping from one foot to another as though trying to stand up taller so the way I'm pulling her hair hurts less. 'Ow, ow, ow.' Her voice is high and distressed and it should bother me more than it does, I guess.

Sophie shouldn't have run off to the door. I have expressly forbidden them from moving. I would have thought that she would listen to my instructions but she didn't. I feel anger surge inside me, and as I pull on her hair, and her face turns pale with pain, I wonder how hard I would have to pull to just yank out a clump of it. A shiver runs down my spine in the warm room as I watch the way her small face contorts. I should feel something but I don't and I don't know why. But I do know it's not my fault. I wasn't always this way.

'Stop wriggling or I will pull out your hair!' I yell and she stands still. I take a deep breath, and my thoughts stray to myself at this age, at five, and then at ten because ten is when I started to become this person, this man standing here, capable of hurting this child and feeling… nothing. When I was ten, everything began to change. I felt it, heard it and I watched it happen – slowly and painfully.

My parents finally got divorced when I was twelve years old. I remember the horrible sadness that hung in the air in our house – after they told me what was happening, but before he actually left. For the first time in a couple of years the house was quiet when they were both home. I was used to angry sniping and snide comments from them. Shouting and crying from her. Lies and denial from him. Both of them kept reassuring me that they loved me and that my life wasn't going to change at all and that the divorce was not my fault. There was obviously some stupid manual they'd read. My life wasn't going to change except my father would no longer be living with us. My life wasn't going to change except my mother and I had to move into a small flat where my bedroom wasn't actually a bedroom but rather an alcove with a hastily thrown up Gyproc wall. My life wasn't going to change except I would now spend every second weekend with my father at his own hideous small flat where we would consume vast amounts of junk food and he would engage in a campaign against my mother that was so pervasive, it's a wonder I ever agreed to go home again.

The reasons for their split have never been fully explained to me but I do know that it involved my father cheating more than once. I do know that money that was supposed to be for our family was used for other women, for gifts and expensive hotels. One Monday afternoon my mother and I stood at the checkout at the supermarket with a week's worth of groceries only for my mother to be told she had insufficient funds to pay for the food. I remember her face, the way her eyes dropped to the ground and she flushed a bright red. Behind us a line of impatient shoppers sighed and clicked their tongues. 'But… I just got paid,' she said. She was working part time in a delicatessen, just to bring in some extra cash, and she was good at keeping track of her money. Not good enough though.

'What do you want me to do?' the woman at the checkout said, boredom painted across her face.

My mother grabbed my hand and pulled me out of the store, leaving all the groceries sitting in bags at the checkout. I felt sorry for her. But I was also angry at her for allowing it.

'He's such a bastard,' she muttered as we drove home. What did she expect me to say to that? How was I supposed to answer her?

She was waiting for him as he walked through the door, crouched in her anger, and she leapt as he said, 'Hello.'

He apologised. He always did, his shoulders rounding and his mouth drooping at the edges. But she was humiliated and furious and she wouldn't let it go even though he got in the car and went late-night grocery shopping with another card. That night the fight went on for hours. I put on my headphones and cranked up my music, disappeared into another space so I didn't have to listen. I hated them both.

Every time I heard them fight, I vowed that my life would be different. I was going to be a different man to my father and I was going to marry a woman vastly different to my mother, who seemed to me to be filled with pretty words about her love for me and empty gestures.

My dad wanted me to come and live with him.

'If you lived with me,' he would say, 'you would be able to eat whatever you want. I wouldn't care about homework; you'd be able to game as long as you wanted.' It sounded as though living with him would be paradise. I was a thirteen-year-old kid. I didn't know any better.

'I want to live with Dad,' I said to my mother. 'He's lonely.'

'He's not capable of taking care of you. He's lonely and I understand that, but it wouldn't be a good idea.' She used her patient voice when she said this. I hated that voice, that smooth, quiet voice that meant she was trying to control herself.

'Dad lets me game as long as I want to.'

'That's exactly why you shouldn't live with him. Rules are there for a reason. You have to get through school and get into university.' There was an edge to her voice as she struggled to keep herself from yelling.

'I hate you.'

That always stopped her in her tracks. I would watch her bite down on her lip and shake her head, holding back on all the things she wanted to say to me. I knew the one thing she really wanted to say was, 'I hate you too.' I felt it coming off her. It was in the air.

Eventually all we did was fight. She wanted to keep me on the straight and narrow. She preached about school and grades and healthy food and he told me that life would be one big party, and even though I had some idea that it couldn't just be a party, he was very persuasive. I kept at her.

When I was fourteen, she gave in. 'Just six months,' she said. 'And you need to call me every day and come and visit every weekend.' She dropped her eyes and I saw defeat.

I was so excited on the first night when I moved in. He ordered pizza and let me drink a whole beer. We talked about how great it would be to be together all the time. 'Your life is your responsibility. If you want to attend school and do the work, that's up to you. If you don't, that's fine. You clean up your own mess and you live your life.' I was in heaven.

I went to school while he went to work, because it was something to do. I was happy. My friends thought I was the luckiest kid they knew, even if my clothes weren't always clean. She rang me every night, and sometimes I took the call and sometimes I didn't. When I didn't, I would see a smile on his face, a small one like he was trying to hide it, but it was there. I understood on some level that he was using me to get at her and it was working, because she asked me to come home every single time, begged me, cried when I hadn't spoken to her for days.

And then he lost his job and it all went to shit.

'Please d—' Sophie moans, her hands reaching for mine as my fist clamps tighter around her hair. Her voice is desperate and there is something, a small tug, a tiny spark of something inside me. But I know if she thinks Sophie has gotten to me, she'll use that. I know her. And I need to know what Sophie said. I need to know if she was clever enough to say something when she ran to the door. Because if she was… Her soft curls are making my hand sweat but I can't let go until I get the truth.

CHAPTER EIGHT

Katherine

'Please just... please...' says Katherine, because she has no idea what else to say. His hands are tangled in Sophie's hair, yanking and hurting her.

'What did you do?' he spits. 'What did you say to that nosy old woman?'

'I didn't say anything,' Sophie says, tears on her cheeks, her hands raised to try and stop him pulling her hair.

'Let her go, let her go,' Katherine says, trying to inject strength into her voice as she rises off the sofa, but he pulls her daughter's hair harder, bunches it in his fist. 'Sit down now,' he says and he points the gun, not at her because it would be fine if it were at her. But he knows better than that. He points the gun at Sophie – small, struggling Sophie, whose tears are streaking down her cheeks.

Katherine feels her body sink back down onto the sofa, the blue sofa that she chose with such care and admired every time she came into this room. This is her favourite room in the house. She loves the family photos everywhere and the large window that looks out onto the garden. When the twins were babies, she and John would sometimes find themselves asleep down here next to two baby rockers vibrating the children to sleep as the sun rose on another day. This is where the twins watch their movies and where she and John binge-watch television series together.

This *was* her favourite room in the house.

She is fighting a surging anger at Gladys for coming over and making things so much worse, and at the same time she feels a small flicker of hope that the older woman might have been suspicious, might have picked up on what Sophie said, although she has no idea what that might have been. Would her daughter have known to tell Gladys to call the police?

He watches her, a ghost of a smile on his face. He is enjoying her pain. She can see that. He is enjoying all of their pain, and it makes her feel sick.

'I'm sitting, see, I'm sitting,' she says, even though it's obvious. But she needs to distract him, to keep him focused on her. Her daughter's brown curls are tightly gripped in his hands and Katherine watches Sophie's hand open and close to try and stop the pain. Her child, her baby. She wants to leap off the sofa and scratch his eyes out, rip at his face.

'She didn't say anything,' says George, quietly.

'No one asked you to speak. And we all know she said something. Now, Sophie, listen to me,' he says. 'You're going to tell me what you said to her or I'm going to rip all of your pretty hair right out of your head.'

'I said I wanted chocolate cake,' says Sophie, her voice thick with tears and pain. Katherine knows she is lying and she is proud of her little girl. Never mind what she has always told them about telling the truth. The rules don't apply today. All the rules have already been broken.

But he believes her. 'Stupid kid,' he laughs and he lets go of her hair and shoves her back towards Katherine, who opens her arms and wraps them tightly around her daughter as she sobs. She feels George start patting Sophie on the back, desperate to help, to somehow make things better, and she reaches out and grabs him to her too.

'Just shut up,' he hisses.

Sophie gulps and swallows the last of her sobs. The room is beginning to smell. The air conditioner is old and doesn't work well in here, not well enough for this terrible heat, and Katherine and her children are sweating out their terror.

'They need something to eat,' she says, a plan forming in her mind. If they can all get to the kitchen, if they can get there quickly enough, then maybe they can get out of the back door. 'Please, let me take them and get them some food,' she says again because he hasn't said no, which she thinks means he is considering it.

He rubs at his face. They've only been in this room for hours but it feels like days.

'Fine, they can get some food,' he finally replies.

'Let me go with them,' she says, hoping that she has kept the eagerness out of her voice.

'Why don't you go alone and leave them here with me.' He grins as though he has made a considerate suggestion.

She takes a breath, wondering what would happen if she did run. His anger is for her, not them, but... he will hurt them to punish her. He will. She knows he will.

'No, no... George, you go, take Sophie, have some... some fruit before you eat anything else.'

George gets up. She catches his eye, stares and nods slightly at him. Will he know to just leave, to just open the back door and run? If George and Sophie are safe, then she can deal with this. She can stay here all day, all night. He can kill her. She doesn't care. She just needs her children to be safe.

George nods back and he takes his sister's hand.

'Oh, and George,' he says casually as they get to the door of the family room. Her son doesn't say anything but he stops dead-still. 'If you don't come back in five minutes, I will shoot your mum in the head.' He sounds so matter-of-fact. So cold. She cannot believe that this is who he really is. She doesn't want to believe it.

George casts a quick glance back at her and she nods her head again, hoping that he will disobey and leave, just leave, but from the way her little boy looks back at her, she knows he's made a decision. She drops her gaze and stares at her hands where she is twisting the simple gold band on her finger, twisting it round and round as though she could unscrew it from her very being.

'They love their mum, don't they?' he says, sneering, when they've left the room.

'You're torturing them. How could you do this to them? I understand to me. I get it – but them? Please, I'm asking you again to just let them go. I will listen to anything you have to say. Just let them go.'

'No,' he says shortly. 'No.'

'Why don't you just say what you want to say? I won't say anything. Just tell me what you want to say.' She tries to conceal the rage that is inside her as she speaks. Rage will not help. She wonders if she could rush at him right now, and if she did, would she get to him before he shot her, and if he shot her, would he shoot them too? She believes him to be capable of this, even though yesterday she would never have thought it possible. Before today she was a different person. Before today she thought that her love could save him; today she knows that for all these years she's been wasting her time.

'Stop doing that,' he says and she realises that she is still twisting the ring.

She can hear the children in the kitchen, packets being opened and something spilled on the floor. She closes her eyes and wishes they would just run but they won't. She is their world, their whole world. They don't know how to exist without her yet.

She picks up the stuffed monkey that Sophie carries everywhere with her when she's home. It started off a rich, soft brown but it's faded now, the face grey, one eye a little wonky where it has fallen off and she has sewn it back on, not quite in the right place.

'I don't think you deserve these children,' he says. 'Some women shouldn't be mothers. Some women are too selfish.'

'Some men shouldn't be fathers,' she says softly and then instantly curses her stupid words.

She glances over at the bookcase where her wedding photo stands. She and her new husband look impossibly happy. From the slight creasing of their eyes, it's obvious they were standing in the sun when the photo was taken. 'Let's turn around,' the photographer said when he noticed, and she and John laughed as he picked up her long train, helping her turn. It had looked beautiful going down the aisle of the church with the white lace roses on the end but was impractical for the reception. She put this picture on display even though she has better ones because of the way he is looking at her, because of the palpable feeling of love that exists in the image. Now, she looks away from it, feeling sympathy for her younger self, for everything she did not know then.

He is standing by the window that looks out onto the garden and the pool. Katherine can see it's shimmering in the sun, perfectly blue and inviting. It's too small for proper laps but she and the children would have spent the afternoon there, waiting for the oppressive heat to pass. He turns away from the window and looks at her and then down at the watch he has on his wrist, silver with a white face and an engraving on the back: *With all my love, Katherine.*

'I don't care about your opinion on fathers. I really don't care at all,' he says softly. 'They have two minutes left and then I will shoot you.'

She has no idea what to say to this, so she just keeps quiet, remembering her joy at finding out she was pregnant and the frisson of fear upon learning that it was twins. She had no idea how she would cope. The utter exhaustion of the early weeks is a surreal memory now, and what she mostly feels is joy that they have each other, that there are two people in the world who will forever be joined. Friendships break, marriages end, even sibling relationships and parent and child bonds can fail, but it must be different with twins. Even when they fight, there is something that she can see between them, some connection that she feels can never be broken. One whole wall of the family room is covered in framed photographs of the twins at every age from scrunched-faced newborns until now. Sophie loves to hear the story of their birth, of the night they arrived.

Katherine had woken from a deep sleep – unusual because she had barely slept in the last month of her pregnancy. She was huge and waddled when she walked, her knees and back struggling with the weight. The twins moved all night, kicking and shoving for space. The night they arrived she had opened her eyes in the dark and moved her hand next to her leg to feel the soaked sheets. She knew what it was but fear had paralysed her as she contemplated the possibility that it could be blood. 'John, John,' she said, hearing her voice catch in her throat as if she was in a bad dream, screaming for help. He sat up instantly. 'They're coming,' he said.

'I don't… I don't know,' she replied. He turned on the light and helped her sit up, throwing back the duvet so she could see that the liquid on the bed was clear.

'Right,' he said. Completely in charge, he helped her up and into the shower so she could clean up before they left for the hospital. The contractions only began when she was in a bed in her hospital room, and she knew it was because she had been afraid to begin until the doctors were close by. 'You were born as the sun rose and light filled the room, and the doctor said that summer babies were the cleverest babies of all.' Katherine always ends the story with these words.

Once upon a time John had sat with her and listened. Once he had enjoyed hearing the story as much as she enjoyed telling it.

'I will love and protect you forever,' he had whispered to them both as they lay cocooned in their clear bassinettes in their hospital room. She had been relieved to hear the words, to know that she and John were in this together. But now… now, her mind goes back to last night's argument with him.

'I'm not going to accept this behaviour, John, I'm just not.' She was walking around the kitchen, putting dishes away and then wiping the counter, scraping crumbs into her hands. She always cleaned like this when they argued, feeling the need to control something, anything.

'And what are you going to do for money without me? How are you going to take care of these kids?' He was leaning up against the sink, his arms folded, watching her, just watching her work.

'I'll figure it out.' She threw the crumbs in the garbage and dusted off her hands.

'You are so ready to toss me on the trash heap, Katherine, so ready to just get rid of me.'

She turned to look at him, reading the despair on his face. 'You're the one who wants to be with someone else.' Her anger rose at her own words and she picked up her cloth again, wiping down already clean surfaces.

'That's crap and you know it. Just let me explain – I can explain if you just stop talking, stop bloody cleaning and listen.' He slammed his hand on the countertop.

'I know what I read. There can't really be any other explanation.' Without another word she walked out of the kitchen, leaving him standing there with his explanation on his lips and no one to listen to what he had to say.

How has her life come to this? She cannot even begin to unravel the threads that have led her here to this day.

He is watching her closely now. 'What are you thinking?' he asks.

She shakes her head. Whatever she says now will be the wrong thing. She can sense that.

The children come back into the room; Sophie's face edged with chocolate. 'I made her eat a banana,' says George, and Katherine nods, swiping at tears that arrive because her little boy sounds, all of a sudden, decades older.

'You always do what Mum says, don't you, George?' he sneers at the child.

George doesn't reply, knowing even at five years old when to keep quiet.

He looks at George and gestures with the gun. 'I'll tell you what my father told me, Georgie boy, something someone needed to tell you one day, and maybe today's the day and maybe you'll listen because you'll always remember me saying it. If you get the chance to grow up and go out into the big, wide world… big if… but if you do, you need to remember: never trust a woman. Don't ever trust a woman.'

CHAPTER NINE

Four hours ago

Logan

Logan drums his hands on the steering wheel as he drives, debating what to do. Is he making more of this than he should be? He doesn't think so. He's been doing this job for a few months now and he's never had a feeling like this before. He stops debating. He'll swing by the house again, try to deliver the computer, just to see if the woman is okay.

He turns right instead of taking the left turn that would get him to his next delivery, shaking his head at his need to check on the woman. It's going to make the day run late. His beer is getting further and further away.

Another text on his phone makes him sigh. She's persistent all right.

You need to call me right now!!!!

This happens every few months. It's usually something to do with money. 'I can't pay the rent, I can't afford petrol for my car, I can't afford to eat.' The news of whatever latest disaster is delivered in a whiny voice, with much sniffing and many tears. The tears are for show and he knows that if he refuses her – and he does refuse her often – she'll just move on to the next one in the family. Good luck to them, as long as she leaves Maddy alone. It doesn't matter how far he pulls away, there is still a connection there and she knows it.

The first time she called him was a year after he'd moved out. Twelve months had gone by and he knows she hadn't thought about him at all. He was only nineteen and struggling, and even though sometimes – like when he had to sleep rough for a night or two – he thought about calling to see if he would be able to go home for a month or two before he got back on his feet, he stopped himself.

He was shocked the first time she called, almost frightened by the desperation in her voice. 'We'll all be out on the street if we can't make the rent, Logan.' He sent the money to help, money he had to borrow so that Maddy would still have a roof over her head.

'They took themselves off for a fancy meal,' Maddy told him two days later. 'She thought it was funny.' He knew the money was never going to help but he gave in sometimes, the cord not quite severed enough between them, her voice still triggering something in him.

Another message comes through.

Call me right now. It's about Maddy.

Logan groans. He'll have to call now. He has no choice. She's probably lying but he can't take the chance.

He turns down a side street and puts the van into park. He doesn't think the day can get any worse.

Before he rings her, he tries Maddy's mobile and gets her voicemail again.

He taps her number, wishing that he didn't have it and that she didn't have his, but there's nothing he can do about it.

'Logan,' she says when she answers her phone.

'Carmella,' he replies.

'You could call me Mother or Mum, you know.'

'Yeah, well, let's not go down that road again, shall we.' His hands grip the steering wheel and he's glad he's pulled over. There is no way he should resume driving until this conversation is done. 'What about Maddy?'

'Aren't you going to ask me how I am? How your dad is? You know he's not been well and I've had to put up with a lot. You could come over and help. That's what a proper son would do. But then you've always had a way of cutting everyone out of your life, haven't you, Logan?'

Logan grinds his teeth, stays silent.

'Everyone is willing to let the past stay where it is, Logan, everyone except you – and you've encouraged Maddy to think the same way. Your dad is right about you, you're terribly ungrateful.'

Logan watches his knuckles turn white and feels his jaw spasm because of how hard he is clenching it. 'What about Maddy?' he asks slowly, menace in his voice.

She sighs. 'Well, I did warn her about that boy, but there you go, she wouldn't listen. I mean she barely speaks to me as it is but I do try with her, Logan, just like I try with you, but the two of you seem to have your own way of remembering your childhood and no regard for everything that was done for you. Your father and I did our best with you kids, but nothing was ever good enough.'

He hears his father's voice even though he hasn't exchanged a word with the man in years. 'Who would want to waste their time with you? You're ugly enough to scare away even an animal. No one likes someone who never smiles. What's your problem?' His parents did not do their best – nowhere near it.

He drops his head onto the steering wheel, his temples throbbing. He knows that he can't react to her, can't give her an opening, can't give an inch because that results in him screaming and her screaming. It's not like she's ever going to acknowledge what kind of a mother she was.

'I'm going to hang up now,' he says instead.

'Fine, fine,' she says, aggrieved that he won't get into an argument. He knows that she thrives on the drama. 'Someone beat her up. They have no idea who but I told the constable who called me I thought it could be that boy. He just beat her up and left her for dead. She's in the hospital and I'm trying to get on a flight down to Melbourne to be with her.'

'What?' asks Logan stupidly.

'Do I need to explain it again?'

'No… no. How badly hurt is she? Will she be okay? Which hospital? When did it happen?' He fires questions at her as his gut churns. *I'll kill him, I'll kill him, I'll kill him.*

'The doctors are hopeful she'll pull through, and… It was… Um… a few days ago maybe,' says his mother, sounding bored.

'Days ago, and you only called me now?' he practically hisses into the phone.

'Yeah, well… I've been… I've called you now, haven't I?'

Irritation runs through his veins at her wounded tone. It's never her fault. She's always *only doing her best.* 'What hospital is she at? Tell me so I can call and… I need to get on a plane.'

'Footscray Hospital.'

'Have they arrested him?' he barks.

'They can't find him.'

'What?'

'They can't find him. Obviously, they're looking for him – the police, I mean.'

'How do they know it was him?'

'Well, I mean, they don't know absolutely but she's in hospital and he's gone and the neighbours said they heard fighting and you know… I told them I thought it was him. It's always the boyfriend or the husband, isn't it?'

'I can't believe this,' he murmurs because he can't. Patrick is a loser, but in the couple of times Logan has met him, he has never gotten a violent vibe off him. He's tall and skinny and he seemed intimidated by Logan, which was how Logan liked it.

'Okay, I'm tired of this conversation now. I called you because I know she would want me to. But the thing is that I need some money to get down to Melbourne. She would want me there. I'm her mother after all.'

Logan feels a scream rise up inside him. He brings a clenched fist to his mouth and bites down on a finger, breaking the skin and drawing blood just so that he doesn't say, 'No, she wouldn't want you there. She hates you because you were a useless mother. Your only job was to protect your children and you failed.'

'How did they know to call you?' he asks, his voice strangled with fury.

'Unlike you, she has me in her phone as "Mum". I guess they thought that would be the best person.' There is a pathetic hint of smugness in her tone as though having the title means anything at all beyond her biological contribution.

Logan takes a deep breath.

'About the money…' she says, and he hangs up the phone, hoping that she's still speaking to dead air.

He sits quietly for a moment, breathing in and out, trying to formulate a plan. Wherever he was going and whatever he was going to do, nothing matters now except getting to Maddy. He needs to get to Melbourne.

'Call Debbie,' he says aloud, because she will know what to do first.

'Hey babes,' she answers, and he explains. 'Oh,' she says, 'poor girl. Poor, poor girl. We knew that Patrick was no good.'

'Yeah, and now I have to get down there. I have to take the parcels back to the depot and Mack is going to be pissed.'

'You leave Mack to me. Now wait a moment…' He hears the sound of her tapping on her computer. 'The planes are full, babes. The earliest I can get you on one is tonight at eight.'

'I need to get there now.' He pushes at each one of his fingers, taking some comfort in the loud cracking sound his knuckles make. He cannot keep still.

'Okay, just wait. You do the next delivery and give me a few minutes. I can call Terri, who I know from school. She's a nurse there. Just give me a few minutes. There's no point in running off to the airport to just sit there for hours going mad.'

'Okay,' he agrees, relieved that Debbie knows what to do, as she always does.

He starts driving, breathing deeply to calm himself, seeing his little sister with her wide smile, her delicate hands that seem to dance in the air when she's explaining something that excites her. If he finds Patrick, he will kill him. He knows that. He really hopes the police find him first. Nightmarish scenarios run through his head, making him sweat despite the air conditioning. He takes two wrong turns.

'Concentrate,' he admonishes himself.

His phone rings, and he looks at the screen on his dashboard, hoping it's Debbie, but it's Mack. Mack checks up on him at least twice a day. Logan knows that he will finally have earned his brother-in-law's trust when the phone calls stop. He takes a deep breath and answers the call.

'Hey Mack.'

He opens his mouth to tell his brother-in-law about Maddy but before he can say anything Mack starts talking.

'So, bit of a weird one. You know those emails that we usually send out after a parcel has been delivered, the ones that ask how our service was?'

'Yes,' says Logan warily.

'Yeah, well, something went wrong with the computer system and the emails went out before deliveries had been logged as done…'

'Mack, why have you called?' Logan cannot hide his frustration, desperate to hear from Debbie.

There is a beat of silence at his abruptness.

'Anyway,' Mack continues, 'that's all sorted but one woman – um, Katherine West – was on your list for early this morning and she clicked extremely dissatisfied on the survey. Now I can see that the parcel hasn't been delivered and I'm assuming that – based on the store it's from – it's a computer, so what I'm wondering, Logan, is… where is that computer?'

Mack's tone is polite, just enquiring. Logan knows that anyone listening would believe that he was just trying to work out where things had gone wrong. But Logan knows that he is being accused of theft. It's not the first time it's happened, and he knows it won't be the last. The matter is always cleared up quickly and his brother-in-law will say something like, 'I knew there was an explanation,' but Logan knows that Mack is waiting for the moment that there isn't an explanation, that things aren't cleared up quickly.

He is quiet for a moment as he gathers his thoughts and forcefully quashes any anger that he knows is rising up inside him.

'I tried to deliver the computer this morning but she wouldn't open the door. I told her it needed to be signed for but she still wouldn't open the door. I told her I'd drop it at her nearest post office at the end of the day. It's still in the van – just a minute and I'll grab a picture for you.'

'Oh,' says Mack, 'no, that's not necessary…'

But Logan knows it is. He gets out of his van and slides open the side door, finding the parcel and snapping a picture so the name of the woman is clear. He sends it off to Mack. 'Did you get it?'

'Yeah, yeah… okay, strange then. She was probably upset that she didn't get it today.'

'Well, I'm hardly likely to force my way into her house, am I, Mack?' says Logan and he tries, he really tries, to keep any menace out of his voice.

Mack clears his throat. 'No, of course not. She may have just hit the wrong button. I'll send her the survey again and maybe give her a call in a couple of days. I'm sure it was a mistake.'

'Yep, sure it was. I'll get on with my day then,' says Logan, any thought of trying to explain about Maddy disappearing, and he hangs up.

He has no idea what to do with himself as he waits for Debbie's call. He was heading for Katherine West's house but from the sound of the survey, she's probably fine and just pissed off that he wouldn't leave the computer. He looks at his delivery list. What else can he do? What else is he supposed to do? He turns left and slaps the steering wheel as he thinks about Patrick's face and his scraggly beard.

He thought the day couldn't get any worse, but sometimes it feels like the whole universe is gunning for him. All he wanted was an ordinary day and a cold beer at the end with his wife. He allows the fury to reveal itself as he drives. He's alone in his van after all. He slaps at the steering wheel a couple more times, the hard plastic stinging his palm and the slight pain tracing its way up his arm, and he mumbles to himself, incoherent vile thoughts that he would never say in front of anyone else, that he has trained himself to never say in front of anyone else. He pictures his father, a smile on his face that is more a sneer: 'You'll end up in prison, boy, mark my words.' His first night in prison had been a torment of noise and fear and his father's face, his father's words.

'A good parent, a parent worthy of a child, wants success for that child,' Aaron told him. 'You didn't get to have that support but you can still find success in your life after this.'

Logan has to keep reminding himself of those words, repeating them when he is furious with the world and himself. He thinks about Maddy and the damage that was done to her. He tries not to allow his imagination to bruise and bloody her face and body. It makes him sick to think of her hurt, to think of her alone in a hospital bed without him there to hold her hand.

He has loved her from the moment she came home from the hospital with their disinterested mother, who cracked open her first beer when Maddy was three days old, sighing, 'Been waiting for that.'

Maddy wouldn't have chosen a man who would hurt her if she hadn't been raised by parents who'd done the same. It's as simple as that.

In his van, Logan opens his mouth and roars his frustration at what his life is, at what he has done to himself and at how difficult every day is because of choices he made, not knowing any better. He roars so loud that his throat scratches, but when he's done, a calm settles over him.

He arrives at his next delivery, unsure as to how he has made it to the right address, and gets out of the van. While he is waiting to be allowed into the block of units he wonders if the woman, if Katherine West, just hit the wrong button on the survey. Was she angry about him not leaving the computer or was it something else? Was she trying, in some way, to make sure that she got a call or a text that she could respond to? Logan shakes his head as he is buzzed in, sure that he's turning this whole thing into something it's not. But he can't help feeling that Katherine West was trying to get a message to someone. In a strange and odd way, she was attempting to alert someone that something was wrong. He is almost sure of it. The feeling that the woman is in danger will not go away, even with everything else going on in his mind.

The door to the apartment he is delivering to is standing open, a woman in a sari smiling in anticipation.

'My spices,' she says, 'what perfect timing, I've just run out.'

Logan smiles and hands over the box, and as he does, he catches the quick glance she gives his hands and face. He feels himself flush, more from embarrassment than from the heat.

'What intricate work,' says the woman softly, looking at his hand where a scorpion sits – its body perfectly drawn so that every part of its skeleton is visible, its tail up, ready to strike. The woman smiles and thanks him for the delivery as she closes the door. Her voice was light and calming, her tone kind, and he feels some of his anger seep out of him. *Maddy will be okay. Please let Maddy be okay. Hang in there, Maddy, I'm coming.*

He heads back out to the van, and his phone lights up with Debbie's name.

'Okay, so I spoke to Terri,' she says when he answers, 'she works in emergency. Maddy is in intensive care.'

'Oh God,' he says, nausea washing over him.

'Terri says she's been put in an induced coma to allow her body to rest and heal. There's some swelling on her brain and they're waiting for that to go down. I've booked you a flight for tonight at eight. They won't know more about her condition until tomorrow morning. I'm trying to find you a hotel near the hospital.'

'Thanks, babe, thanks,' he says and he's a little ashamed of the tears that fall. His sister, his baby sister. *I'll kill him. I'll kill him.*

'Come home,' says Debbie.

Logan sees himself pacing up and down the living room of their small flat, waiting for the hours to pass. 'No, I'll finish up here. I won't be much longer and I need something to take my mind off it. Can you call them every hour, your friend… Terri, can you call Terri every hour and get me an update?'

'Absolutely. Try to stay calm. She's getting the best care. There isn't anything you can do.'

'I love you,' says Logan, an uncharacteristic statement. It makes him feel weird to say the words.

'Ah babes, I love you too, and it's going to be fine. She'll recover. Just get through your day and I'll pack for you.'

After Logan hangs up, he starts planning how to get Maddy back to Sydney so he and Debbie can take care of her. Looking at a future where she's okay focuses him, and though he hears a text on his phone again, he doesn't look at it until he's at the next delivery.

You're next.

Logan doesn't recognise the number. The words are shocking in their simplicity. Next for what? Is the text meant for him? Is it a mistake?

He stares down at the two words. There are a lot of people in his past who are capable of sending a threatening text. People he stole from, people he met in prison, even people he once considered friends like Nick, who he thinks is still in prison. He hasn't spoken to Nick since that fateful night, refused to see him even when he tried to visit him in prison before Nick himself was caught and jailed for his crimes.

An unexpected laugh bubbles up inside Logan. He cannot believe that this is somehow still the same day. He finds himself laughing out loud as though someone has told him the greatest joke he's ever heard. It's only when he realises that his cheeks are wet that he stops and takes a deep breath.

What am I next for? He studies the text, trying and failing to recognise the number.

Maddy is in a hospital bed and now someone says he's next. That can't just be a coincidence. Is it a text from Patrick? Surely not. He's in Melbourne, far away from here. But maybe Patrick has nothing to do with what happened to his sister. Faces and names flash through his mind. Everyone he has ever associated with knows he has a little sister who he loves. Even if Nick is still in prison, he knows everything about Logan's life and maybe he hasn't taken kindly to being ignored for the last few years. Maybe he's talked about the things they did more than he should have. Nick knows people everywhere. The list of possibilities gets longer the more Logan thinks about it, his heart racing with all the things he's done wrong.

What if this is payback? He thinks he's left the past behind him but what if someone he stole from is making sure he understands his mistake? Hurting someone he loves would be the best possible choice. Whoever hurt his sister would know that the first thing he would do would be to get on a plane and go and see her. Hurting her would lure him down there to face whoever is waiting for him. 'Oh God,' he whispers, feeling his stomach churn, his forehead bead with sweat. Maddy has been hurt because of something he's done.

Tonight, he'll get to Melbourne and his past will be waiting for him.

He slaps at the steering wheel again, fury rising inside him as all he can think is, *I'll kill him, I'll kill him.* He just isn't sure who exactly he is thinking about.

CHAPTER TEN
Gladys

'I'll tell you what they should do,' says Lou, pointing at the television set, where a variety programme is on. 'They should add a dog performing tricks to this.'

'I'm sure one of the contestants did have a dog a few weeks back,' says Gladys, 'they voted him out.' She doesn't take her eyes from the television even though she's not really watching. Occasionally she glances out of the large bay window where she and Lou have their small round breakfast table and two chairs. Sunshine streams in, colouring the timber table orange, and even though she doesn't want to be out in the heat, the sharp green of the grass against the bright blue of the sky begs to be experienced.

'No one appreciates true entertainment anymore.'

Gladys hates the variety programme but Lou refuses to watch anything else, despite every streaming platform available to them. He doesn't seem to be able to concentrate on a movie long enough to keep the characters straight, and he nods off during series, waking only to get angry at her for continuing to watch without him. She is only sitting with him in the cool living room because he has been calling for her all morning. He seems to need her right next to him today. She thinks it may be because his routine with Peter has been interrupted. He prefers Peter to help him bathe and shave and Gladys has not made a good job of it. There are two cuts on his chin from the razor.

'Don't you think?' he asks, and she realises that she hasn't replied to him.

'Probably not,' she agrees. 'It's time for your medication, Lou. Do you want to have a snack with it?'

'I wouldn't say no to a nice peach. Do we have any peaches?'

'We do,' says Gladys, and she hears the small sigh from Lou. He wanted there to be no peaches so that he could protest and fuss. Before he can say anything else, she leaves the living room and goes to the kitchen, where she selects and washes a peach, cutting it up into pieces that are easy for Lou to eat but big enough for his trembling hands to pick up. She pops a piece into her mouth, savouring the tangy sweet taste that always feels like summer in a mouthful. Gladys feels the peach stick in her throat at the idea that there is nothing to look forward to except the loss of Lou. *Stop being silly*, she admonishes herself.

She takes the peach back to Lou and hands him his pills, watches in silence as he swallows them like a child.

'Where are you going now?' he asks when she leaves again.

'The tumble dryer is done. I'm just going to take the linen upstairs and put it away.'

'You never sit still for a second,' he says irritably.

Gladys bites down on her harsh words. 'I'll only be a minute,' she says.

Once the linen is safely and neatly put away, she goes into the guest bedroom to see if Katherine has finally opened the blinds in the children's rooms but they remain closed, the house silent and glowering in the hot morning.

She studies them for a minute, wondering why this is bothering her so much. She can think of a hundred reasons why she should not even be thinking about this but something keeps niggling at her and she has no idea what. What did Sophie mean by something strange going on in the house? Has the child also felt the tension between her parents?

Gladys rubs at a spot on the window. Are the Wests planning to divorce?

Does Katherine want the divorce or does John? Or both of them? She hopes they don't do it, if only for the sake of the children. Katherine would put the twins' needs first. Gladys knows that she's a very passionate and loving mother. She'd had the help of her own mother until the middle of last year, when Janet lost her life to a heart attack. Katherine was devastated. Perhaps losing her mother has made her question everything in her life. Losing a loved one can make a person look at everything differently. Even the understanding that Lou will not be around for many more years has changed the way Gladys approaches her own life. Nothing seems to interest her that much anymore.

One of the blinds twitches a little and, to her amazement, as she watches, two small hands appear holding a white piece of paper. There is something written on the paper in thick blue marker, but Gladys can't see what it says. She needs her glasses for everything but she left them by the television set. She looks frantically around the guest room and is overjoyed to remember that Lou keeps his birdwatching binoculars in the guest room cupboard. 'Don't go away, don't go away,' she repeats as she frantically untangles the strap and puts the binoculars against her eyes, adjusting the lenses until she can see what's written on the paper in shaky letters.

Halp Us

Help us. It says help us in a child's handwriting. A chill goes through Gladys as she pulls her phone out of her pocket – meaning to take a picture to show Lou so he believes something is going on – but the little hands with the sign disappear abruptly and the blinds remain closed.

Gladys waits, her heart thudding in her chest, but there is no more movement from the house, and the longer she stares at the closed blinds, the more she questions what just happened.

She goes back downstairs on shaky legs. 'You won't believe what I've just seen,' she says to Lou.

'The linen cupboard, I imagine,' says Lou, a spark of his old humour flaring up.

'No, I'm being serious, Lou. I was in the spare bedroom checking if the blinds were open in Katherine's house—'

He frowns and interrupts her. 'What is your obsession with her blinds? You sound a bit mad, Gladys. She's keeping them closed to keep out the heat, it's a simple thing. Why won't you leave it alone?'

'Now you listen to me, Lou Philips, stop interrupting me! You're being very rude,' says Gladys, her voice sharp and high.

Lou's shoulders bow a little and he sinks further into his chair. He hates it when she shouts at him. 'Sorry, old girl,' he mumbles, an unusual thing for him to say, and Gladys feels a familiar tap of guilt on her shoulder. He doesn't mean to be like he is.

She goes over to sit next to him in her own leather chair. 'It's fine, love, but I wanted to tell you what I saw, so let me explain.'

'All right, then.' He gives her his full attention, still contrite about yelling at her.

'One of the children held up a sign in the window, a hand-written sign, and it said, "Help us." I mean "help" was spelled incorrectly but it definitely said, "Help us."' She takes out her phone, wishing she had a picture, and then shoves it back into her pocket, stands up and sits down again, the image of the sign appearing before her. Did she see what she thinks she saw?

'That's a bit odd,' he concedes.

'I know,' says Gladys, relieved that he believes her even as she questions herself. 'I told you something odd was going on over there. I think I should march over and demand Katherine open the door, or maybe I should just call the police.'

'Listen, love,' says Lou kindly, 'I know that it's hard being here with me all day, especially when you would rather be out. I know that but I think that you might need to take a little walk or something. I'll be fine on my own for a bit.'

Irritation flares in Gladys at being dismissed as simply imagining things because she's cooped up in the house. She thought he was on her side in this now. She struggles for a moderate tone, knowing that he is attempting kindness. 'Something is happening in that house. I just know it.' Gladys twists her hands together, anxiety gnawing at her. Yesterday –the thing she didn't tell Lou about – comes back to her. But it's obviously nothing to do with what's happening at Katherine's and she sees no reason to worry Lou when there is little he can do about it.

'Maybe she and John had a big fight and they're all just having a day to calm down. That might be why the kids are unsettled and making a game out of it. Remember when you thought I was flirting with the new secretary at work?'

'That was years ago, Lou.' She sighs and rubs at her forehead where she can feel a headache coming on.

'Yes, but we fought all night and then the next day we both just took the day off and sorted ourselves out a bit. Sometimes a couple needs space to sort themselves out. The children may just be playing. If you call the police, I don't think Katherine and John will appreciate it. No one in the neighbourhood ever does when you get involved.'

'But John is out, isn't he? You heard him leave this morning, you said.'

'Did I say that?' asks Lou, looking confused.

'I should call Katherine…'

'You're just interfering. People will start to think you're crazy.'

'Lou, John left early this morning, just screeched off, making enough noise to wake you, that's what you said before. Maybe they had a big fight. Maybe he… maybe he hit her or something…

I don't know. Maybe she needs help and that's why the children made the sign. Surely you can see that something may be wrong?'

She pulls her mobile phone out of the front pocket of her apron, spilling a couple of tissues onto the floor, which she then has to bend down to retrieve.

'Well, just call Katherine, then.'

Gladys is quiet.

'I said just call her, then,' repeats Lou.

'Yes, well, I have done,' she admits, 'four times already and she hasn't answered.' She looks down at her phone, biting her lip. *What is the right thing to do?*

Lou's eyes widen. 'You're going to get arrested for harassment, Gladys. Imagine you in jail! What will I do then?' He pulls at the fabric of his shirt and shakes his head as he speaks. 'What will I do?' he moans again.

She moves quickly to reassure him, resting a hand gently on his fidgeting fingers.

'That's not possible, Lou,' she comforts him. 'I won't call Katherine again. I'll just call John at work quickly and then I can put this whole thing out of my mind. It will only take a minute. I'll just ask after the children and… Oh look, I don't know, I'll make something up. I'll call him at work.'

'How come you have John's work number?'

'I don't have it, but I know he works at Barker and Partners, don't I? Katherine gave me a whole collection of notebooks from his company because she said they were changing their logo. I'm going to call, and if he sounds even a little cagey on the phone, then I'll march back over there and see what's happening.' She doesn't look at him as she speaks, but down at her phone instead. She's not going to give him a chance to talk her out of this.

Lou folds his arms and waits.

Gladys peers at her phone through her glasses, slowly typing the name of John's company into Google. 'Ha,' she says triumphantly when she finds it and presses on the number on the webpage entry. Katherine was very proud when she told her that John had made partner in his firm. It's a big company with over a hundred employees. Gladys knows because she looked it up.

'Yes, hello,' she says to the woman with a very competent voice who answers. Gladys clears her throat. 'I'm hoping to speak to Jonathon West.'

'May I ask who's calling and what it's in reference to?' says the woman.

Gladys contemplates the truth but decides that a quick lie would probably get her further. 'I'm his next-door neighbour and I think that there is a pipe leaking in his backyard. I can't get hold of his wife and I'm worried that it's going to flood the house.' Gladys crosses her fingers. The truth would have sounded very strange. The convenient lie just popped out. She did once have to phone Katherine because they had left the hose on for hours while they filled the swimming pool, and the water level just kept rising. Gladys had looked out of her bedroom window and seen that it was going to overflow. 'Thanks goodness you called,' Katherine told her afterwards.

'Just a moment, I'll see if he's available.'

Gladys looks over at Lou and he nods his head. He's interested now as well. They both need to know that Katherine is okay. She feels sort of motherly towards the young women in the neighbourhood. Katherine's mother is no longer here to protect her daughter, and sometimes younger women need the help of an older and perhaps wiser woman.

'I'm sorry, Mr West didn't come into work this morning,' says the woman, returning to the call.

'Oh, are you sure he's not just in a meeting? I'm happy to leave a message.'

'I'm afraid not. As I said, he didn't come in today at all.'

'Well, where is he then?'

The woman hesitates. 'His assistant did not give me that information,' she says.

'Oh, perhaps I'll call him directly. Can I get his mobile number?'

'Didn't you say you were his neighbour?'

'Yes.'

'Then don't you have his mobile number?'

'I ah… no.'

'I'm afraid I cannot give out personal numbers for staff. Thank you,' says the voice, and she efficiently hangs up.

Gladys turns to Lou and says, 'If he didn't go to work today, then where is he?'

'At home, maybe,' suggests Lou.

'But he left this morning, you said so. If he'd come home again, we would have heard, and why would he have come home again in the middle of the day?'

Her husband shrugs his shoulders. 'He did leave very quickly and he made a lot of noise and I thought… I thought…'

'You thought what?' asks Gladys, trying to hide her impatience at his trailing off in the middle of a sentence.

'Heavens, Gladys, I've just remembered he came back. He did, he came back about ten minutes later and I thought, "What's he doing home again?" I heard the garage door go up. I heard his car pull into the driveway. He came back, Gladys, I just forgot.'

'Oh, Lou,' she says gently, 'why didn't you say so?'

'I forgot, love, just forgot until right now. I mean it's not something we usually pay attention to, is it? I'm sorry.' He is apologising again and she doesn't like to hear it. Strangely, she prefers it when he's gruff. It means he's feeling more like his old self.

She sighs. 'It's not your fault, it's just… things feel so strange today.' She frowns, crossing her arms. 'So how long did he stay after he came back? Is he still there?'

Lou turns to stare at her, the look on his face telling her he's bewildered by her question.

'I don't know,' he says, 'I must have drifted off again.' He turns back to the television. 'I'm sure it's nothing, love. We're making a mountain out of a… molehill, that's it. It's nothing. They're just having a day at home.'

'I really don't think so,' says Gladys, standing up. She goes to the window, looks out onto the quiet street where nothing moves in the heat. Even the lorikeets have found some place out of the sun to sleep away the day.

She looks at her phone. Does one call the police because they are worried about a neighbour simply because her husband is not at work and the children haven't gone to school?

Lou watches her quietly. 'Look, maybe they had a tiff and they're sorting it out now. Maybe she decided to keep the kids home from school because of the heat. Any number of things could have happened. I say we watch one of those crime series you like, the one with the doctor, you know. What about that, old girl?'

Gladys turns to stare at the television, where a new kind of mattress is being advertised. Lou is right. No one ever appreciates a visit from the police. But that's what they're there for, to maintain law and order. It's not as if she calls them that often. She didn't call them after the little incident yesterday. She wanted to, but she didn't.

A news break comes on and the story of the young woman who was attacked in Melbourne is the headline. 'The twenty-five-year-old woman assaulted two days ago is in an induced coma in Melbourne's Footscray Hospital. Neighbours report hearing arguing in the days prior to the assault.'

Do you hear that? she thinks. *They heard them arguing and did nothing and now look at that poor girl, look what's happened to her. People are so quick to recommend you keep your nose out of their business but what if they need help? What if they really need help?* She doesn't say any of this to Lou because there's no point. She tunes back into what the dark-haired reporter on the television is saying.

'Police are appealing to the public to help identify and locate this man, last seen leaving the apartment on the night of the assault.'

A grainy image of a young man in a red baseball cap is shown leaving the building on the CCTV.

'That could be anyone,' says Lou.

'Yes,' agrees Gladys, although there is something about him that looks vaguely familiar. She has no idea why.

A stern-looking policeman appears on the television, his hat shading his eyes from the sun. 'All we are asking for is help in locating this individual. We can neither confirm nor deny his involvement in the assault of the young lady. We are hoping he will come forward himself to assist police with their enquiries.'

'Good thing he's not here in Sydney,' says Lou.

'Yes,' agrees Gladys, 'a very good thing. That poor girl.'

It's strange that the man on the television seems familiar. She shakes her head. Maybe the heat is getting to her despite the air conditioning. As the news changes to another story, the image of the man on the television lingers. Just like the problem of Katherine's silent house and what on earth she should do about it.

CHAPTER ELEVEN

I was surprised by how easy it was to get a gun. An illegal one. A legal gun requires far too much paperwork and you need to use it for hunting or you have to be a member of a gun club, or a whole lot of other things that I would never have been able to lie about. I never imagined that I would know people involved in a world where illegal guns could be procured. It came up in conversation one night at a bar. 'If I could, I would just shoot him in the head,' my friend Derrick said, talking about his boss after a bad day at work. 'I would,' he muttered, 'I really would kill him.'

'Where would you get a gun?' I asked. I had a smile on my face but I was listening for the answer. I wanted to know. I really wanted to know.

'Well,' he began, 'I know this guy who knows someone...'

I don't know what Derrick would say if he knew that I used that information to actually get a gun, nor do I know what he would say about what I'm doing now. He and I stopped talking a while ago. 'You've changed,' he told me, which was code for, 'You bore me now.' I didn't care then. I preferred being home. Home sweet home. Funny how quickly that changes.

Yesterday I knocked on a door in Kings Cross. It was in a nice building, and on my way in a man taking his dog out for a walk greeted me like I had every right to be there. I assume he has no idea what is going on in his building. I knocked on the door, paid my money and left with something that can end lives. The man who handed me the gun barely even looked at me. He could have been handing me a cup of coffee.

But lives end every day and people just go on living. That's what I felt when she told me we were done – that my life was over. It felt like a death.

My life was supposed to be different to my father's life. I was not going to follow in his footsteps and end up on a sofa with a drink in my hand. It has to be different. The idea that our relationship is over is not something I can accept. I didn't accept it. I don't accept it but I can't see a way back to what I had. Not anymore.

The gun is heavy in my hand, the metal cool against my warm skin, and it is the very essence of fear itself. I believe if I didn't have it, she would have tried to get away already. She would have sent her two little angels out of the house without question. But the gun changes things. She doesn't know how quickly I could use it to hurt, to wound, to kill.

They are all watching my every move.

I can see her thinking, plotting. She has tried reasoning with me, begging me, appealing to my humanity, but she won't get through. It's too late for that. I had a plan for my life and, after everything I went through, I deserved to have it work out the way I wanted it to. I was in love – whatever that is. It felt like love. She was in love too once, but now she claims she's not and it's not fair.

My father was right about some things. He was right about women and control.

But I'm not going to be controlled, and if I cannot have the life I wanted, then no one gets to have a life. I check myself for feelings about this thought but there's nothing. I could be reading a newspaper article that has nothing to do with me or looking at a row of numbers. I have taken my grief and anger and locked them away. It's better this way.

'Can they get their iPads?' she asks, so politely, so carefully that I acquiesce. I'm being generous and kind.

You are generous and kind to those you love. I think she would say she has treated me kindly, that she's been generous with me. I used to see her love for me in her eyes. I should have taken note of when that changed. I know now that when someone stops loving you, it doesn't happen quickly. It's a pulling away, a distancing, a creating of space between you and them, and then one day you realise that the love of your life no longer thinks you're the love of her life.

'The love of my life,' I mutter.

'What?' she asks but I don't repeat myself. I take myself back to an earlier time, a better time.

I met her on a cool autumn day when the wind whistled through the city. I was walking to work, my head down, my eyes streaming from the gale, and I bumped into her, just like that.

'Oh, sorry,' I said and I took a step back.

'It's all right,' she smiled, 'no need to cry.'

'Oh, I'm not, the wind... it's...' I stuttered because she was so pretty and I wanted to touch her brown hair where the weak autumn sun was catching thin streaks of gold. She laughed at me then because I hadn't seen the joke. And then I laughed with her.

'Have coffee with me and I'll feel better,' I said, and she said yes. I couldn't quite believe she'd agreed. The coffee shop was right there and there was a table inside, out of the wind. The air tasted of sugar and the coffee machine roared and clanked. We sat opposite each other for a few moments after ordering our drinks, just looking at each other, smiling as we became aware that the attraction was mutual.

'I should get back to work,' she said.

'Where do you work?' I asked, but she shook her head. She wasn't ready to tell me yet and I understood. You never know what's going on in a stranger's head. She's known me for a long time now, but she still has no idea – or at least she had no real idea. She knows now.

After that first half-date, I remember walking out of the coffee shop and looking up at the sky and sending a silent prayer of thanks because it felt like this was what I had been waiting for through all the painful years of my life. Here, finally, was the reward I deserved. I was certain she would be different to every other woman I had ever known. Absolutely certain and, of course, completely wrong.

And so here I am and the gun seems to be getting heavier as the hours pass. I am becoming a little unsure about my plan but I can't do anything about that now.

'Be like a shark, son,' my father told me. 'Never stop moving forward or you die.'

He was really good at giving idiomatic advice. Pretty crap at listening to it.

After my father lost his job when I was fifteen years old, he used the time available during the day to drink and hate my mother – and, by extension, me.

That sounds simple and it seems like it would have had a simple solution. I could have moved back in with her, but he was a drowning man and every time he did something that made me threaten to leave, he would hold up his hands and cling to me as he cried about how badly his life had turned out.

By then I had been living with him for over a year and I didn't want to go back to rules and regulations. I didn't tell her the extent of what was happening with my father. 'She will love the fact that I've lost my job. It will make her so happy to see me suffer,' he told me, his green eyes droopy with fatigue and alcohol, his hair greasy because there was no reason to shower if he didn't have work.

'I won't tell her.'

'You're a good kid. I'll get back on my feet again soon.' He was positive about getting a job after his fourth beer. Not so positive after his seventh. He lost the job because the manager of an appliance store needs to be able to account for missing stock. And because a beautiful woman is always worthy of an expensive gift. I only put those things together later. He could have bluffed his way into a new job but he turned up to a few too many interviews slightly hungover because,

'Your bitch of a mother has sapped my confidence. If it weren't for her, I would have had my own shop.'

He aged as I watched him, day by day and week by week, only happy when he had enough beers in him to point out all the things my mother had done to screw up his life.

'And she wouldn't have another kid.'

'And she hated cooking.'

'And she was just lazy and didn't want to get a proper job.'

'And, and, and.' He never ran out of complaints about her.

I could see, on some level, that he was blaming her for his mistakes, but then I would go visit her and she would say, 'You don't want to turn out like your father. You need to study to get somewhere in life. I want you to have choices. You need to stop hanging out with those boys, they're not good people. Maybe you should get a haircut, perhaps you should join a gym…' and on and on. I didn't care if what she was saying was right or not. Telling someone else how to live their life is never right, and I imagined that once I found a woman who I could be with, she would not be that kind of woman. Children are not chess pieces, but back and forth I went between them, until that wasn't possible anymore.

Now, as I tear myself away from the past forever boomeranging in my head, I realise that the kids have been gone for a while, longer than they should have been. She is quiet on the sofa, watching me.

'They're taking a long time,' I say to her.

'Oh, you know… they put the iPads down and forget where they are.' She swallows quickly, swallowing down the truth. They are not just looking for their iPads.

'They're not stupid.'

'Of course not, they're just looking for their iPads and maybe… I don't know, going to the toilet. They're just little.'

Her eyes dart to the door of the family room and I know that something else is going on up there. They ran up the carpeted stairs *together but they're quiet now and they should only have been gone a few minutes.*

'I might just go and see what's happening,' I say.

'No, please, they'll be back in a minute. You don't have to.'

'I know I don't have to,' I laugh, 'I want to.'

CHAPTER TWELVE

Katherine

She sits on the sofa, cradling Sophie's stuffed monkey. 'Stay here,' he warned her, and then slowly, horrifyingly, he followed them up there. She stands up and sits down again quickly. He told her to stay.

She is trying to think of a prayer, any prayer beyond the words 'please God'. She wants to say something different but her mind is incapable of forming proper thoughts right now. She closes her eyes so she can hear better but only silence wafts down from the children's bedrooms.

He has taken the gun with him. She could, theoretically, run now. She could get up and race to the front door and outside. Theoretically – but as if she would leave the children, as if it would even be possible. And he knows this.

She looks over to the window that faces out onto the garden. If it were closer to the street, she could open it and call for help, but all the houses in this road have large gardens and thick walls. And it would only anger him further if he heard her.

Glancing at the shelves above the television, she studies the rolls of wrapping paper, waiting to be used. The twins will be six years old in three days. She drops her head into her hands. They have a party planned for Sunday afternoon. They have hired a jumping castle for the garden. Her pantry is filled with party bags and last night she wrapped the first of the presents she had bought them. She has possibly gone overboard this year because as she was shopping for them a few weeks back, she thought, *What if John and I are no longer together next year?* A stray thought that shocked as it appeared. This is not a space she expected to be in, not now. She believed she had chosen John so carefully, been so sure. This shouldn't have happened.

But by last night she was certain that she was headed for a divorce, that it was only a matter of time, and John knew it as well. 'You can't do this,' he'd said to her a week ago, when she first suggested that they take some time apart. 'It's starting to affect the children,' she'd said. 'We need to just give this marriage some space to breathe. You're always angry at me.'

'You make things so hard.' His jaw clenched; his crossed arms locked out any real discussion.

'I understand you think that. I know you're unhappy and I'm unhappy too and… maybe we need some time.' She had rubbed her eyes, keeping away tears, needing to show strength.

'You can't do this,' he'd said, shaking his head. 'I won't let you do this.' What had she felt then? Relief, she thinks. She had assumed it meant he wanted to really talk, to understand her concerns.

And then everything changed. Last night's argument, over texts from another woman, and now Katherine is here… her world upended.

Standing up, she goes to the door of the family room. She's not going to sit here any longer. But then she panics at what he might do if she disobeys him. If something happens to the children… *I will not be told what to do.* Easy to say if there were no children involved. They make a woman, a mother, so vulnerable. She is terrified to disobey him. Terrified for her children. Quickly, she sits down again.

Last night's argument repeats itself, John pulling at his dark hair, frustration making him grit his teeth.

'Your fault, Katherine. You're the one who's been pulling away.'

'I have twins to take care of.'

'And I have a job. We're both busy!'

'So you're texting another woman?'

'It's not like that, it's just a friendship. I don't get anything from you anymore, not even that.'

'Rubbish. Friends don't end their texts with heart emojis.'

There is a shriek from upstairs followed by a scream and she leaps off the couch and runs to the bottom of the stairs. 'Sophie, George… Sophie, George!' she yells, the words a strangled squeak, but then he appears, points the gun at her. 'Stop right there.' She freezes.

He turns around, snarls, 'Get out here, you brats,' and the children appear from Sophie's room. They are holding hands and they are also each holding their iPads. George's cheek is flaming, a bright, deep red.

'What… what happened?' she begs.

'Get back in there,' he hisses at her and she darts back into the room, her eyes falling on the wrapping paper again and the blue handle of the scissors underneath the rolls. She grabs at them, scraping her hand on the blade as she does so, and sits back down on the sofa, pushing the scissors down between the two seat cushions, feeling the blade catch and rip the fabric. Her heart pounds as she tries to breathe evenly, to give nothing away, when he comes back into the room with the twins. *What have you done? What if he sees? What have I done?*

They run to her and cling on to her, their arms around her waist, little bodies shaking, such fear she thinks it may break her.

'Sorry, Mum,' sobs Sophie.

'What happened? What happened?' she repeats, her voice high – terrified – and she's panicking that he will somehow figure out that she has the scissors.

'Just shut up,' he commands and they do as they have been told, all three of them scrunching up together on the sofa that

Katherine decides she will throw away, should she and her children make it out of today alive. She gulps down a moan of despair as she realises how impossible that idea is beginning to seem. What on earth could scissors do against a gun? The children are silent, disbelieving, as they watch him.

'George tried to make a sign to alert the neighbours, didn't you, Georgie boy?' he says, and he sounds amused that a child should try something so stupid.

George nods his head slowly and Katherine knows without a doubt that he has taken the fall for his sister. Sophie is a child of invention and ideas: 'What if we… why don't we… let's try.'

She remembers walking into the kitchen when they were three years old, after having left for just five minutes to put on a load of washing, and finding the whole floor covered in white flour.

'I did it,' George said immediately and she simply laughed at the mess. Then Sophie, knowing there would be no consequences, said, 'I saided we should try to do baking.'

It is so like him to say it was his fault, so protective of him, and her heart melts for her child. As the redness on his cheek begins to fade, a clean handprint is left. He has been hit with a lot of force. He has never been hit before and she can see from his red-rimmed eyes just how shocked he is. Her children are lectured, given time out, their misdemeanours explained. They have never been hit. Not until today. They have never been hurt. Not until today.

'I'm so sorry, baby,' she says.

'Just play on the stupid things,' he says and both children obediently open their iPads to games they like. She can see little hands trembling, can feel their shock and horror. He has hurt George and she has not protected them. A mother needs to protect her children against everyone, even against their own father if that becomes necessary. She should have done a better job of that.

She wonders if they are both thinking about this now, about her failure to do the one thing all mothers are supposed to do.

She watches their hands move across the screens in lacklustre fashion. They are not interested in the games that they would so willingly play at any other time.

'I want to tell you a story,' he says.

Katherine looks up at him, noting the change in his voice. Is he regretting this now? Is he trying to find a way to reverse this situation? His tone is softer, his body more relaxed. Perhaps he has shocked himself with how terrified George and Sophie are.

'It's a story about this boy who found a girl that he thought he could love forever. She was pretty and funny and clever and all the things a woman is supposed to be, and the boy treated her with great kindness.'

Flowers for you and chocolates too because I love you – yes, I do. The words written on a card return to her now, and she feels her smile inside her, hears the joyous laugh that had bubbled up at the time. He did love her as she loved him.

There is a ping from George's iPad, which is synced with her computer, and she turns to look. Her son panics and mistakenly touches the email to open it and she realises it's a survey about a parcel, the attempted delivery of the computer from earlier this morning. She lifts her hand to close it but George taps on one of the numbers and then quickly gets rid of the email.

He gets up and grabs the iPad from George. 'What are you doing?' he roars, bending down to yell in her son's face, furious at being interrupted. All softness gone, all possibility of her finding a way out of this disappearing.

'He didn't do anything, it was just an email!' she yells, needing to be as loud as he is. Needing to keep his attention on her.

'Nothing is just anything with you. I can see you planning something. Do you think I'm an idiot? Do you?'

'No,' she says, shaking her head frantically, 'no, I don't, I don't.'

He lifts the iPad above his head and then he throws it down on the ground, the glass splintering. Lifting his foot, he stamps on it two or three times until the screen is completely shattered.

'See what happens?' he shouts as he stamps. 'See what happens?'

'Stop it, stop it...' she yells, standing up, 'you're scaring them.' *Please let the scissors be far enough down in the sofa. Please don't let him see.*

'Am I?' he yells and then he lifts the gun and cracks her across the cheek. She falls backwards on the sofa, feels her mouth fill with warm blood. 'Oh,' she says, a numbing shock of pain rendering her speechless.

'Mumma, Mumma,' shouts George, a word he hasn't used since he began school and settled on calling her Mum.

'You hurt her. You're being mean!' screams Sophie, her little face red with indignation.

'I'll do the same to you too if you don't shut it.'

Katherine's head spins, she feels woozy. She, too, has never been hit. She cannot quite believe it of him... and yet it's happened. She would like to close her eyes for a minute, just rest and let the pain fade so she can think, but if she closes her eyes the children will not cope. The rich metallic taste of blood coats her tongue, and she suppresses the urge to spit it out, to rid herself of the thick, gluggy feeling.

She pulls up the white T-shirt she is wearing and uses it to wipe her mouth but the blood keeps coming. She doesn't want to take off her T-shirt, doesn't want to be half-dressed in front of him, even more vulnerable than she is.

'I need a towel,' she says, her voice garbled because of the blood in her mouth, vomit rising in her throat. There is a sharp pain where he hit her and she can feel that a tooth has been cracked, slashing the skin inside her cheek.

'Get her something,' he says, pointing with the gun, and George dashes out of the room and returns with a large pale blue towel from the bathroom. Blood soaks into it, changing its colour, changing everything.

'Oh, Mumma,' whispers George. He has never seen her bleed before. Even when she gets sick, she conceals it from them, taking all sorts of over-the-counter medication to stop a runny nose or bring down a temperature so they still believe that she is able to function no matter what. She can see that George's view of her is changing, altering – and with it his view of the whole world. If your mother can be hurt this way, then what else is possible? It is this that brings tears to her eyes. He still needs to believe that she is invincible. He still needs to believe in this and the tooth fairy and Santa Claus but mostly he needs to trust that his mother and father and home are his safe space. It's not true anymore and her children have lost something huge, something unseen and enormous that will forever alter who they are.

Katherine holds the towel against her mouth. Things feels out of control, surreal. She needs to reassure her wide-eyed, stunned children. 'I'm fine,' she says and then she repeats it, 'I'm fine,' because George and Sophie are pale with shock. They don't believe her but she repeats it, hoping that repetition will help, will convince them. 'I'm fine, I'm fine, it's okay.'

'She's fine,' he says and he returns to the recliner.

She presses the towel against her mouth with enough force to cause pain, hoping to stop the bleeding.

'I hate you,' hisses George, standing beside her, little shoulders back, small and fierce.

He laughs. 'Yeah, well I'm not fond of you right now either.'

She grips her son to her side with her free hand, as if by doing so she can absorb the hurt. So cavalier, so selfish – how can it even be possible? How can someone look at a five-year-old child in distress and not care at all?

She takes the towel away from her mouth and is relieved to see that she is no longer bleeding as much. There is a sting on the side of her cheek and she lifts her hand to touch where it hurts and feels that it is cut but only bleeding slightly.

'It's time to stop this now,' she says. 'Let them go and tell me what you want me to hear.'

She looks out of the window where she can see plants and flowers in their garden beds wilting in the heat. She would have given the garden a sprinkling of water by now, just enough to keep everything alive, just enough to stop leaves browning and drooping flowers dropping their petals. But it's too late for that. The merciless heat has taken hold.

'You know what, I think I'll take my time. I'm actually kind of enjoying this and I haven't enjoyed anything in a very long time.'

'There's something very wrong with you,' she whispers.

'Yeah, well,' he sighs, 'you would know.'

CHAPTER THIRTEEN

Two hours ago

Logan

Logan is walking back to his van from another delivery when his phone rings, and he curses when he sees it's Mack. He cannot deal with another call from his brother-in-law and boss today. He answers as he clenches his fist, ready for what's coming.

'Logan, Debbie just called. I am so sorry, mate, so sorry to hear about Maddy. Anna and I think the world of her and she's... I mean she's going to be such a great teacher and I... we're just...'

Logan is surprised to hear Mack's voice choke up, as though he's crying.

'Th-thanks,' he stutters, 'she'll... I mean, she'll be okay we hope.'

'Bring everything back now and just leave, Logan. I'll do the rest.'

Logan considers this for a moment. 'Mack, I'll finish up if that's okay. I'll go mad just waiting to get on a plane, and Debbie is in touch with her nurses. I'm okay to work another couple of hours.'

'Okay... okay but if you feel... I'm here, Logan, we're all here for you.'

'You're a good mate,' says Logan, feeling himself getting choked up, everything he once thought about Mack disappearing with the man's kind concern. Mack keeps talking and Logan listens, thanking him when the conversation is done.

He gets into his van, determined to finish the day so Mack can start tomorrow with a clean docket.

A text pings in from Debbie:

Just spoke to Terri. She says Maddy's stable but critical. Even if you could get there now, they probably won't allow you in. They may have to operate to relieve the pressure on her brain. I think you should come home.

I think I'll go crazy if I do. I only have a few deliveries left. I spoke to Mack – he's signed me off until the end of the week.

Good. I've booked you into a motel. It's not exactly luxury but it will do.

Logan allows himself a chuckle at Debbie's last text. All he needs is a bed and a locked door. He doesn't care about anything else.

He picks up the meat pie he bought from a service station ten minutes ago. He takes a few minutes to force down a bite, parked on a side road with the air conditioning on because the thought of being outside is not pleasant. Every time he climbs out of his van and feels the furnace blast of heat hit him, he stares up into the perfectly blue sky, hoping for a slight gust of wind or a slight darkening to grey that would mean a storm was on the way. But the sky remains achingly blue, the sun a fiery yellow. He would welcome a storm – a giant gust of wind and pounding rain would be better than a day this beautiful while his sister lies in a hospital bed.

The temperature has reached thirty-nine degrees and every suburb he drives through is silent, as though the whole of Sydney has decided to take a collective nap. He's passed lots of houses with dogs lying by front gates, their tongues lolling as they watch the street for movement.

He doesn't mind the quiet. In prison, what bothered him the most was the constant noise. It never stopped, not even at night. Men in prison don't talk normally. And underneath the loud voices, the noise... he could always hear the fear. All he wanted to do was get through the years and start again. There were others who wanted the same thing, but there were many more for whom prison was a way of life they never anticipated leaving. Those were the most dangerous men of all, because they had nothing left to lose.

Prisoners aren't supposed to have access to mobile phones but they are smuggled in and available to those who want them enough. Logan pictures Nick's face, tries to see him as he would look now. He looks at the text again, his fingers hovering over the number. He could just call and find out who it is.

He touches the number, his heart hammering in his chest as it starts ringing.

But the ringing continues until the call is answered by a robotic voice. 'You have reached the message bank of 614—' Logan hangs up, knowing the robotic voice will just repeat the number.

A yellow Porsche roars past him, the noise startling him as it spins its wheels in the quiet street where he's parked. Maddy once bought him a toy Porsche for his birthday. It was his seventeenth and she'd been telling him for months that she was getting him a car. She had presented the small toy car to him with such love and hope in her face that he hadn't even managed to laugh at the joke, only to give her a long hug. She was the only one to give him a present. He still has it somewhere, is holding on to the desire to give it to a son one day.

Cars have always been his passion and he feels at home around an engine. Engines can usually be fixed – people, not so much. It was his plan to get work as an apprentice mechanic when he was released from prison, where he'd taken classes, but no one wanted to hire him. His record follows him like a dog. He has to put the truth in his cover letter – no point in hiding it.

'Just keep trying, babes,' Debbie told him. 'Put in an application everywhere you can and leave the rest to the universe.' Debbie is big on leaving things to the universe but then she comes from a life where the universe seems to be on her side. She and Mack grew up with loving parents who gave them what they could materially but made up for any lack with complete love and support. Debbie's father, Paul, is a quiet man. The first time they met he barely glanced at Logan's tattoos, shaking his hand and avoiding looking down at the letters 'H A T E' inked across his fingers. Logan knew that Debbie must have briefed her family on him but her mother, Ruth, couldn't hide the surprise in her eyes. Before the meeting, Logan had debated what to wear and then he had purposely chosen a T-shirt, reasoning that he may as well be upfront from the beginning. At the table, while lunch was being served, he carefully moderated how quickly he drank his beer, how he held his knife and fork. But he wasn't able to control the tapping of his knee on the underside of the table, hadn't even known he was doing it until Debbie placed her hand gently on his leg and squeezed. The only member of the household who seemed unfazed by his appearance was their Labrador, Betty, who dropped her golden head onto Logan's knee and stared at him with soulful eyes while he stroked her soft ears.

After lunch, Paul called him aside and he felt his heart sink to his stomach. He understood he was going to be asked to leave Debbie alone, to give the beautiful, smart young woman a chance to find someone more worthy of her.

In the garage, Paul picked a spanner up off his workbench and searched the wall for its correct placement. Logan waited, his heart pounding. He knew that he wouldn't even be able to argue with Paul about his unsuitability. He was thirty years old and he had already spent three years in prison for break and enter and assault. He had no job and no money. He was a waste of a human being. As these thoughts circled in Logan's head, Paul found the place for the spanner and smiled, clapping his hands together to get rid of imaginary dirt. 'She's always been the best judge of character, you know.'

'She's really smart,' Logan replied.

'As smart as any Labrador, I imagine,' Paul said and Logan started laughing. Paul was talking about Betty. Paul joined him in his laughter.

'I know my daughter, Logan,' he said. 'If she thinks you're an okay bloke, then that's good enough for me. I've always been a fan of second chances. It seems that you've been given one. See that you don't stuff it up. We love her dearly and would hate to see her hurt.'

'I won't hurt her, Paul, I promise,' Logan said, hoping like hell that he would be able to keep that promise. 'I won't waste this second chance.'

Paul nodded and Logan breathed a sigh of relief. He smiles now as he thinks about Betty, who always sits right next to him when he and Debbie go over for a visit. His own personal dream is a house with enough of a garden for a kid and a dog. It's not much, but right now it seems an impossible goal. It's what Maddy always said she wanted as well – a house with a yard and dinner on the table, and kids who weren't scared of their angry parents. She'd thought she'd found it with Patrick, and even though Logan didn't understand the attraction, what bothers him is that his radar never picked up on the man being capable of such hideous violence.

He looks down at his hands. He is so much bigger than Patrick. He could kill him with his bare hands. This thought is satisfying.

Another text comes in and he looks down at his phone to see a message from his mother.

Just thought you should know that what happened to her is on the internet.

Logan doesn't reply. He looks up a news site and straight away sees an article about Maddy.

'Neighbours heard arguing and a woman begging someone to stop,' he reads. Pinpricks run up and down his arms. They heard her begging. He can hear his sister's voice, her tears, her cries for help, and the bite of meat pie threatens to come up again. He rubs his hands together; the desire to hit something, hurt something, hurt himself in place of hurting Patrick is overwhelming. When he lived at home, he did his best to protect her, stepping in front of a careless slap for no reason from their mother or a more deliberate hit from their father. He took the beatings for her, because he could. But then she was too far away for his protection. He holds his hands up to his eyes, pushing against them, trying to focus on the darkness he creates, but the chaos of his thoughts will not be calmed, even as he tries deep breathing and counting.

Maddy, Maddy, Maddy.

When he gets to Melbourne tonight, he will visit his sister and then he knows that at some point he will leave the hospital and search for the man who hurt her and then… he doesn't want to think about it. Once he gets there, he will call the number again and again until Patrick answers. Or until someone else does. It has to be from the same man who hurt Maddy – it has to be.

He looks at the article again, sickened by the bare reciting of facts. He reads articles like this every day, but it is different when it's your sister being written about. The neighbours heard her screaming and begging and they did nothing? What kind of people live next door to Maddy? Who hears a woman asking for help and does nothing?

He rubs his hands through his hair, damp with sweat. It's killing him that he wasn't close enough for her to call.

There's a chance it wasn't Patrick who hurt her, but his mother is right – it's always the husband or the boyfriend. Logan met quite a few of them in prison. That's where Patrick belongs, although Logan would prefer him dead. He clenches his fist, imagines the feel of it smacking into Patrick's cheek, imagines pummelling the flesh on the young man's face.

'Stop it, stop it, stop it,' he growls, trying to rein in his own rage.

His thoughts return to the neighbours who heard something and did nothing. What is wrong with people? If he thought someone was in trouble, he wants to believe he would help, that he would step in. All it would have taken was a knock on the door. A call to the police would have been even better.

The woman from this morning comes back to him, and he feels a wave of shame. He thinks something is going on in that house but he's done nothing. How would he feel if tomorrow he read about her on the internet – and he could have stopped it?

On impulse he decides to swing by her house again. It's out of his way but it doesn't matter.

The drive takes fifteen minutes, and when he gets to the house he sits in his van for a moment, watching the waves of heat shimmer off the asphalt.

This is not a good idea. But I'm here now.

As he walks up the path to the front door, he notes that the house is still silent, no noise coming from inside. He rings the bell again, clutches the computer in his hand, holding it up, covering his face, when he hears what sounds like a chair being dragged and then the sound of the peephole sliding open again.

'Thought I would just see if you can accept this now,' he says, clearing his throat, knowing that this is not standard procedure, knowing that there is no way he should have done this and that if the woman complains, he will lose his job. But he's made the decision and so he waits for a reply from whoever is looking at him through the peephole.

'There's a real gun,' whispers a child's voice.

'What?' Logan says, straining to hear better.

'No wait, ow…' yells the child. Logan hears a short scuffle and the chair being dragged away.

'Look, mate,' comes a male voice, low and menacing, 'she doesn't want it today. Don't come back here or I'm calling the police.'

The peephole closes and Logan stands on the front step, debating what to do.

Outside in the street, emptied garbage bins – some of their lids left open, some lying on their side where the truck has dropped them – contribute to the rotting heat smell. Sweat beads on his upper lip. He runs his hand through his hair and it comes away wet.

The door remains resolutely closed. He looks around anxiously. He shouldn't be here. The last thing he wants is for the police to be called on him. He knows that they'll see him for who he is and what he's done.

'No one saw,' he mutters as he makes his way out of the front garden.

He has kept repeating that mantra to himself ever since that last time. The time he doesn't want to think about. It was months ago, before he went to Mack for a job. Months before and one desperate night, one desperate moment, but thankfully, mercifully, he stopped himself.

It was still cold that night, the wind biting as he stood in front of the house. It was so easy to get inside. It took no time at all. Even now he can still see the sleek black laptop, light and expensive, in his grip. The house was empty. He had the laptop and some diamond earrings abandoned carelessly on the side table in the main bedroom. He cat-walked through the rest of the house, picking up small things – a digital camera, an iPad, some loose cash in a drawer – and then he made his way back to the broken back door, where the lock had given way with a small shove. And then he stood there as his heart thumped and his lungs seemed unable to inflate. The caged-in feeling of his small cell hung over him and he felt himself begin to shake in the cold night air. Debbie's disbelief, Maddy's disappointment and his father's smug, 'Told you so,' assaulted him, one after another.

And then he put everything down on the kitchen table and left, closing the door behind him.

It woke him up at night, the horror of what he had almost done to his life, all over again. Did he leave a print, some DNA, some evidence? He was wearing gloves and he's sure he kept them on, but he can't remember. He is on the database for life. Did he leave a clue that it was him? Would the owners have reported it if nothing was taken? When the nightmare wakes him, he prays to a god he's not sure he fully believes in that he will be forgiven and that one terrible, desperate act won't come back to get him. So far, it hasn't.

But can he let his fears over repercussions from that one night stop him from helping this family?

There's a real gun. That was a strange thing for a kid to say. Were they playing a game – cops and robbers or something? But why was the man who spoke to him so aggressive? Why wouldn't they just open the bloody door and take the computer so he didn't have to think about any of this?

What if the man who spoke to him was the husband and father, and he has a reason for not wanting the door to be opened? A series of horrible images of battered and bruised faces assaults Logan, Maddy's face crowding out all the other pictures in his head. What if the woman inside was hiding the beating she got from the man there – and then what about those kids? Has the woman in the house been hurt the way Maddy has been hurt?

In prison there was a group of men who hung around together because they were all there thanks to the 'bitches' they had found themselves married to or sleeping with. They muttered about these women all the time, about what they would do once they got out and got their hands on them. They were forced into counselling and sometimes it helped. Sometimes a man saw the light and realised that putting his hands on a woman was assault even if he was married to her, that he couldn't take his anger at the world out on the woman he claimed to love. Sometimes they didn't see the light.

Logan knows that there are flats in their building where, every now and then, a woman emerges with a bruise on her arm or a black eye, and he also knows that he mostly doesn't interfere. He can't. He would hit the man who hit the woman, and that would mean back to prison for him. Debbie sometimes takes the opportunity to slip some pamphlets under the door, pamphlets that let the woman know help is out there. It's not easy to ask for help. His own sister is in a hospital bed right now because of a man who hurt her. And he's determined to do something about that.

Back in his van he thinks about what Debbie has said about the universe: 'Just keep an open heart and an open mind, babes. The universe will put you where you need to be.' Why did the universe put him here, today of all days?

He tips his head back against the seat and closes his eyes, curses this day, curses everything that has happened because now he knows what he has to do. Looking at his phone, he considers the ease and simplicity of simply calling triple zero and giving them an anonymous tip. But he's not sure he would be able to explain it on the phone, that he will be able to make it clear enough that there is definitely something happening in the house. Would they even take him seriously? And if they didn't, if they dismissed it as a crank call, what then?

He has no choice. He feels like he's driving to his own execution, happily taking himself off to hand himself over to the enemy. But something is happening in that house where he knows there are at least two children, small children who may need protecting from their parents. He pulls over and looks at his GPS, locating the nearest police station.

You're going to regret this. You know you are.

CHAPTER FOURTEEN

Gladys

'I thought you might like to try a different flavour today,' says Gladys, putting the bowl of salted caramel ice cream down on the tray over Lou's legs. Her shoulder is aching a little where he leaned heavily on her on the way into and out of the bathroom. Peter is a large, strong young man, muscles bulging, and he never has a problem helping Lou. Peter is also fond of a game of chess, and Gladys knows that Lou misses this today, but she doesn't know how to play and she fears that Lou would be more irritated than grateful if she asked him to teach her.

The ice cream should pep him up a bit. He is sitting in his chair in front of the television, watching the news break, his wheelchair next to him in case he wants to use it. 'They think it was that girl's boyfriend who hurt her,' he called to her when she was in the kitchen.

'Yes, well, it's always the case, isn't it? People can be dreadful,' said Gladys.

'What flavour is this?' Lou asks. 'You know I only like choco-late.'

Lou hits out at the bowl, tipping it over and spilling it on the carpet. Gladys rushes to get a rag, unable to help the few tears that appear. 'I just wanted to give you a change,' she says while she is down on her hands and knees, mopping up the mess. She feels herself pushing down her own anger. It's a lump in her throat, and in her mind, she watches it move down into her stomach where it can't force out damaging words. She takes a deep breath and wipes away the tears, not wanting Lou to see.

Lou is quiet. 'I'm sorry, old girl,' he says eventually. 'I'm a bit of a difficult old man, aren't I?'

Gladys sniffs and returns the rag to the kitchen. She brings Lou a bowl of chocolate ice cream and takes a serving of the salted caramel for herself. The news ends with the promise of a cool change that will drop the temperature by ten to fifteen degrees in an hour. 'That'll be a relief,' says Lou quietly but Gladys cannot muster a reply. She allows the cool ice cream to slip down her throat, swallowing her feelings with the sweetness.

Gladys can't concentrate on the TV – she can't stop thinking about what to do about Katherine and the children.

Should I call the police? Should I go over there again? What if this is all in my head? What if I need to simply leave this family alone?

Your imagination is going to get you into trouble, she admonishes herself silently.

On the wall the air conditioner rattles as it pumps out cold air. Occasionally, Gladys glances at it, daring it to choose today of all days to break down. She's sure she's never heard it rattle like this before.

A trailer for a crime series plays during the advert break. A dead body, blue lips and twisted limbs, being studied by two police officers. Gladys moves in her chair, uncomfortable with the image.

'Why do they keep showing the story of that young woman on the news here if it happened in Melbourne?' she asks, needing to clear the air because she can feel Lou's silent sulking.

'Ah, you missed that bit,' says Lou. 'They're saying that the man they want to talk to, the one in the red hat, might have left the state a day or two ago. They're not sure, you see, so they're showing it everywhere. He could be in Sydney by now or Perth or Adelaide, anywhere.'

Gladys takes another spoon of ice cream but it feels like too much; she swallows, feeling a sharp, cold pain from her teeth to her ears. Something about the man in the red hat bothers her more than it normally would and she has no idea why. Probably because the young woman in the pictures is so pretty. Rebecca, her niece, has just started dating a new man, and she and Lou have only met him once. He seemed nice but you never know. Most people seem nice enough but who knows what people are hiding from the world.

Inspiration strikes and she says to Lou, 'I might just whip up a batch of chocolate muffins to take next door. If everyone is sick, it will be appreciated.'

'You can never leave well enough alone,' he says.

'Yes, but… I won't be long.' She gets up from her chair and picks up the empty ice cream bowls to take to the kitchen.

'They won't want muffins if they're not well,' says Lou as she leaves the room, 'leave them alone.'

'It won't take more than a few minutes,' she sings, determined not to let his admonishments stop her, and she continues to the kitchen. 'Something is definitely not well over there… Something is very unwell,' she says as she takes out her muffin tray and finds the chocolate chips.

It takes no time at all to mix up the muffins, and Gladys slides the filled tray into the oven, anticipating the delicious smell of chocolate that will soon be floating through the house.

'How about that crime series? There's one on now,' Lou says when she returns to the living room.

'Yes, good idea,' she agrees, knowing he's being kind. It's an episode she's seen already but it doesn't matter as she's unable to concentrate as she waits for the timer on her phone to go off. She's never felt like this before – well, once, when Rebecca was in Europe. She remembers waking one morning and wondering which country Rebecca was in as the tour was moving to a different place almost every day. She felt terribly uneasy about her niece, and after waiting until she could no longer stand it, she called her sister, Emmaline. 'I'm worried about Rebecca,' she said.

'Well, you must have a sixth sense,' Emmaline replied. 'I've just had a call. Their bus crashed on the way up the mountains and she's hurt her wrist. They don't think it's broken but she's having an X-ray just in case.'

Rebecca was fine but Gladys had been right about something not being well. She feels the same way about Katherine now, even though she's certainly not as close to her neighbour as she is to her niece.

She watches the timer on her phone, willing the minutes to pass. In the episode, someone shoots someone else, startling Gladys, who hasn't been concentrating.

'Why are we watching this violence?' she asks Lou.

'It's a good story and you like it, you always say you like it,' says Lou, and Gladys checks her phone again. She knows he only suggested the series for her but if he's enjoying it and managing to stay awake, she supposes that's a good thing.

Picking up her phone, she checks the timer again, and then, with one eye on the television, she looks at the news site she likes to read. The top story is about a man in America being sentenced for killing his wife and children. Gladys remembers the man on television months ago when his family went missing, crying and begging for help in finding them. He claimed to have no idea where they were, but it was all an elaborate lie. Gladys had known not to trust him as soon as she saw him. He had shifty eyes and he cried too much.

A small shiver runs through Gladys. How well does she know John really? Not very well. She's never had more than a casual chat with him. She reviews the facts she has. This morning John screeched off and then returned, and he isn't at work. The blinds are closed, the house silent. The children are home and one of them put a sign in the window asking for help. Katherine wouldn't let her in. It all adds up.

Gladys does not want to be one of those neighbours who claims that they didn't think anything was going on when something dreadful happens in their street, does not want to be one of those people on television who claims they are shocked and horrified. She knows something is going on – she knows it.

The timer on her phone goes off and Gladys leaps up, relieved that her excuse for going over again is ready. Katherine might think she's interfering – or she might be eternally grateful that Gladys wouldn't leave well enough alone. Either way, she is taking the muffins over.

As she pulls the tray out of the oven, the man that the police are searching for crosses her mind. The red hat is just a red hat and it's hard to tell anything other than the colour from the CCTV footage, but for some reason she knows that on the front is a Nike logo in raised stitching in the same red. Gladys puts the muffin tray on top of the stove and takes a deep breath. She's seen that cap before. She saw it yesterday.

'There must be hundreds of those caps,' she mutters. It must be just a coincidence. It has to be.

CHAPTER FIFTEEN

There is too much blood. It turns my stomach. It's dribbling out of her mouth and onto the towel George got for her and dripping onto her T-shirt, and truthfully, I've never liked the sight of blood. Especially not my own. It's interesting watching the kids and how protective they are of her. Sophie is mostly afraid, but George wavers between being afraid and furious with me. Now he is watching me, his green eyes narrow and focused on my face. If looks could kill…

I have no idea why they thought I wouldn't catch them trying to send a note to… well, there's no one who would see something like that, and it wasn't in the window long enough anyway. But still, they tried. You have to give them credit for trying, and I had to do what I had to do.

I didn't think I had hit her that hard, but the gun was in my hand and it gave the blow some extra impact. My hand is hurting now. I rub my fist slowly, keeping the gun trained on the three of them.

I have so much to say, so many things to tell her. 'Do you want to hear a story about when my father died?' *I ask.*

'I know that story,' *she says but the words are a little garbled because her mouth is filled with blood.*

'What?'

She spits some blood into the towel and I check myself for feelings of guilt or remorse but I am pretty sure I feel nothing. The ability to shut down my feelings about other people is probably something I inherited from my father. In the end the only person he really cared about was himself.

*My father got worse and worse as the months went by after he
lost his job. A lot of the time I came home from school and found
him asleep on the sofa. But sometimes I came home and he would be
awake and he would ask about my day. When he asked me what I
had learned at school, I always told him, 'Nothing.'*

*Usually, he let it go, but once his anger flared up out of nowhere
and he leapt off the sofa and grabbed my shirt, pulling me towards
him. 'Now you listen to me, son, because I know what a harsh world
it can be,' he said. I was fifteen and tired of his shit so even though
his hands were twisted in my school shirt, his breath too close to
avoid, I rolled my eyes and sighed loudly. He twisted harder, his nails
scratching my skin. 'You think you're so clever, don't you?' he spat and
then he delivered a hard slap to my cheek. It wasn't the first time he
hit me. He liked hitting me. Sometimes it was hard enough to leave
a slight bruise, but it was never hard enough to make me see him as
anything other than pathetic. I wonder now if I had shown fear, real
fear, if he would have felt better about himself. Their fear, the fear
that I can see in the way they watch me, in the way they keep trying
to move further back into the sofa, squashing the soft fabric cushions,
lets me know I'm the one in control. Things have gotten messy but I
still have control.*

The blood has stopped seeping from her mouth now. I can see her
moving her tongue around the inside, checking for a broken tooth.
There is a cut on the side of her cheek that's oozing a little and I
squelch a desire to tell her to get some ice for it. I used to want to
take care of her.

'Do you know that when my father died, I waited two days before
calling the police?'

Her brown eyes widen in horror. 'No, you never told me that.'

'Well, I did.'

'I'm so—'

'Please don't tell me you're sorry for me. I am so tired of hearing
the word "sorry" from you.'

CHAPTER SIXTEEN
Katherine

Her twins are very different children and Katherine often thinks about who they'll be when they grow up. George is quiet and thoughtful. He sticks to the rules and always has done. He walked after Sophie did, but he never had any of the bruises and bumps she ended up with. Sophie rushes at life, leaping first and thinking and looking later. It's why she's already getting into trouble at school while George would never dream of disobeying his teachers or breaking a rule.

'Why would you have taken the dolls to school if you knew that they were not allowed?' she asked her last night.

'How come marbles are allowed but not my dollies? Marbles are boring,' was her petulant reply.

Katherine didn't quite know how to answer that. Sophie was right. Rules can be very arbitrary. But she needs to learn to take her time, to think things through, and this is what Katherine has been trying to teach her – to try and anticipate the consequences of her actions. She knows she is failing at this but it has never really mattered as much as it does today.

The blood is only seeping a little now and she thinks it could have been much worse. George has taken the blame for Sophie but her impulsive daughter could have really been hurt.

Think, think, think, she instructs herself. Is it possible that this is the worst he will do to them? Will he leave now or at least let them leave?

When the bell rings and Sophie leaps off the sofa to run to the door, she doesn't even have time to open her mouth before he goes after her, spitting, 'Don't you dare move,' at her as he leaves the room.

Katherine sits, her body hot and cold, with her arm around George. She hears Sophie shout, 'Ow!' and then there is silence. When he returns, he is holding her in one arm, his hand covering her mouth as she struggles and kicks. Because he doesn't have enough of a hold on her, he drops her and then, in a fury at losing control, he shoves her down onto the floor where she bursts into noisy tears.

'Stop!' shrieks Katherine. But he is already right next to her, the gun in his hand touching her temple.

'Shut up, shut up, all of you. You need to shut up. And you better not have said anything to him.'

Katherine looks at him, bewildered. 'Who?'

'The delivery guy from this morning. He really wants you to take that computer,' he says. 'Shut up, Sophie, or I swear to God…'

'Please, Sophie… please, sweetheart,' she begs her daughter, 'just be quiet, okay? It's okay, Mum's here, Mum's—'

'Oh my God, you never shut up. Why do you never shut up?' he asks as though the pain of hearing her speak is actually physical. He pulls at his hair and rubs his chin, frustration in the movement.

'Sophie,' says Katherine, the word a warning. She needs her to stop.

Sophie closes her mouth and Katherine can see her biting down on her lip to keep quiet. She climbs back onto the sofa, rubbing her arm where she landed on the carpet. Katherine pulls her children close to her, holding tight. Their bodies are damp with sweat as is her own. The air conditioner cannot blow away their terror.

'Now listen to me,' he begins, menace in every word, 'if anyone tries anything stupid like that again, this is what's going to happen.' He picks up Sophie's stuffed monkey that has fallen on the floor and shoves the gun into his waistband, and then they watch as he pulls at the stuffed toy, grunting with the effort of it until the head rips off nearly completely. It's a display of power, a show for himself, an ugly demonstration of what he's capable of.

I don't know this person. Perhaps I have never known him.

'Oh, my baby,' wails Sophie and it is the utter despair in her young child's voice that forces Katherine off the sofa, her body standing without any thought, just a need to show him that he cannot keep doing these things to them. And as she moves, she is aware that the gun is not in his hand but in the waistband of his pants and she has just this moment to try and get it from him if she is quick enough.

Make a noise. Make some noise.

She shouts as she moves, hoping to distract him enough so that she can go for the gun.

'How could you? How could you? It's her favourite toy. That's awful, you're awful. What is wrong with you? What is wrong with you?'

As she gets to him, he looks up and she lunges – not for the toy as he first thinks but for the gun.

Her hand goes around his waist and he shouts, 'Hey!' and drops the monkey, then he grabs her arms and pushes her away.

She falls backwards and he looms over her. She starts to stand up and he grabs her hand.

'Just what do you think you're going to do here?' he hisses and he bends her wrist backwards, forcing her to sink to her knees as he bends it further and further back. The pain shoots through her hand and arm and she cannot even voice it. He keeps bending it, pleasure on his face at the agony he is causing and then there is a pop sound, a crack, and he lets go. She drops onto the floor and lies there for a moment. Her body is a mass of tingling nerve endings, the pain forcing her breath from her lungs. There is a buzzing sound in her head; a hot flush of pain covers her body in sweat. But she needs to get up. She needs to get up and sit next to her children. She cannot believe they've had to see something like this, that they are witness to such a thing. But she knows she needs to get up because even though she has not succeeded in getting the gun, she still needs to find a way to save them. The scissors are still between the seat cushions, but if she tries to do anything and he stops her, what might he do with the scissors?

Get up, Katherine. Get up!

She moves awkwardly, cradling her wrist as she wriggles up onto her feet and then sits down next to George and Sophie. Both children have been stunned into silence. They are staring at him, their mouths open.

'See what happens?' he says casually and then he goes to stand by the window. 'It's hot in here. Why haven't you got this air conditioner fixed?'

'I should have, I know.' Katherine takes a deep breath and tries to calm herself, to slow her beating heart.

He pushes open the window and hot air from outside rushes in so he closes it again.

'Can I get Mum an ice pack?' George asks quietly.

'What?' he says.

'When I fell down and hurt my knee, Mum put an ice pack on it and it felt better. Can I get one from the kitchen for her?' A carefully asked question, uncertainty in every word.

'It's okay, George,' she says. The air in the room feels thicker, heavier and harder to breathe in and out. Pain in her wrist ricochets around her whole body as she trembles in an effort to stay upright when all she wants to do is lie down.

'Can I?' George repeats, determined to do this one thing. George is a thinker, a planner, and as she watches him, she understands that her son is the key to the children being saved. She cannot see how she can make it out of this alive but if she can figure something out and somehow communicate it to George, then that is all that matters.

'Fine, whatever,' he says, bored with anyone else's pain.

George darts from the room and returns quickly with a soft ice pack that he drapes over her swelling wrist and hand with delicate care.

'Thank you, sweetheart,' she says and he nods.

'I'm sorry, Mum,' he says.

'It's not your fault, baby,' she replies as tears begin to course down his cheeks.

'But it is,' says George.

'No, George,' he says, his voice soft, almost kind, but his teeth are clenched, his top lip curled, 'it's not your fault. In fact, if it's anyone's fault at all, it's hers. She's the one to blame for everything that's happened here today. Blame her, blame Mumma.'

CHAPTER SEVENTEEN

One hour ago

Logan

It's the most innocuous-looking police station Logan has ever seen. It reminds him of the foyer of an office building, with its white melamine counter and some fake leather benches against a light blue wall, a vibrant potted plant in the corner. Everything about it tells whoever walks in that this is not a threatening place. There are no drunks asleep on the couches and no jittery junkies waiting for their ride home, just an empty space and one policewoman standing behind the counter, looking at a computer, engaged in what Logan thinks may actually be a game of Solitaire. It's a suburban police station in a suburb where cats go missing and sometimes parties run past midnight and the neighbours can't get to sleep on time. The only smell is of a pine-scented disinfectant mixed with a sweet fragrance from the flowers blooming in pots outside the door.

Logan wonders if the police who work here have ever seen anything scarier than a domestic disturbance over who parked over whose driveway. But then he thinks about the woman in the nice house in the nice street quite close to here. There is something scary going on over there. He knows that sometimes the nicest houses belonging to people with the widest smiles conceal the worst horrors. He met some people in prison who had all the manners of the private-school-educated, who were sharp and clever, and who were in prison for murder and rape.

He shivers a little as he walks inside, as much from the cranked-up air conditioning as from an old learned fear about the nature of police stations and their life-changing sinister magic. Six years ago, he walked into one a worried man with a bandaged hand and was driven away a charged criminal, and his life will never be the same. He loiters in the front for a minute without approaching the counter, fighting the urge to turn and just run. *I didn't leave any prints. No one knows.*

The woman in the big house is not his problem, she really isn't. His fear over having to deal with the police tells him to just leave it alone – but instinct will not let go. The woman in the big house is in trouble and he knows it. Why would the kid have mentioned a gun? What made him or her say 'ow' and who is the man who told him to go away? He feels like he's playing one of those detective games, piecing together clues, but this is not a game. Even if he could dismiss the woman, he can't dismiss the kids. Maybe if one of the neighbours in his suburb or one of his teachers had noticed something off about him – had spotted a bruise or two, had clicked that his loner behaviour was not normal and stepped in – he would have grown up an entirely different human being. Someone has to look out for the kids.

He keeps thinking about Maddy in her hospital bed. He asked Debbie to get her friend to send him a picture. 'Why would you want to see that?' Debbie asked over text. 'I need to,' was the best he could do.

The shock of her bandaged head and the tube coming out of her mouth had stolen the air from his lungs. There was no real way to tell it was his sister in the bed but he knew it was. In his van only minutes ago he had dropped his head and closed his eyes. *Please let her survive this.*

Now he pushes his shoulders back and strides up to the counter. He's done his time and he's trying to help. And no one saw his one last sad desperate act. No one saw it and no one knows about it and he's not going to let that prevent him from getting someone help.

The policewoman is dressed in a uniform with a tactical vest and a gun at her side. Logan is sure that without the air conditioning she would be sweating buckets. It's a lot of weight to have to carry, and the short, blonde-haired policewoman doesn't look like she weighs much.

'Can I help you?' she asks, her face neutral as her eyes dart up and down assessing him, his size and the coloured edges of his tattoos peeking out of his sleeves at his wrists, the words on his hands, the words on his face. He watches her lips move slightly as she reads the tiny letters under one cheekbone that spell out: *I refuse to sink.*

He imagines she think he's lost.

'Um yeah… it's kind of strange… I'm not really sure how to explain it.'

The policewoman's hand goes to her side, rests on her gun. 'Start at the beginning?' she suggests.

'Okay, so I'm a delivery driver with Pack and Go, as you can see,' begins Logan, pointing to the logo on his shirt, where a smiling box is circled with a clock, hoping that it gives him a reasonable amount of legitimacy, 'and I went to a house this morning at around seven thirty to drop off a computer but the woman wouldn't open the door. She needed to sign for the package but she wouldn't open the door…'

'Don't you have procedures for that sort of thing?' the woman asks and Logan can see her stifle a yawn. Right now, he's the most interesting thing she's seen all day and she's already bored with what he has to say. He's not used to being dismissed so easily.

'No,' he attempts to keep his frustration in check, 'I'm worried that there is something going on in her house, something that's stopping her from opening the door. I think she's in trouble. Her name is Katherine West.' Logan feels his shoulders relax a little. He's told someone who can actually do something about it now.

'I went back to try and deliver the parcel again and a kid said something about a real gun through the door, and then the kid said, "Ow," and some guy told me to go away.' Logan feels his certainty wither as he speaks. He sounds like he's a bit mad.

'Is it usual for delivery drivers to return a second time to try and deliver a parcel? Don't you just leave a note and drop it at the post office?'

'Yeah, we do usually, but I feel like something is going on at that house.'

'Sorry, what did you say your name was?'

'I didn't. What difference does it make?' Logan's stomach turns over just once – this is not good.

'What is your name?' the policewoman asks very slowly and clearly, making sure he understands the question, a small smile playing on her lips.

Logan considers lying but she could just call the company. She knows where he works now and Mack only has ten drivers. He also thinks about just telling her to forget it but he's piqued her interest now. He's done a very, very stupid thing by coming in here.

'Logan Clarkson,' he says softly, 'but I have no idea why that matters. I can give you the address of the woman's house and you can send a car to check it out. All I wanted to do was tell you that I'm concerned about her.'

'And how long have you known Ms West?' she asks, her fingers tapping on her keyboard.

Logan feels his hands form into fists. He knows exactly what's going on here.

'I don't know the woman. I am a delivery driver. I tried to make a delivery and she wouldn't open the door and I found that strange. I'm concerned for her welfare.'

'Is Katherine related to you in any way?' Her tone is flat, her voice devoid of interest or emotion. But he knows she's asking the questions this way so that he will slip up and give her an answer he doesn't mean to give her.

'Look… no… no, I told you, I'm just doing my deliveries.' He struggles to keep his frustration out of his voice. 'I don't know anything about her. She's got nothing to do with me.'

The policewoman throws him a look and then reads her computer screen, her lips moving as she does so. She looks up at him. Her hand goes back to the gun at her side. There is a small twitch right next to her eye. He can tell she's a little – just a little – unsure now and worried about what he may do. He's big enough to leap over her nice white counter.

'Well, we will certainly send a car, Mr Clarkson. Am I correct in saying that you have served three years in prison for break and enter and assault?'

Logan knows that she's stopped listening to him about anything at all. She is more concerned about his record. His past is not going to let go.

'Yes,' he replies, polite and careful. He knows that even the smallest misstep could land him back in jail.

'We've had a few break-ins in the houses around this area over the last few months. You may be right to be concerned.' She gives him a half-smile and even though he is a lot bigger than she is, his skin pricks with fear. He is a mouse to her cat and one wrong word will allow her to catch a hold of him.

'Okay, and the address of the house you tried to get into is…?'

Logan registers the words; registers the way she has phrased her question. 'I didn't try and get into it. I just wanted her to sign for a parcel.'

'And the address was?'

'It's um…' Logan swallows. The policewoman's face is making him nervous. 'It's twenty-four Hogarth, no sorry Holborn, twenty-four or twenty-six…' He shakes his head. He's been to the house twice today. How could he possibly have forgotten the address?

'It's on my phone, but I…' He searches in his pockets. He has left his phone in the van.

'I understand,' says the policewoman, a hard edge to her voice. 'Perhaps you can wait here while I go and get a detective. You can explain it to him. And then we can go and get your phone together. Please don't move, Mr Clarkson. I'll be back in a minute.'

'Fine,' says Logan.

The policewoman turns and walks to the back of reception, where there is a door. She opens it and looks around, perhaps hoping to catch someone's attention. She looks back at him quickly and then she steps into the back area, leaving him alone at the front.

Logan feels himself starting to sweat in the frigid space. He's going to get hauled back there and then things are only going to go one way after that. He won't be able to control his temper, he knows he won't. He was just trying to do the right thing. *And they may know something.*

He shouldn't be here. He should be waiting at the airport, hoping to get on an earlier plane so he can be with his sister. This woman has nothing to do with him and he bears no responsibility for what is happening in that house. He bounces on the balls of his feet, desperate to run. He takes a deep breath, hoping to calm himself, but his heart rate speeds up and he can't stop himself from turning around and bolting out of the police station, down the concrete stairs and across the road to where he has parked his van. His body moves without him forming a plan. He knows he needs to run.

'Mr Clarkson,' he hears as he climbs into his van. He starts the engine and drives off before he's even put his seat belt on, panic making his hands shake.

Debbie was right. He should have just left it alone.

'You're such an idiot!' he shouts as he slams his hand on the steering wheel. When he feels he's put enough space between him and the police station, he pulls into a side road and, sitting in his seat, he rips open the long-sleeved shirt he is wearing, ignoring the buttons that go flying, hitting the floor and the window with light cracking sounds. He takes it off and throws it on the floor and pulls a T-shirt he keeps in the van over his head. His tattoos are clearly on display. It doesn't matter anyway. It doesn't matter how hard he's trying to live a good life, how tightly he is clinging to the straight and narrow, or who he fundamentally is. He will always be a man with a criminal past first, last and every time.

He's going to get on with the rest of his day, and when they come for him, he'll lie like the criminal he is and say that he actually made a mistake and tried to deliver to the wrong house or some other rubbish. He hopes they send a car and knock on doors in the neighbourhood. It was Hogarth Street, he's sure. They'll probably go and check. They'll find the house. He's sure they will. They have her name as well. It will only take minutes to figure out the right address, although they may question why he gave them the wrong one.

'Enough,' he rebukes himself. 'Enough, enough, enough.'

He is done being concerned about the woman. Debbie is right. It's really not his problem.

He only has a few deliveries left and then he's done – done with everything that has happened today.

She has his name now. That was stupid, but all his record will show is that he's done his time. His fingerprints are on file too. Would they dust for fingerprints if nothing was taken? *Moved but not taken.* He caught himself just in time. But was it just in time, or has he now alerted the police so they will take the time to check?

He can't go back to prison. There's just no way. A ball bounces into the street in front of his van and he registers it but doesn't think, and only when a small child races onto the road does he slam on the brakes, the tyres screeching to a stop and filling the air with a burning rubber smell that comes in despite the air conditioning being on high.

'Get a grip, Logan!' he shouts as a panicked mother darts into the street to retrieve the child and the ball, waving her apologies as she does. It could have gone another way. He's not concentrating. Life changes in a split second. He doesn't have the luxury of split seconds anymore.

CHAPTER EIGHTEEN

Gladys

Gladys turns out the chocolate chip muffins, inhaling the sweet, dark smell of the cocoa and melted chocolate chips. She gently breaks off a corner piece, burning her fingers a little, and blows on it. When she feels it's cool enough, she pops it into her mouth. It's delicious, just the right amount of moist and chewy but with a little bit of crust around the edges. Chocolate muffins are one of her specialities.

She puts one of the muffins on a plate to give to Lou for his tea and keeps the broken one for herself. The rest she arranges on a green plate with a pretty white doily underneath. No matter what Katherine is going through, there's no way she'll refuse a plate of muffins. Gladys admires her work, loving the way the colours work together.

'Just dropping these muffins off at Katherine's,' she calls to Lou.

She opens her kitchen back door before he has a chance to answer and walks out of the house and around the side to the front gate. The heat is a thick blanket, settling over her shoulders, as the cicadas scream. She immediately begins to perspire but she walks quickly, hoping that Katherine will invite her in.

At Katherine's front door she rings the bell and takes a deep breath. She will just leave the muffins if they won't let her in, but she's sure this time the door will be opened.

She waits for a few minutes and, when nothing happens, she rings the bell again and then she calls through the door, 'Yoo-hoo, just dropping off some of my famous chocolate chip muffins.'

Feeling somewhat silly, she steps up to the timber front door and puts her ear to it. She can't make out any sound but it is a very thick door. She steps back and waits again. Next to her the marigolds in their large pots are wilting in the heat. *Poor things*, she thinks. They need some water.

She decides she will press the bell just one more time and then, if no one comes, she will give up and leave the muffins at the side of the door. She shakes her head a little, annoyed that she has not thought to cover them. If she leaves them on the floor, the ants will get them, and already large flies are buzzing around her head. It's probably too hot to leave them anyway. She will just have to take them home and try again later. She reminds herself that the muffins are a ruse to get Katherine to open the door. If she does, Gladys tries to think of questions that she could ask that would allow Katherine to tell her she needs help without actually telling her.

Do you need to see a doctor? I can call one for you, is the best she has come up with so far.

She presses the bell and waits another minute. Just as she's about to give up, she hears the sound of the safety chain moving and the lock turning, and the door opens.

CHAPTER NINETEEN

Things are starting to unravel in my head because I'm getting tired. Control is slipping away but I clutch the gun tighter. I will not let go. I take in great big lungfuls of the stifling air coming in from outside and try to calm myself. I try to remember the plan that I had this morning, the plan to make her listen and understand. That's what I need her to do, listen, understand and then acknowledge her part in all of this. Then we can move forward from there. But I'm not sure what forward would look like. Who will we be after today, the two of us, the four of us?

'Why?' she asks me, utter confusion in her voice. 'Why are you doing this?' She is cradling her wrist as it puffs up and her eyes scrunch with the effort of fighting the pain she is in.

I shove the gun into the waistband of my pants and clap my hands together, then wipe them on my jeans, getting rid of the sweat. It's easier if I don't look at her. I don't want to see her pain because I know it will sway me. Even a monster has some feelings.

'On with the story of my father dying,' I say, and I see George watching me. He is too little to conceal his facial expressions and so his thoughts are obvious. He thinks that the gun is less accessible because it's in the waistband of my pants. I reach behind me and pull it out and his little shoulders slump. 'I'm not stupid,' I tell him.

'I didn't say you were,' he says, with more anger creeping into his tone than I like.

I take a step forwards and crouch down right in front of him, so close he can feel my breath. 'I can hurt you like I hurt her, like I hurt Sophie and that stupid toy. I can, you know,' I say, my voice low.

He wrinkles his nose and sits back further on the sofa, pushing his body into the cushions to get away from me. I can't help the small thrill of power I feel. My father would have benefitted from believing I feared him, rather than that I found him ridiculous. Perhaps all fathers like to be feared instead of loved.

'Tell me why you didn't call the police when your father died,' she says quickly, forcing my attention away from George.

I stand up and go back to the window. I don't like the heat but the air in here is starting to get a stale smell. In fact, it stinks.

'I came home from school and he wasn't on the sofa, where he usually was. There was an empty bottle of whisky on the coffee table along with at least seven empty bottles of beer, but I didn't think much about that.' I can still see the label on the bottle of whisky, slightly torn at the corner. It was a cheap brand, even I knew that. I was grateful he wasn't there. I thought he had gotten himself so drunk that he'd stumbled off to bed and I looked forward to having control of the television and being alone for the night. I moved the bottles aside and put my feet up on the ugly fake wood coffee table, something he hated me doing. I kept my shoes on.

'I thought he was sleeping, just sleeping,' I say.

'It wasn't your fault,' she replies.

I shrug. 'I could have checked on him, but I was so sick of his shit. I just left him to it and had myself a good night. I even opened one of his precious beers and drank it while I ate my two-minute noodles.'

'You couldn't have known,' she says.

'Yeah, I don't care what you have to say about it,' I say mildly, and then I point the gun directly at her. 'I think it would be best if you just shut up.'

She sags down and the children huddle closer to her.

'Perhaps they can go and get something else to eat. It would be better if they didn't hear this.'

'Actually, it's time they learned about the real world. This,' I say, gesturing around the room with my gun, 'is not the real world. This nice *garden and the nice house and everything that goes with it isn't the real world and they should know that. My childhood was the real world.'*

'Most children are not held hostage by someone who's supposed to love them,' she says, 'by their—'

'Just shut it,' I say. If she understood anything at all about love, then I wouldn't be doing this. I thought I understood love but it turns out that even when I think I understand it, I can't have it. All I can have is heartbreak.

I wait in case she's going to argue with me but she doesn't. She's hurt, that's fine. I've been more hurt than any human being should be. Physical pain heals; it's the mental shit that kills you.

'I didn't check on him the next morning. Just got up and went to school. It was only when I came home that afternoon that I thought something might be wrong. Do you want to know why I thought that?'

'Why?' she asks but she's only asking to placate. I don't think she really cares.

I laugh, a dry laugh. 'Because there weren't any more empty bottles on the coffee table. It was still the same ones from the day before, the same whisky bottle with the torn label and the same seven beer bottles. It was then that I thought to check on him and I went and opened his bedroom door and, man, the smell… well, I can tell you it was pretty bad. He'd lost control of himself in the moment he died.'

'What does that mean?' asks George.

'It means he'd pooped in his pants, just like a baby,' I say.

'Don't…' she begins.

'You know what the trouble with you is?' I ask and then I answer my own question because I know the answer. 'It's that you think you have any control of this situation at all, Katherine, and you don't, you really don't.'

'I know I don't have control,' she says. 'You're the one with the gun.'

'I am,' I agree.

I freaked out when I saw my father on his bed, where the sheets were crumpled and stale-smelling before his death, because he never thought to wash them. I don't say this aloud but I did. I grabbed him by the shoulders and shook him and slapped his face and shouted, 'Dad, Dad, wake up, Dad.' I checked for a pulse. We'd been taught how to do that when we had a lifesaving class at school and I checked, holding my breath, hoping for something, anything, but his skin was cold and his eyes were glassy, his face grey. I knew he was dead. I would like to say I felt his spirit in the room, that there was a cold draught and I knew it was him saying goodbye or any of that other rubbish people say when someone they love dies. But I didn't.

I sat on his bed, the smell not bothering me anymore, and cried for a long time. I think I was crying because there was no hope left. Before he killed himself, I'd had moments of believing that something would change one day, and he'd get himself together. Once, when we happened to watch a programme on addiction together, he said quietly, his voice slurring, 'That's probably me.'

'You could get help,' I said. 'Those people got help.' My heart fluttered at the possibility of things being different.

'I may just do that,' he agreed, but then he opened another beer.

His death meant that my life would only get worse. I understood that. Like every kid of divorced parents, I had been hoping that he would man up and get better and then somehow, she would take him back and we would get to be a family again. It's ridiculous for a fifteen-year-old to think that way, but I'm pretty sure that most kids hold on to that small sliver of hope.

His death meant all hope was lost. It might have been hours that I sat there but then my tears stopped and I felt, as strongly as I would a punch to the stomach, a shutting down of part of me, a closing over. He wasn't worth my tears or my time and all he had ever done was let me down. I went through his wallet, took what little cash he had and left. I started walking and I just kept walking. I wanted to call my mother. I knew that I should call her and the police but I didn't do any of that. I bought myself dinner and I waited. It was spring and it was still cool in the evenings but I slept on a park bench that night, curling up small.

I shake my head as I think about this. 'I felt like I had no one to turn to when he died,' I say, 'that's why I waited.'

When I returned the next day, the smell had seeped out of his bedroom and into the flat and I knew I couldn't wait any longer so I called the police. Once they arrived the whole thing was set into motion and by that night I was back with my mother, back in the last place I wanted to be, because it was all her fault and he'd said as much.

He left a note. I never told anyone but he did.

Dear son,

Sorry about this. I know you don't want to hear anything I have to say anymore so I'll leave you with one last thought. Don't trust women. They'll make you the happiest man in the world and then they'll break you into pieces so you can't imagine living through another day. Don't ever trust them.

Dad

I should have listened to him on that one, and I did for a while. But then I met the woman I thought would be the love of my life, and I fell so hard and so fast that I didn't stop to think about what would happen when she was tired of me.

And so here I am in this room. As I look at this woman, I realise that I hate her with such a visceral force it's a wonder I haven't killed her already.

'I don't want to talk about this anymore,' I say, and I go back to looking out of the window, at the green grass in the perfect garden that doesn't tell the whole story of who she is and what she's done.

CHAPTER TWENTY

Katherine

When the bell rings again her heart lifts a little because it's possible – because anything is possible – that someone has come to help.

'This shit never stops,' he complains.

He's getting tired and she can see that. They all are, but he's been holding that gun for hours now, hurting them all by degrees for hours now. George's face still has his handprint vividly visible on his cheek. Sophie keeps rubbing her head where Katherine is sure he must have pulled out some hair. And the throb from what she is certain is a broken wrist is an agony that she feels right throughout her body.

When she first saw the gun, she hadn't imagined that he would use it, because it felt impossible.

But now she knows that it's not impossible. She believed that if he wanted to kill her or the children, he would have done it already, but perhaps his intention is to make them suffer for as long as possible, knowing that watching George and Sophie suffer is hurting her more than any bullet might.

She is trying to formulate a plan, any plan beyond the simple thought of throwing her own body at him, attempting to stab him with the scissors, forcing him to shoot her and hoping that the children get away before he has a chance to fire the gun again. She cannot guarantee that they will get away or that they will know to run, and she cannot think of how to indicate to them that this is what they should do.

'I think it's Gladys at the door,' she says now, grasping at straws. 'She'll be concerned because I didn't invite her in. You should let George talk to her – he can tell her we're sick, I'm sick. I already told her that… I think I did, but maybe… She makes things for us. Maybe she's brought over a cake.'

'Yoo-hoo,' Gladys calls, 'just dropping off some of my famous chocolate chip muffins.'

Katherine shrugs her shoulders as if to say, 'I told you so,' but she doesn't say anything else. If she pushes, he will refuse to let George open the door, but if George can open the door to Gladys, then maybe, just maybe…

He rubs his head, forcing his hair to stand up. He looks suddenly younger, less threatening, and she can see that he is losing focus now. It's not easy to kill someone, even though it looks easy enough in the movies and on television, but he's intelligent enough to realise that the taking of a life is a permanent thing. He lost his father too young and has suffered for it. He knows what death means for those left behind.

'If you don't let George talk to her, she'll just keep returning,' she says.

'Fine,' he says, 'go tell the old bat that everyone in the house is sick. And I swear to God, George, that if you say one other thing, if you so much as even sigh, I will rip your sister's head off the same way I ripped that stupid stuffed toy.'

George glances at her, his eyes wide, disbelieving. No one has ever spoken to him like this. He cannot understand what to do with these terrible threats of violence. And she senses that even though it would be easy enough for George to tell Gladys to call the police, now is not the time. She is not strong enough to fight him off if he goes for Sophie. The pain is making her weak.

The risk is too great. She gives her head an imperceptible shake. He blinks and she knows that means he understands. It's a wonder to her, even through the fear and the pain and the simmering anger that is underneath it all, that she is able to speak to her child like this, that he understands. She closes her eyes and sends up a small prayer that she will get to see him grow up and become the extraordinary man she knows he will be.

George gets off the sofa and goes to the front door.

She hears him open it, struggling with the lock that is at shoulder height for him. She listens to the murmur of voices, Gladys and George, and she can hear her son's hesitancy. He is considering what to do. *Just tell her we're sick, my darling. Now is not the time. Just tell her we're sick.*

'Why's he taking so long?' he asks, and then he gets up and goes to the front door and she hears something but cannot make out any words. She assumes he's warning George to keep his mouth shut. Adrenalin floods her body, fear for her little boy drowning out her own physical pain. *Don't hurt him, don't hurt him.* Her muscles tense as she gets ready to run to the front door if she hears anything except the soft murmur of voices.

She turns to look at Sophie, who is subdued, watching her game rather than playing it. They are alone with access to the outside world.

'Give me the iPad, sweetheart,' she whispers, her eyes darting to the doorway, but her daughter is slow to respond.

Even though movement is agony she begins to reach for the iPad, hoping that she can access her email before he comes back into the room. But seconds later he returns with George, and she hurriedly shoves the iPad back at Sophie, who instantly finds her game again. Katherine feels the throbbing in her hand increase with the beating of her heart.

He is holding her son by one arm, almost dragging him. George is trying to carry a plate filled with chocolate muffins, and the care behind the gift makes Katherine want to cry. Gladys is probably worried that Katherine is angry with her because she was so abrupt this morning. She silently blesses the older woman who is dealing with so much herself, but who is still working to maintain neighbourly bonds.

'Look, chocolate chip muffins,' he says, grabbing the plate from George and shoving him back on the sofa. 'Eat one,' he commands and both children look at her.

'Go on,' she says, 'you must be hungry.'

Usually when Gladys gives them a plate of muffins, she warms them up for the children, melting the chocolate and filling the house with the sweet cakey smell so she can almost pretend she baked them herself. The twins adore Gladys's muffins, but now they reluctantly take one each. Sophie pinches off a small bite and puts it in her mouth.

'What about you?' he asks Katherine. 'Aren't you hungry?'

'No,' she says weakly, and she lifts her hand a little, still wrapped in the ice pack that is now warm, hoping to reach some part of him that can feel something for her. He hasn't looked at her wrist, at her really, and she convinces herself that this is because he doesn't want to see how much pain he has caused her. Perhaps if she can get him to acknowledge it, he will come to his senses and realise what he's doing.

But instead, he stands up and grabs a muffin from the plate, charging towards her. 'Open up,' he says, almost jovial.

She shakes her head. 'I'm not hungry.'

'Ah well,' he sneers, 'too bad,' and he grabs her head while still holding the gun. With the other hand he shoves the muffin into her mouth, crumbling it and filling her mouth until she can't breathe, even as she tries to chew.

She struggles, kicking her legs out at him.

'Stop it!' shouts George.

'Mumma,' cries Sophie, and they both begin hitting him with their small fists.

He starts laughing at their futile attempts and then he does let go, throwing the remains of the muffin at her as she chokes and coughs and spits out as much as she can. And then as she leans back against the sofa, her chest heaving, eyes watering as she struggles to breathe, George says, 'I'm going to kill you.' Her son's voice is filled with an eerie menace, the sweet tones of childhood gone. He is a man in this moment, an angry man.

'Not if I kill you first,' he replies and then he grabs a muffin and shoves it into his own mouth. 'Not if I kill you first,' he repeats as he chews with his mouth open and swallows quickly.

And Katherine realises that she's been asking herself the wrong question. She has been asking how someone who once loved her can hurt her this much, how he can watch all of them suffer and feel nothing, but what she should be thinking about is all this deep, vicious anger he is filled with. All this violence that he has been hiding from her. There is something that she doesn't know, something that could provide a clue as to why he is doing this, and if she can just find out what it is, what has triggered him, then perhaps she can find a way out. There are things she does not know, things she hasn't understood about him. She just needs to keep him talking.

'You need to finish your story,' she says quietly.

'Yes,' he agrees, 'yes, I do.' He looks at her, his green eyes meeting hers. 'I wonder…' he says.

'You wonder,' she prompts.

'How it ends.'

CHAPTER TWENTY-ONE

Thirty minutes ago

Logan

Logan rubs his face, feeling the stubbly growth that appears through the day. In the mirror he can see bags under his blue eyes, and his lips look cracked and dry. He doesn't want to call Debbie again because he knows that she would tell him if there were any updates on Maddy. He is worn down by the day, by the early-morning delivery that went wrong, by his attempts to help when he should have just left things alone, but mostly by his fear and worry over his sister.

He cannot lose her. She is essentially the only family he has.

And now he has to worry about the police looking for him and what that might mean if they decide to take him in and question him. He's exhausted by the heat, by everything. He needs to get to Melbourne and be with his sister; that's all he wants right now.

He only has three more deliveries and then he's finished, and that can't happen soon enough.

'Just bring them back here and I'll do it,' Mack said when he called again, worry in his voice over the fact that Logan is still working.

'It's fine. All the earlier flights are booked out.'

'Don't they keep some seats aside for compassionate reasons or something like that?'

'Debbie's looking into it, but even if I get there now, I can't see her because she's in a bad way. If it's all the same to you, I'll finish up and then go home.'

'Whatever works, Logan, and if you need to talk to someone, I'm here.'

'Thanks, mate.'

Driving, the act of watching the road, of checking street signs and of glancing at the GPS, allows his mind to run through his past. He lists those he once called friends and those he only regarded as acquaintances and even those who he may have threatened or who have threatened him. The person texting him may or may not be connected to what happened to Maddy. It may or may not be Patrick. There are some who he knows are in prison, some who he's heard have been released. Nick keeps returning as a possibility but Logan knows he was serving his sentence somewhere in Sydney, although he had a girlfriend who lived in Melbourne. Logan brakes at a red traffic light. 'Shit,' he mutters. Nick had a girlfriend who lived in Melbourne. Are they still together?

As he turns a corner, he allows a nightmarish scenario to play out: Nick being released and moving to Melbourne, bent on revenge. *You're overthinking*, he tells himself. The sender of the text must be Patrick.

Needing to distract himself, he turns on the radio to listen to the news, wondering if what happened to Maddy is something that could make it to the radio. A song about a broken heart irritates him and he switches stations listening to the weather report for a moment before switching stations again. He knows how hot it is. The news comes on and he turns it up.

'Police are asking for help in locating the partner of a woman badly beaten in Melbourne two days ago. They are asking the public for help in finding Patrick Anderson. It has now been confirmed that Anderson left Melbourne two days ago, bound for Sydney.'

Logan pulls over the van, his heart racing. He touches his hand to his chest. He's too young for a heart attack but there is a pain down one arm that makes him think it's possible. He cracks his neck one way and then the other, wanting to climb out of his own body.

You're next.

He turns the news up louder, trying to concentrate even as he cracks his knuckles, twisting his fingers for the relief of the pop.

'Is he treating you okay?' he once asked his sister.

'Yes, big brother, he's fine – a little clingy but fine. He has some issues, but don't we all? I told him that you're watching him. I mean, it was a joke but he's scared of you.'

'Good. I don't like him. He's using you.'

'But I like him and he knows how you feel about him. You made that clear last month when we visited you. He's trying to get a job. He can be so sweet. You don't get it. He tries to tidy the apartment and cook for me. It's not his fault that finding work is this hard. He's not good with authority, but then neither are you.'

'And if he doesn't get his act together? Then what?'

'Then it may be time for me to move on.'

If Patrick Anderson hurt Maddy and now he's here, Logan knows there's only one reason for that. He doesn't need to think about who sent the text anymore. He knows.

He curls his hands into fists, reading the word 'HATE' on one hand and 'PAIN' on the other. 'Come find me,' he mutters, fear being replaced with fury warming up his body. He relishes the man coming to find him. It would obviously be self-defence, and that's allowed – isn't it? He shouldn't be thinking like this. That's the thinking of a man he never wants to be again. But he cannot help the images flickering across his mind, a silent movie of violence.

He wonders when Patrick will show up, if he'll accost him at work or out in the street. And then, as he imagines meeting the man in the street, sees how that would play out, he realises…

Patrick knows where Logan and Debbie live. He winds down the window because he can't seem to catch his breath. *He knows where we live. He knows where we live.* He scratches at his chest, where itchy sweat covers his skin. Fury is replaced by panic and for a moment he has no idea what to do.

Maddy brought him to Sydney for a visit last month and the four of them endured an uncomfortable dinner as Logan questioned the man dating his sister over roast chicken, asked him about his plans over chocolate mousse and suggested he get a job after they'd all had coffee.

'You were rude,' Debbie told him. But Logan hadn't cared.

He knows where we live.

'No, no, no,' cries Logan. Debbie's at home, alone, in bed with a cold, in bed and weak. Debbie is at home. Terror dances through Logan. If Patrick is looking for him, he will find Debbie first. *Don't just sit here, idiot.*

Logan swears and picks up his phone. 'Listen, Debbie,' he says when she answers.

'Oh, hey babes,' says Debbie, 'hang on a second, there's someone at the door.'

'Debbie, wait! No – wait!' he shouts, starting the van and pulling off with a screech of tyres, the phone slipping in his clammy hand. He's too late. He should have just gone home and he would have been there now. He's too late.

'What are you doing here?' he hears her say and then, 'Oh no, no…'

'Debbie!' he screams as he turns a corner, cutting off a Mercedes Benz and nearly hitting a car parked on the street.

'Debbie, Debbie, Debbie!' His voice fills the van, breaking with hysteria, his pulse pounding in his throat, his hands slick on the wheel. 'Debbie,' he moans.

CHAPTER TWENTY-TWO

Gladys

Gladys cannot sit down. Her steps around the living room are short and rapid, the rattle of the air conditioner setting her teeth on edge. 'I'm telling you, Lou, something is very wrong. "Thanks for trying to help," that's what he said to me. He knew that I know that something is wrong. I mean he's five years old, Lou. What kind of a five-year-old says something like that?'

'Can you please stop pacing, old girl, you're making me tired. Maybe he just meant thanks for the muffins and it came out wrong. Children get things mixed up all the time.' But Lou's voice is uncertain. He is no longer as convinced of his own position. Gladys pushes, needing an ally to her own thoughts.

'George is a particularly clever little boy. He was trying to give me some sort of message, I'm sure of it.'

'Maybe but what exactly can you do about it?'

'Well, I shall telephone the local police station and demand that they investigate.' She nods her head. This is the right thing to do.

'Yes, I suppose you could do that, but Gladys, didn't they ask you to… I don't know, stop calling or something?' He is hesitant, unsure of her reaction.

Gladys feels her face flame. 'I only call for good reasons, Lou. Constable Auerbach just asked if I could give people in the street more time to respond before I called her.'

'Please try talking to your neighbours before you call us, Gladys,' is what the constable said, but she had smiled kindly when she said it. 'You've called us twelve times this year already,' she said, then she reached out and patted Gladys on the arm, soothing an old woman. It had taken all of Gladys's will to not pull her arm back, refusing the kind gesture.

Gladys didn't think it could have been that many times anyway, but if it was, it was certainly not her fault that dogs barked all night or at least until 10 p.m., or that people parked in the incorrect manner or that sometimes the teenagers in the neighbourhood seemed to be exhibiting signs of being hard of hearing, so loud was their music. Every neighbourhood needs someone watching, making sure that things are all in order.

She reflects now that this is probably why she didn't call the police after yesterday's little incident. She had thought about it. She had definitely thought about it, but then she had imagined Constable Auerbach smiling kindly at her again and telling her, in a slightly condescending manner, that people have a right to do their jobs. But today she has tried to speak to Katherine. She's tried over and again.

'Look at that,' says Lou, turning up the news, obviously hoping to distract her. 'That young man has come to Sydney. They know he's here now. They'll get him, they will.'

Gladys glances at the television, sees the red cap again and she sinks into a chair, realisation creeping up her spine. 'I've seen him,' she says, placing her hand over her heart that is beating faster with each breath she takes.

'Well, yes, there on the television.' Lou gestures with the remote.

'No, Lou,' she says, wringing her hands. 'That man, wearing the same red cap, was here, in our garden. He was here.'

'Oh, Gladys, listen, I think…'

But she tunes her husband out. The red cap with the raised stitching in the same colour is seared on her mind. You can't see the stitching in the CCTV footage but she knows it's there. She knows it's him. The facial features are blurry on the television but they sharpen as she thinks about him. She's seen him. She can just make out the slight beard on his chin. She remembers that beard, knows she thought, *If young men can't grow proper beards, they should remain clean-shaven.* A passing thought as she looked at him.

If she hadn't wanted to hang the washing out then and there, she would probably not have seen the young man in her back garden at all, but there he was, looking straight into her kitchen when she came outside with the heavy plastic basket, filled with Lou's shirts. He does seem to drop food on himself a lot these days. She is forever running for the stain remover.

'What are you doing?' she shouted at the young man, fear causing her voice to sound high and squeaky. He was dressed in jeans ripped at the knee, a black T-shirt and the cap. *Red cap. Raised stitching on the front.*

'Gosh, I'm so sorry,' he said politely. 'I'm gardening next door and I wondered if I could place a ladder in your yard so I can trim the tall hedges on this side as well. I won't, of course, if you would prefer me not to.' He had a nice smile and he spoke very well so Gladys relaxed a bit.

'Are you from Mark's crew?' she asked because the Petersons next door were very proud of their garden and had Mark and his gardening crew in at least once every two weeks to keep everything looking shipshape. One of them usually came over to ask if he could cut the tall hedges from Gladys's side of the garden and of course she always said yes.

'I am,' he said and he smiled widely at her.

'Well, of course you can, I always allow it,' she said and then she realised that she'd forgotten her peg bag and had to go back inside. When she came back outside, he was gone, but she expected him back with his ladder at any moment. She darted to the front of the house quickly and saw that Mark's van was indeed out the front of the Petersons' house, so she assumed all was well.

She had been surprised when the young man hadn't returned with his ladder and even more surprised when Hamid, one of the regular gardeners, turned up to ask if he could trim the hedges only half an hour later.

'But I already told the other man that it was fine,' Gladys said.

'I'm the only one here today,' Hamid said. And Gladys just nodded and smiled, feeling very stupid. Especially when she realised that Hamid wore a khaki brown shirt with 'Garden Gurus' on the pocket. The other young man had not been wearing any sort of uniform. Of course, she dashed around the house for a bit, grateful that Lou was having a nap, checking her purse and Lou's wallet and the computers. Nothing had been taken or even moved. All was as it should be. She thought about calling the police, but then she imagined Constable Auerbach and her smile asking what exactly the problem was, and so she left it.

What was he doing here? Looking for money? Will he be back? Gladys imagines trying to sleep with the thought that a violent man is loose in her neighbourhood. No number of locks on her doors could make her feel safe. She needs to tell the police. It's important that they know so they can begin looking for him.

'I'm telling you, Lou, that man was here yesterday.' She repeats herself, her hands twisting with worry.

Lou reaches forward and touches her leg lightly, softly – his concern for her communicated through his fingers. 'Gladys, maybe you need a bit of a rest, you know, just for twenty minutes or so. It's really hot.'

She shakes off his touch and stands up, returns to her pacing. 'You have no idea what could be going on, Lou.' She feels her body heating up as she moves, her mouth dry and thoughts crashing into each other. 'Maybe the young man has something to do with John?' she says.

'Gladys, John is an accountant and he—'

'We don't know anything about what he does.' Her voice rises so that he will keep quiet. She paces some more and then stops in front of her husband's chair. 'Maybe John is involved in something nefarious and the man is holding the whole family hostage,' she says, grasping for the plot of some movie they once saw.

A look of real fear settles on Lou's face. She knows that he thinks that something is really wrong with her. He is afraid for her mental wellbeing but she knows she saw the man, and she knows that she cannot stand by anymore and just let what's happening at Katherine's house go on. Maybe the two are connected. Maybe not but she needs to get some help from the police.

'I'll be back,' she says to Lou, because she means to do something about all of this. Once and for all.

She will make the call outside after checking Katherine's house just once more. A little spark of hope inside her imagines seeing Katherine and the children out the front, the hose sprinkling over the twins as it did last Sunday.

'Maybe it's all fine,' she says aloud as she leaves her house. 'Maybe everything is fine.'

CHAPTER TWENTY-THREE

'I know that you've carried this around with you for a long time. I understand how much it would have hurt you and how difficult it was for you to live with your father and then for him... but you're not there anymore.'

I am eating my way through an apple. The strange thing about being given free rein over what you eat is that your body starts to cry out for something more after a few months. I started to crave fruit when I lived with my father, the same way some kids lust after junk food.

After he died and they sent me back to live with my mother, I could see she thought the problem had been solved.

'We can start again,' she told me. 'I've found a good counsellor and we can go together and we can just start again.'

But I didn't want to spend any time with her. I was failed by both of them and the only thing I wanted was to leave my past behind and start my life again. At fifteen, I just wanted to move on. I imagined that becoming an adult and having control of my life would make everything different, but here I stand because of a woman who made a decision, who broke my heart and unravelled whatever life I had built for myself. Here I stand because exactly the same thing that happened to my father has happened to me.

I carried the guilt of my own part in his death with me all the time. It weighed me down and made me tired and apathetic about my own existence. If I had only listened to him when he lectured me, or maybe if I had found a way to get him some help... If I had been a better son, then he would have believed there was a reason for him to stick around, to try and give up the alcohol and get off the sofa. But I wasn't and I knew it was my fault he was dead.

'I don't want to live with you,' I told her. 'I would rather go into foster care.' I enjoyed the way those words hit her, shocking her so that she crumpled a little and sank into a chair.

'You hate me that much?' she asked.

'He wouldn't be dead if you had taken him back.' Such a simple thing for a wife to do. Forgive. Listen, understand and forgive.

I stare at the three of them on the sofa now. The children are dozing in the heat but she is still watching me, her one cheek swollen, her wrist puffed up, watching and waiting for a chance to get away.

'Only a few weeks ago, I was happy,' I say. 'I thought I had everything figured out.'

She is quiet, seeking refuge in silence, afraid of what I may do if she says something wrong. I like her like this.

I think about falling in love, about that first rush of excitement when all you can think about is that person and you spend your whole day just waiting to see them. Those first few months, we couldn't keep our hands off each other. When she asked me to move in with her, I was like a kid at Christmas, so excited I couldn't sleep the night before. The first night I moved in we stayed up all night talking, planning, even naming our future children.

I had already told her about my father dying and I had explained that I was estranged from my mother. One night, a few months after we met, I told her about my childhood as we sat in front of a fire in a pub on a cold night. It was pouring outside but we had braved the weather to go looking for a good burger and we found ourselves in an old-fashioned pub with a dartboard on the wall and a large fire roaring in a stone fireplace, blackened with age. The burgers were pretty good and we were the only two in the place.

'Why don't you want to talk to her?' she asked me that night in the pub.

'I can't,' I told her. And then I explained about my father. She listened quietly, occasionally touching my hand, her eyes shining with unshed tears for my tragic childhood. I thought that was the end of it. I thought we would never have to discuss it again, that I would never have to think about it again.

I felt completely accepted by her. Once you've shared your childhood demons with someone, there is a connection that shouldn't be broken. I knew in the pub that night that I'd found a woman who would never break my heart and who would always understand me and what I needed. I feel really stupid about that now because I was warned by my father, but I somehow thought that it would be different for me.

The longer we were together, the more she lectured, argued, tried to control me. That's what she was doing. She was trying to control me. My father's note came back to me again and again. I should never have allowed myself to fall in love. I could see it coming, a slow-motion movie of my life and how it would play out. First, she would try to change me and I would grow frustrated with her. My father cheated on my mother and maybe somewhere deep inside me was the gene for that, the need for that. I used to imagine scenarios where I did meet another woman, where I could be with someone who didn't need me to be a different person to the one she had liked in the first place. And then I saw her telling me it was over and kicking me out and I didn't even need to think about what that terrible spiral down into addiction and depression would look like. I had watched it, been part of it and I couldn't stand the idea that it was going to happen to me. I felt trapped by how much I loved her and how much I knew she was going to hurt me. I should have left then but I kept hoping. In some weird way I'm still hoping that it can all be fixed, that it can be put right. I just needed to do something drastic, something big. I needed to make her understand that leaving me, that our parting, was simply not an option.

But I'm not sure now. I'm not sure where I go from here or what I do, and strangely, I would like to be able to ask my father what I should do. But he's gone because it all got too much for him and I can't let that happen to me. I have to see this through.

I have no choice.

I drop my apple core on the floor, watching her eyes widen at the gesture. It's laughable that something that ridiculous still has the ability to affect anyone considering where we all are now.

'My life wasn't meant to go like this, you know,' I tell her.

'That's not my fault,' she says, frustration in her voice.

'Then whose fault is it?' I ask as I rub the gun against my shirt, ridding the handle of my sweat.

'It's…' she begins, but I shake my head at her.

I don't care to listen to her answer.

CHAPTER TWENTY-FOUR

Katherine

Her mouth is gritty with bits of chocolate muffin, her throat dry, but she doesn't want to ask him for water. She doesn't want to ask him for anything except that he just go, just leave her and her children alone. There is mounting anger inside her but she knows that she needs to control it. His behaviour is not just unpredictable and violent – it feels like he's on the edge of something worse, something that she will not be able to recover from. The room is warmer with each passing hour, filling up with the heat of their combined bodies, and she longs for the outside, for space to breathe and move. She can feel that there must be a way out of this beyond just sitting here and waiting for him to decide it's over.

'It's getting late,' she says. 'Do you understand? This can't go on.' She speaks softly, gently. He is back in the recliner, the gun resting on his knee, pointed at the three of them. He is getting tired. It's hard work to maintain the rage that's keeping the gun pointed in their direction.

'I don't…' he begins.

'I understand. You don't know what to do,' she says. 'But if you just get up now, just get up and leave, I won't report you to the police. I won't say anything at all. Take whatever you want and just go.' She is in pain all over her body but she feels herself rise above the throbbing and the sharpness of it as she speaks. She has to end this. She cannot give in to the pain because she has these children to save.

He snorts, derision in the sound. 'Of course you're going to report me. I would report me.'

'No one needs to know about what happened here today. I can say that I fell and hurt my wrist. The kids will keep the secret, won't you, George? Sophie?'

The children rouse themselves from their light sleep. She knows they have been listening. 'We can keep this a secret, can't we?' she repeats. They both nod, but cautiously. They've been told that lying is bad. She hopes to have a chance to explain this all to them, to be here still and to have them with her so she can explain.

'It would be so easy to leave now. You can go anywhere you like. Where would you like to go?' You have to keep a person threatening you talking. That's what she's read and heard. Keep them talking until you can see a gap, a space, a moment to change the balance of power and save your own life.

She keeps her tone light. He has responded to her a little, and all she needs is a little. The children watch her as she speaks. They don't understand her calm voice when they know she should be angry or scared.

Outside the cicadas are screaming and inside the air conditioner rattles and wheezes. It is afternoon and the heat is thick and heavy, hanging in the air, the sun burning the grass brown in places. And he is tired. She can feel his exhaustion in the air, as though it is part of her. If she keeps watching him, there will be a moment, just a moment when she can make this work. She rests her damaged wrist on her knee, wincing at the continual pain there, and she slides her good hand between the seat cushions, surreptitiously, slowly and carefully. She feels the slightly rough plastic handle of the scissors and she grasps it tightly. Any minute now.

CHAPTER TWENTY-FIVE

Fifteen Minutes Ago

Logan

'Debbie, Debbie!' he keeps screaming as he drives, weaving in and out of traffic, other cars hooting their anger. He can hear muffled conversation from the other end of the line but he has no idea what's going on. It sounds like she's dropped her phone. He feels like he cannot control his speed. His foot is pressed on the gas pedal and the van goes faster and faster and he is powerless to make it stop. He roars through a stop sign, narrowly missing being hit by a car that had the right of way. The driver holds their hand down on the hooter, long and loud, indignant at his behaviour, but he is moving so quickly, too quickly, and the sound is only momentary before he's left it behind.

He needs to slow down or he's going to get pulled over and then he won't get to her. He won't be able to save her. Debbie is small and light, and although she's stronger than she looks, she won't be able to defend herself against an enraged man. Patrick's hands on his sister, Patrick's hands on Debbie, the two women he loves most in the world. This cannot be. He cannot let this happen.

'Logan,' he hears, 'Logan, why are you shouting my name?' She yells the words, sounding hysterical.

'Debbie…' he says again, pure relief running through his veins, making him feel almost high. He lifts his foot off the gas, the van slows down and he searches for a space to pull over for a moment. His whole body has broken out in a sweat and there is an ache in his jaw from clamping his teeth together. His hands slip a little on the steering wheel. 'Who's there? Who's there?' he yells as he pulls the van to the side of the road.

'Stop yelling,' she says, even as she's shouting herself. 'Stop yelling and listen. It's my dad, just my dad,' she says, her voice still raised. 'He came over to bring me some soup and he dropped it all over the carpet. We're cleaning it up but you're yelling like a crazy person. What on earth is wrong?' Her voice softens and with her explanation he feels his body relax, his muscles release, and he takes a deep breath. It's her dad, just her dad.

He would like to reach through the phone and grab his wife, hold her to him. He could have lost her. She could have been taken from him and he will not let that happen.

Logan rubs his eyes, creating the dark space he needs, knowing that if he doesn't calm down, he will not be able to explain himself.

A white cockatoo lands on the front of his van, cocks its yellow-crested head and stares at him. 'Put your dad on the phone,' he commands, and he is grateful that she doesn't question him. He watches the bird as it climbs onto a windscreen wiper and perches there, making eye contact, before spreading its white wings and flying onto a tree in a garden near where he's parked.

'Logan,' says Paul, concern in his voice.

'Listen, Paul, I don't think I can explain it to her without freaking out, but Patrick is here, in Sydney. He's here and I got a text saying that I'm next and I think he's here to hurt me because of…'

'Because of what happened with Maddy? Debbie told us. Surely not.'

'I think so. Please just take Debbie with you. Take her to your house. I'm getting there as fast as I can.' He squeezes the steering wheel, watching the bird as it struts up and down a tree branch.

He looks around and pulls out into the road again, keeping to the speed limit, concentrating on what he's doing.

'All right, son. You calm down and drive carefully. I'll take her with me and text you when we're at my house. You come there and we'll call the police and explain. Now just calm down. Everything's going to be fine.'

'Thanks, Paul,' says Logan and he is ashamed that he's shedding a few tears.

He watches the road, tries to orient himself because he's gotten himself a bit lost.

She's with her dad, she's with her dad.

He can handle this because Debbie is safe and that's all he needs to know. He spots the name of a road he recognises and turns the van around. 'She's safe,' he repeats aloud. 'She's safe.'

After driving for a few minutes, Debbie calls him. 'We're on the way to my parents' house. There wasn't anyone there, like in the street or anything. Maybe he isn't coming after you.' In the background he can hear the classical music that Paul always plays in his car. Just after Logan asked Debbie to marry him – getting down on one knee on a beach, embarrassed that he couldn't think of a less clichéd idea but so excited he dropped the ring with a small diamond it took him months to save for – Paul took the whole family to hear a string quartet at the opera house to celebrate. The music was beautiful at first, but soon Logan found himself drifting off and Debbie had to keep nudging him awake. 'Guess it's not for everyone,' Paul said afterwards and he remembers the way Debbie and her mother laughed at him but he also remembers that the laughter was gentle and inclusive and that for the first time in his life he didn't feel judged. *This is family*, he thought and he couldn't believe he was lucky enough to have found a woman like Debbie with a family who accepted him. He doesn't deserve Debbie, he knows that. And he will give his life to keep her safe if he has to. It's not even something he has to consider. It's just the truth.

'I think he is, Debs. Just get to your parents' house and make sure everything is locked. I'm on my way.'

He takes a few shortcuts, hoping to make his trip to Debbie's parents' place shorter. He looks around at the houses in the street where he's driving and realises that it's the street from this morning, the street where he started his day – where he first understood that it was going to be a really, really shitty day. He could never have imagined how bad it was going to get.

How is it that he's back here? How is it possible? He wasn't thinking about a particular route, just about getting to Debbie's parents' house as soon as he could.

Why is he even thinking about this woman? It doesn't matter. He's sure the police will check on Katherine West and her family.

But dammit, the niggling feeling is there again and just won't go away.

Without knowing why, or what he plans to do, he cruises to a stop in front of Katherine's house and gets out of the van.

A large tree on the pavement rustles in the silent afternoon and he looks up to see a whole host of cockatoos resting in the heat. One of them peers down at him and then spreads its wings and leaps, landing on the front of his van.

'Okay, universe,' he grumbles. 'I understand.'

CHAPTER TWENTY-SIX

Gladys

She marches out of her house and into the street, where a white van with the words 'Pack and Go' is pulling up. As she watches, the door opens and a tall man, covered head to toe in tattoos, gets out. Gladys feels like she might just faint away. She opens her mouth as a flock of cockatoos takes flight from the tree in front of Katherine's house, startling her and disturbing the still air, creating a tiny gust of wind, and then everything is quiet again. She squares her shoulders and takes a deep breath. 'Excuse me,' she says, holding her chin high. 'Excuse me!'

CHAPTER TWENTY-SEVEN

I feel my eyes growing heavy, my body slipping as though I'm falling, and I jerk myself awake, lifting the gun in case they were thinking about trying anything.

I sit up straighter and then I get up and walk around a bit, watching them, trying to generate a little more energy. Her wrist is grotesquely swollen and bright red. I notice for the first time how pale her face is, how she keeps biting down on her lip. I think she must be in a lot of pain. Somewhere inside me, I feel something twisting, something churning – maybe it's guilt. Is it guilt? My arms are heavy holding this gun; my body wants to sink to the floor. The walking isn't helping and I drop down into the chair again. I could leave now, just get up and leave. Start over somewhere else, maybe try to find another woman to love me the way I deserve to be loved. I think about leaving this house, walking out into the stifling heat and finding my way to a main road. I imagine holding my thumb out, getting a lift to the ocean where there would be a breeze coming off the water because there is always a breeze. I could wade into the sea where it would be cool and quiet and it wouldn't matter that I have no one who loves me. I could walk out until the water covered my head and then I would be alone in the floating space and it would feel better.

I am so tired, so incredibly tired. I put my hands against my eyes, the gun hurting my temple. I shove it into my waistband and rub my eyes, rub them hard so black dots appear. I need to get rid of this fuzzy exhaustion. I have to think clearly now.

Taking a deep breath, I pull my hands away from my face. And she's standing there, holding a pair of scissors above me, small blue-handled scissors. She holds them high up and I can see that she wants to hurt me but at the same time she doesn't want to hurt me. She has never caused anyone physical pain. But she's pretty good at mental torture. I want to laugh at her silly attempt to stop me. Me! I have a gun. I'm bigger than her and yet she thinks she can do this. And I am no longer tired. I'm furious at her stupidity and at her tiny, stupid moment of hesitation.

'This has to stop,' she says and she brings the scissors down, going for my face, but I'm too quick for her. I leap up and grab her hand, pull the scissors away and chuck them across the room, and then I backhand her hard, as hard as I can. I feel the power in my hand as it connects with her face and I could roar with fury. I cannot deny how good it feels.

Sophie screams. She opens her mouth and screams loud and long.

I put my hands over my ears because the scream has been waiting inside her all day. I know it's the scream of a terrified child. It fills the air and tears at my eardrums.

She lies there, still. I think I may have killed her, but then she moves and rolls on her side.

'Sophie, stop,' she commands and the little girl closes her mouth. Her voice is thick with pain but still trying for calm.

The room is silent. George is watching me, his fists clenched. Sophie is huddled on the sofa and she is on the floor, trying to get up without hurting her wrist. I go over to her and extend a hand. 'Let me help you.' I would like to touch her kindly, just one more time. I want to help her as she struggles and there is something inside me that regrets hurting her.

'Get away from me,' she spits. 'Just get away from us and get out of here.'

She's angry with me but it wasn't my fault. I watch her, sensing the shift in her, the change. She's been trying to appease me all day, but now she's finished doing that. I remember this about her as I watch her struggle to get off the floor. She tries and tries but she reaches a point where she's done. I can see she's reached that point.

She's the one who attacked me. It isn't my fault that we're here. It's because of her, because of decisions that she made, and now she thinks she gets to be angry at me. 'I don't think so,' I mutter.

She climbs back onto the sofa, slowly, painfully, her breathing heavy and her face twisting with the pain. They all slump together in a heap, pure hatred evident on all their faces. Even her. The kids' faces are dirty, grimy with chocolate and food and sweat. She has blood dribbled onto her white T-shirt and large sweat patches under her arms. I can smell myself and it's not nice. We are an unpleasant bunch to look at, to breathe in, but we will not be here much longer. They will not be here much longer.

I never thought I would see hatred on her face. Anger and frustration, yes, but not actual hatred. I never thought she would feel the way about me that I have come to feel about her. I don't like it. My legs feel heavy, the weight of my sadness too much for them.

I never wanted her to hate me. I only ever wanted her to love me for who I was and not who she thought I could be.

The three of them look drained of energy. But they're still willing to fight. That's fine because they have no idea how far I'm willing to go.

I'm also tired now. I would like to rest, to sleep, but in order to do that I have to be done with this. There is no way out except the only way I imagined this would end.

'Be a shark, son,' my father said and so that's what I will be.

I nod my head as though he is watching me. I understand what I need to do now. I start to count. I count down from one hundred in my head, slowly, carefully, knowing that when I get to one, this will all be over.

CHAPTER TWENTY-EIGHT

Katherine

Defeat makes her want to cry. She has no idea how on earth they're going to get out of this. There is a ringing in her ears. Her body has never been hurt like this before. She cannot comprehend pain without a purpose. She remembers the feeling of pushing her babies into the world, the overwhelming sensation of agony that ran through her, but she could harness it and use it for the energy she needed. Something has changed in her. Something has superseded the fear she has been fighting all day long. It's a wonder to her as she gazes out of the window that it is still light, that night has not arrived and the wind that was supposed to bring the cool change has not blown through the open window, chilling them all.

They have been in this room forever but she's not going to be here forever more. She is not going to let him hurt her and the children. Not anymore.

Last week she had taken the twins to the shopping centre for groceries and they had walked past the pet shop and stopped to look at the puppies cavorting in the window, little white balls of yapping fluff. 'Oh, please, Mum, please,' Sophie begged, as she did every time they saw a dog, 'I will love it forever.'

'When you're old enough to really take care of one – I promise.' She is planning a puppy as a Christmas surprise. She has already been in touch with a breeder. How can it be possible that they will not be here for Christmas? An impossible thought this morning; a very real possibility now unless she does something.

He wants this to end as well. She has to make sure the children survive and so she has to fight through the pain she is feeling, the physical agony from her wrist, her cheek, her ear where he hit her, and the anguish in her heart of someone who is supposed to love her, to love them, hurting them. She and she alone has to end this now.

Help isn't coming.

CHAPTER TWENTY-NINE

Now

Logan

He slides open the side door, taking the computer box in his hand again, but as he starts for the front gate a woman stops him.

'Excuse me,' she says, ownership and judgement in just those two words.

Logan looks at her. She is an older woman, dressed in batik-print, three-quarter pants which are a riot of flowers and colours. She is also wearing a blue sleeveless top, revealing muscled, ropey arms. Her short brown hair is pinned back with a child's butterfly clip.

'I was just going to deliver this computer,' says Logan.

'You don't look like a delivery man,' says the woman, eyeing his tattoos. He knows exactly what she's thinking. He shouldn't have ripped off his shirt but there's nothing to be done about that now.

'Well, I am,' he says flatly.

'Yes, well,' huffs the woman, pursing her thin lips. 'I live next door and I can tell you that Katherine receives lots of deliveries but I've never seen you or your van. I'm concerned for my neighbour, so I'll thank you to show me some identification.'

Logan sighs, contemplates getting back into the van and driving off, heading to his in-laws' house and sitting across from his wife, smiling into her beautiful face. *The neighbours heard screaming.*

The words come back to him and his sister's voice calling for help sickens him.

'Look, I—' he begins.

'Now I'll have no arguments from you, thank you. I have my phone right here and I am happy to call the police, and believe me when I tell you that they will be here in two ticks.' The woman holds up her mobile phone in its red and white spotted case and Logan clenches his jaw, trying to resist the urge to hand the computer to this ridiculous woman and leave. He's done all he can, he really has, and he's encountered nothing but obstacles in his desire to help whoever the woman inside the house is, and by the time he finds out if something is or is not going on, he will be back in jail just for daring to exist after a prison sentence. He needs to get to Debbie because she is his priority. If Patrick comes looking for him, he wants to be ready. He has his own family to protect. Katherine West is not his family.

The woman puts her hands on her hips and Logan glances at the house that she says belongs to her. It's as big as the one next to it and the neighbour obviously knows the woman he is concerned about.

'Actually,' he says slowly, 'I would be grateful if you'd call the police.'

'What? Why?' Her open-mouthed surprise is almost amusing.

'Okay, lady, I'm going to level with you. I know what I look like and I know who I am, but here's the thing. I tried to deliver this computer this morning and she wouldn't open the door. Now, that's not a big deal but it's a computer and I told her I would wait so she could get dressed or whatever. But she still wouldn't open the door and she sounded… I don't even know how to describe it.'

'Scared,' says the woman. 'She sounded scared?'

Logan looks at the lady. That's an odd response. Why would that be her first guess… unless… unless she's noticed something as well. She reminds him a bit of Mrs McGuire, who lives on the ground floor of their building. Her windows face the street and Debbie believes that there is not a thing that goes on in their building that she doesn't know about. If she catches him as he's leaving for work, she will tell him how many deliveries there have been that week, how big the parcels going to number twenty-four are, where three young women share a flat, and what time the gardener for the complex will be arriving. Debbie thinks she's nosy but Logan doesn't mind her watching things. Someone has to.

He takes a chance that the woman he is looking at is this street's version of Mrs McGuire, and that she's also noticed something amiss.

'I guess… scared or worried or something. I could be completely wrong but I would be grateful if you'd ring the bell and maybe she'll let you in, and then I can just give her the computer and I can stop worrying about her.' Logan holds out the computer, desperate to just be done with this. 'I tried to deliver it again a couple of hours ago and some kid inside the house said something about a gun and it's just… You probably think I'm insane but if you call the police…'

'What's your name?'

Releasing a sigh, he says, 'Logan.'

'Logan, I'm Gladys, and as I told you, I live next door. Now normally, Logan, I wouldn't believe a word you've said. I mean I would assume that you're some sort of… Look, it doesn't matter. The point I'm trying to make is that I am also worried about Katherine and the children, George and Sophie.'

Logan feels a small shiver run down his back. He notices the strong, almost rotting smell of the honeysuckle on the fence dying in the heat, and the scream of the cicadas is suddenly too loud for him. He has not been imagining this.

'Okay, Gladys… look, I'm really pleased I ran into you. I've got to tell you, I went to the police this afternoon to try and get them to send someone but they didn't seem interested in what I had to say because, well…' Logan holds out his arms so she understands that he is referring to his tattoos. There is no reason for the woman to hear about his past right now.

'Well, I've never judged a book by its cover, I'm sure. You sound like a concerned young man and I share your concern.'

Logan wants to laugh at the lie. He's willing to bet she would normally cross the street to avoid someone like him. But he stifles a smile – shocked that he can smile on a day like today – and decides he doesn't care what this woman thinks of him, as long as she gets the police to come.

'Great, so perhaps you can call the police and ask them to do something called a welfare check? They'll come if you call them.'

'Of course, they will,' says Gladys, her shoulders going back, 'that's a very good idea. I was going to anyway, you know. I am very worried about Katherine as well. I've called the police a few times this year... well, maybe more than a few. Rhonda from down the road flits off here and there at a moment's notice and leaves her two teenage sons in the house and you can imagine what they get up to.'

'I'm sure,' says Logan, fighting the urge to wrench the woman's phone away from her. This is taking too long. He needs to go. Debbie is with her parents, probably tucked up in her childhood bed with a cup of honey and lemon tea. She's safe but for how long?

Gladys finally stops talking and she taps the number for the local police, stored in her phone – and, Logan imagines, at the top of her contacts list. He closes his eyes as she explains her concerns in minute detail without, he's pleased to hear, referring to him, and he thanks God for interfering neighbours.

'They're sending someone over in the next twenty minutes,' she says. 'The nice young man told me not to try and get into the house but just to wait, so they are obviously taking my concerns very seriously.'

'Great, that's great,' says Logan. 'I might leave you to it. I'll drop off this computer at the post office and she can pick it up another time. I'm glad you're on to it, Gladys. She's lucky to have a neighbour like you.'

'Yes, well, she's never said so but I do believe you speak the truth,' says the elderly lady.

Logan turns away from her and puts the computer back in the van. He feels the weight of the day lift off his shoulders. He can leave now. Gladys has things under control. He imagines that if the police don't arrive soon, she will call again and keep calling until they do. She seems like the type.

He breathes in, catching the scent of the coconut sunscreen that Debbie uses and perhaps this woman uses as well. He sighs with relief.

His day is not over. His worries are not over, but at least if he and Debbie are at her parents' house, they can take a small break before he heads to the airport. Paul will have beer in the fridge and he can pop open a bottle and figure out what to do about Patrick, about Maddy.

He slides the side door of the van closed and leans his head briefly against the warm metal.

And that's when he hears a scream.

CHAPTER THIRTY

Gladys

The scream is long and loud, desperate and sad all at once. Gladys looks at Katherine's house and then at the man. Her mouth drops open, words failing her. Logan takes off running and she watches as he darts to the side of the house, pushing at the side gate and then heaving his shoulder into it. The wood gives way, the gate swinging open with a crunch.

Who screamed? Was it George or Sophie or Katherine? Gladys covers her mouth with her hand. *Who screamed? Who was it?*

'Oh, Lou,' she says, remembering that her husband is waiting for her.

She walks quickly back towards her own front door, steps inside her house, just a step, and shouts, 'Are you okay, Lou?'

'I'm fine,' shouts Lou. 'What was that scream? I heard a scream.'

Gladys looks back at the street, where she can see if a police car approaches. *Come on, come on.* She wants to go back to Katherine's house and see what's happening. She can't see much through the green hedging that is between her front garden and Katherine's front garden. But first she needs to reassure Lou, who's still in the living room.

'It was… I think it was one of the children,' yells Gladys so that he can hear her. 'Now you stay right where you are. I've called the police and it's all going to get sorted out, just stay where you are, Lou.' She waits to hear his reply, her gaze concentrated on the road.

'Don't tell me what to do, Gladys. If something is happening over there, you need to stay here until the police come. You need to be safe.'

Gladys marches back into her house and into the living room, wagging her finger as she sees Lou, who is peering at the door. 'Now you listen to me, Lou Aaron Philips, I'm fine. All I need is for you to keep yourself safe while I figure this out.'

'No need to be so strict, old girl, I'm just worried about you.' He sags a little in his chair and she is immediately sorry, but her worry over Katherine and the children is making her horribly jumpy.

'I'll be fine, love. Do you need anything? I may be a few minutes.'

'No, no, I'm all right… but, Glad, please be careful.'

She plants a quick kiss on top of his head and marches back down her front garden path to stand outside Katherine's house and wait for the police. As she goes, she dials the station again. No reason why they can't hurry themselves along. No reason at all.

'Yes, now listen here,' she says when the call is answered, and she explains again, although this time she adds in the scream she and the delivery man just heard. It was not a normal scream, not a child playing or just doing themselves some minor injury. That scream held fear and pain. Gladys has no idea how she knows this, but she does.

She paces up and down, looking down the front path to Katherine's house. What if the man who has gone into the house is the dangerous one? *Should I follow him inside? Should I stay here? Will Lou be okay if something happens? Who will take care of Lou if I get hurt?*

The delivery driver is such a frightening-looking man, every inch of his skin covered in violent tattoos, but his voice is deep and calm and he has nice blue eyes. Can she trust him? She thinks she can but she has no idea why this is. He is not the sort of person she would normally trust. He's the sort of person she would call the police on. She almost did, but it was the way he said, 'I'm going to level with you,' that made her pause. The world needs more people like Logan.

It's unnerving how quiet it is, how the silence has draped itself over the suburb after the last few minutes of noise. Gladys looks around at the other houses on the street, wondering exactly what is happening inside all of them. Katherine's house looks the same today as it did yesterday but she has obviously never had any real idea of what is occurring behind the beautiful timber front door that is meant to keep people out, but which may very well have kept people trapped inside today.

CHAPTER THIRTY-ONE

'I'm asking you one last time,' she says, interrupting my counting. 'I'm asking you to leave, just leave.' Her face is a mess and I have to listen carefully when she speaks because her cheek and lips have puffed and it's affecting her speech, the way she sounds. I did that. How did I do that? But then again, I've done worse than that. I've crossed other lines and I can feel myself stepping over another one.

My father's grey face and staring eyes are there as I count. 'Don't trust a woman, boy.' If I leave, if I don't finish this, I know it will only be months before those staring eyes are mine. Except I won't just lie in some bed in a small apartment for a couple of days. I won't just be there until my son, who loves me, opens the door to the terrible stench of my death. I will lie there undiscovered and alone because at least he had me. However shitty a son I was. At least he had me. As of today, as of the end of this countdown, I will have no one. But I will not be the only one to suffer.

'No,' I say to her because she is still hoping to get through to me with her pleading. 'No, I don't think I'm going to do that.'

I resume my counting at fifty. Halfway there and it will all be over.

CHAPTER THIRTY-TWO

Katherine

She nods her head at his final refusal. She will not ask or beg or plead again. He's made a decision. Well, so has she. These children may grow up without a mother, but at least they will grow up. If she moves quickly enough, uses her whole body to block the gun and shouts at the children to run, she may just give them time to get away. She has no other option now. He's taken all of her choices away.

She glances at her weary babies; at the way their little bodies are slumped on the sofa. Sophie's curls are limp with heat and sweat, her green eyes dull with the exhaustion of hours and hours of fear and confinement. George's hair is slicked to his forehead but his eyes have an intensity that bothers her. He is staring at him as though trying to annihilate him with just a look. He wants to hurt the man who has hurt them and she can feel her little boy, the person he is, slipping away.

There is no question about what she has to do. She's made her choice. She's chosen them.

CHAPTER THIRTY-THREE

Logan

Logan stands at the back door of the house. It's a standard back door with an easily opened lock. It wouldn't take much to push it open. The gate at the side gave way easily enough with just a small lift and shove, the old wood splintering. Logan hesitates. If there is nothing going on in the house – if he's just imagining this and he gets inside, actually breaks in – then he is going back to prison for a long time.

But the scream sounded like it came from a child. That was a few minutes ago. It's all quiet inside now. Maybe she saw a spider? Debbie screams blue murder when she sees one of the huge huntsman spiders that stalk the Australian summer. They're harmless unless they give you a heart attack. Maybe that's all it was. The neighbours on either side of him have kids and sometimes it literally sounds like someone is being tortured. Debbie has gone over to check once or twice, only to be told, 'Oh, he just didn't want to eat his carrots,' by a harassed parent who would rather she hadn't interfered.

He presses his ear against the door, hoping that he will hear something that can give him a clue as to what is going on inside. But there is only silence. He has left Gladys out the front waiting for the police and he hopes, actually prays, that they turn up soon so he doesn't have to do this.

Pushing up against the door, he covers his other ear with his hand so he can hear better. The sun is relentless and he can feel it burning the skin on his arms and face. A large blowfly lands on his arm and he swats at it irritably, trying not to make a sound.

No one is in the kitchen behind this door, he's sure of that. He's assumed this is the kitchen. It may be the laundry. It would be better if it were the laundry because then it would be less likely that anyone is in there right now.

Taking a deep breath, he turns the handle, meaning to lift and shove as he does so but knowing he needs to be very quiet about it. And the door opens.

It was never locked.

This is an expensive house in a nice suburb. People don't need to lock their doors, but sometimes, the threat is already inside the house.

Logan steps in, holding his breath and freezing as the door opens and there is a sound like a click. He listens for something, anything, calling on all his instincts, unsure and a little scared at what he's going to find.

CHAPTER THIRTY-FOUR

Gladys

Gladys has no idea what to do. She is at a tennis match, her head swivelling from her house to Katherine's house, her ears listening for any sound. Sweat soaks through her shirt. The heat is heavy and thick in her lungs and still the police don't come. 'Please, God,' she prays aloud. What is happening inside that house? Is Logan inside already? Should she go around the back and check? She has no idea what to do and she feels like screaming in frustration herself. And still, the police don't come.

CHAPTER THIRTY-FIVE

*I gulp in the heated air. I'm covered in sweat but I'm nearly there.
Ten, nine, eight... I slow down but I'm getting there. Who will I be
after this? Where will I go? I know I will have to run. I will have to
let others find them, others walk through this house and discover three
people who were and now are not. Three people that I should have
loved enough not to do this. I imagine myself somewhere far away,
living out my life, holding on to the memory of this day of heat and
hate. Can a person live like that, I wonder? Can they wake up in the
morning and drink their coffee and know with each passing minute
that they are the reason that others are no longer here? I began this
believing that's possible. I would make sure everyone who has ever
caused me pain has paid for it and then I would move forward into
a new life, free of years of baggage. But I know it's not really possible.
I am weighed down by it all and weary of how heavy it is.*

*Seven, six... I feel tears pressing, my throat thick with grief, as I feel
the truth inside me, as I understand what I have known all day long.
Whoever comes into this house, whoever uncovers what has happened
here, will discover four people. Not three but four.*

I want this done. I want it over with.

CHAPTER THIRTY-SIX

Katherine

His lips are moving, counting, and she knows she has to move before he gets to zero, just before.

Glancing at her children, she tries to take in their little faces, to breathe in their sweaty, sweet smell. She has so much more to tell them, to teach them, so much more love to give them. If only she had written some of it down so that they could find it after she's gone. She looks at their faces and tries to picture the man in George, the woman in Sophie, and understands that the best she can hope for now is that they remember how much she loved them and that they understand her sacrifice. *My life for theirs*, she sends up in a silent prayer, and to her it seems a fair enough trade. *My life for theirs.*

George will blame himself. Her little man, her deep thinker. He will blame himself. They are not allowed to open the front door without an adult present. It's a rule of the house, even in this safe suburb.

'Do not open the door without me,' she has shouted whenever the bell chimes. But children are impulsive; George is controlled but always interested. Who might it be? Is it a delivery, a box with contents to guess at? Or is it Gladys, who comes bearing cake?

This morning his curiosity got the better of him, and she was in the laundry, the washing machine filling, rushing water drowning out the chiming of the bell.

George opened the door.

But even if her son hadn't let him in, Katherine knows she would have. She would have welcomed him into her home.

Please don't blame yourself, George. I would have done the same thing.

She closes her eyes and assesses the pain in her body, her cheek, her mouth, her wrist. She has to find a way to get her children out of this house. Tears prick at her eyes and she takes a deep breath because she doesn't want to cry in front of her two silent, frightened children. She must find a way to get them out.

As she breathes out, she hears a click, just a small click from the kitchen. It is the sound the kitchen door makes when it's opened. There is a small piece of wood at the bottom of the door that has split away. John is going to putty it up at some point but he hasn't done it yet and so whenever it opens, no matter how quiet the person opening the door is trying to be, there is the small click of the wood catching. She doesn't even hear it anymore. It's simply become one of the sounds that are part of her everyday life. But she has heard it today, with her eyes closed and her heart filled with despair. She has heard it today. She opens her eyes to find George staring at her, his green eyes wide, his fist clenched, and she knows, without a shadow of a doubt, that her son has heard the click as well. He pays attention, that's who he is. And right now, as the heat strangles the air, he has heard what she has heard.

Someone is in the kitchen. Someone has opened the back door.

She can see George rising a little from the sofa. He wants to run, to see who it is, but she knows they need to wait.

She has no idea who it could be and she wonders if it's actually someone breaking into the house. There have been some burglaries in the area but mostly those take place at night when the homeowners are out. The irony of it is that she would welcome a burglar right now.

George opens his mouth a little and she gives her head a slight shake. 'Wait,' she mouths. She mouths it three times before he nods that he has understood.

They need to wait.

CHAPTER THIRTY-SEVEN

Logan

The kitchen is empty; a white marble countertop gleams in the afternoon sun. Shiny black cabinets sit below the counter and stark white ones above. A black-and-white checkerboard floor of tiles adds to what should be a magazine-perfect look but there are too many things out of place for a magazine. The sink is filled with dirty dishes. A trail of ants marches along the countertop that is covered in cracker boxes and half-eaten pieces of fruit, on which fruit flies converge and gorge themselves. Disinfectant wipes lie unopened next to the mess. He glances at the large fridge, which is covered in photos and children's drawings held up by animal magnets.

He takes a step forward, hears a crunch under his foot and silently curses as he looks down to see a spilled bag of crisps. He knows that this is not how this kitchen usually looks. He takes a deep breath and steps around the crisps, looking down, his feet careful as he listens for movement in the house.

CHAPTER THIRTY-EIGHT

Gladys

Gladys waits, hating the heat and the sun and this day more with each passing minute. 'Where are you?' she mutters, peering down the street. 'Where are you?' She looks at her watch and sees that Logan has only been inside the house for a minute or so. The heat is oppressive and the cicadas are maddening whenever she tunes in to them. She looks at her phone again, waiting, hoping – for what, she's not sure.

CHAPTER THIRTY-NINE

When I get to five, I slow my count, leaving the space of one breath in between the numbers, because a life can change in just one breath, because I'm going to take a breath and change their lives.

I'm not sure I'm ready for this. I've fired a gun before. My father once took me to a shooting range. It was a present for my fourteenth birthday. He didn't tell me where we were going. He wanted it to be a surprise. It was a rifle range and I found the gun unwieldy to hold. I wasn't very good but my father was. He hit the target every time. 'I've always had a good eye,' he told me. I think it was one of the last good days he had. I wonder if you can miss if you shoot with a handgun in a small room. I wonder what the kickback will feel like, if there will be a smell in the air.

There is no way back and nothing else to do. I feel that; my broken heart knows that. And when I'm done with her, with them, I'll make sure that I don't have to feel anything anymore or ever again. I believe that was the plan all along. I never meant to make it out of this alive. Maybe there was something else I was going to do today but not anymore. It is easier to leave pain behind, easier to not have to feel. I tried it one way, I really did, but I failed the same way my father failed. I am my father's son, but I am going to do one thing differently to the way he did it. I am going to take those who hurt me with me.

CHAPTER FORTY

Katherine

Her thoughts are a chaotic whirl as she tries to figure out how she's going to do this. She can feel the presence of another human being in the house. Her senses are heightened, fear making her hyper-aware of everything. Maybe Gladys is in the kitchen. Perhaps the older woman has sensed something, knows something. Perhaps it is someone even more dangerous than what she is dealing with here – but she doubts that. Nothing makes a man more dangerous than hate.

She needs to tell George what to do and she needs to figure out her part. *Think, Katherine*, she silently admonishes herself. She would like to give in to the agony of her body, the exhaustion of her mind. She would like to curl up on this sofa and stay very still but mothers don't get a choice like that.

The children need to get away and they can only get away if he's distracted. She needs to be the distraction. No matter what is going to happen to her now, she needs to be the distraction. She leans forward and puts her head on her knees in a gesture of defeat, praying that her daughter and son will react the way she thinks they will. She breathes in and out slowly, one breath in, one breath out – how many breaths until her last?

Sophie moves right up to her and drapes herself over her mother, and George leans down and puts his face next to hers. 'Don't cry, Mum,' he whispers.

'How touching,' he sneers.

She lifts the arm with the broken wrist and pulls George to her, feeling his surprise at how tightly she is holding him, ignoring the searing stream of pain right up into her neck, and she whispers, barely moving her mouth and hoping that he will hear what she has to say. 'When I say "now" you need to run to the kitchen.' His body relaxes against her and she breathes out with relief. One more breath? Two more breaths? How far is he into his countdown?

She sits up and looks at her son. 'George loves Captain America, don't you, George?' she says. He loves the character, and has seen all the movies with his father. He has a dress-up with a shield and a mask that he puts on whenever he gets the chance and he stands up taller when he's in the costume, believes he is capable of more. Captain America is brave and strong and she wants George to know that this is what he must be. She watches as his little back straightens and he plants his feet firmly on the carpet, his body tilted slightly forward. He is getting ready to run and this is what she wants.

She can't wait any longer.

'I know what you're doing,' she says. 'I can see you counting. You think that this is the solution to your broken heart, that this is how you make it stop hurting. But it's not going to happen, because I'm not going to let it happen. I will not allow you to hurt these children.'

'You made me lose count,' he says slowly, 'now I have to start again.' There is a lilt to his voice, a note of gratitude almost. He is happy he's lost count.

'Maybe you don't want to do this.'

'Maybe it's the only thing I want to do. It's what I came here to do and you can't stop it now. You simply can't.'

She stands up slowly.

'Hey…' He raises the gun.

'Now, George!' she shouts. 'Now!' And she launches herself at him – her whole body goes for him. She swings her arms and kicks her legs, a whirling dervish of fury, distracting him, forcing him to lift his hands. She attacks as her children run.

CHAPTER FORTY-ONE
Logan

He hears the sound of running feet. 'Get back here!' a harsh voice shouts, and then a woman screams and there is a gunshot. He knows it's a gunshot. He's heard gunshots before. People think it's a single, contained sound but it has a slight tail of noise after the initial, shocking explosion.

He looks at the kitchen door that leads to the rest of the house and watches as two children burst through the doorway. When they see him, they freeze, only their small chests moving up and down as they become frightened statues. The little girl is clutching a stuffed monkey, its torn head lolling backwards, some of the stuffing leaking out. They are holding hands so tightly that he can see their fingers are white with the effort of it. He watches the little boy take in his appearance; his face grows pale and he swallows once, twice. A tear slips down his cheek, and Logan feels his heart break for the child.

He crouches down, wishing he was still wearing his long-sleeved shirt. The boy's eyes dart all over his skin, taking in his tattoos, and there is not only fear written on his little face but defeat as well. He thought they were getting away. Now he thinks they are not.

He can see the girl's eyes darting from arm to arm as well and he knows the fanged snake is visible at his neck.

Crouching down further, he makes himself smaller. He raises his finger to his lips. 'Shhh,' he says and the boy nods. He hates that they are scared of him. But he needs to get them out of here. How long until the man who shouted comes after them? Seconds slip away in the hot kitchen.

'My name is Logan,' he says, 'and I'm here to help, okay?' He tries to keep his voice soft and even.

The children regard him warily and then the little girl glances at her brother, her face full of love and trust, and Logan knows who it is he has to convince.

'Is your name George?' he asks.

The boy nods, his big green eyes filling up with tears that he can't wipe away. He needs his hand to hold on to his sister. Logan can see that the other hand is bunched into a little fist. This kid means to protect his sister no matter what. He's her brother and that's what brothers do.

'George, I'm here to help you and your mum. The police are coming. Gladys told me all about you. I want you and Sophie to go out of the kitchen door and run to Gladys. Do you think you can do that?'

'We can do that, can't we, George?' stage-whispers the girl. She looks hopefully at her brother. He will be the one to make the decision. Logan wants to shout at them to run. How soon until the man with the gun comes? Time is a solid thing in the kitchen, his heartbeat racing the tick of the clock on the wall.

Standing up, Logan takes a step to the side, clearing a path for them. The little boy stares at him, unsure, untrusting.

Logan wonders what he could say to this kid to get him to move. He thinks about Mack's son, Chris, who is seven, remembers walking up and down the aisles of Kmart with Debbie looking for a present for his birthday.

'Anything to do with Captain America, Mack told me,' Debbie said and then they found the costume, complete with shield. Chris loved it.

He takes a chance that Captain America is someone this kid knows about. He has to get them to move or he will have to lift them both bodily and take them out of the kitchen, but that will take too much time.

'I bet Captain America couldn't run as fast as you,' says Logan, attempting to keep the desperation out of his voice.

George's mouth opens, amazement on his face. Logan knows he's said the right thing. He nods his head furiously and then the children glance at each other and they take off through the open back door, their receding footsteps the best thing he's heard all day. Relief floods Logan's body – if the kids are safe, that's one good thing.

'Keep going,' shouts Logan, and he starts to run towards the room where the gunshot came from.

It only takes him a few steps through the dining room to get to the room at the back where the sound has come from.

And as he bursts in, he looks at what has happened, at who is there, and he knows that whatever you do in your life, you can never outrun karma. Karma never loses an address.

CHAPTER FORTY-TWO

Gladys

Gladys hears the crack of sound that fills the air. It's come from inside the house but that's not possible because it sounds like a gunshot, an actual gunshot. She holds her hand over her mouth and she turns to look at the front door. It was a gunshot, she's sure of it. 'Oh God,' she moans, 'oh God, oh God.'

She should have called the police earlier. She feels like she might hyperventilate as she forces air in and out of her lungs. Someone is hurt and she could have prevented it.

And then she hears footsteps, and she sees George running, pulling Sophie along behind him. They come from the side of the house and they keep running through the open gate and then George launches himself at her, tears staining his face. Gladys nearly falls over but she puts her arms around the two trembling children and says the only thing she can say: 'It's all right, it's okay.' They are both damp with sweat, their hair limp in the heat and their cheeks red. They are dressed in their school uniforms because they were meant to leave for school, that was what was meant to happen.

'It's all right,' she repeats, hoping that's the truth.

They bury their faces in her stomach and they are both crying and trying to speak at the same time. She hears the words 'he' and 'gun', and Sophie says something about her stuffed monkey. Their small bodies shudder and Gladys feels a whole day of terror in the way they cling to her. She has no idea what's happening inside the house. But she needs to get them away from here, they need to be somewhere safe.

Where is Katherine? Was that a gunshot? Who was shot?

'Shhh,' says Gladys as she holds the children and begins moving backwards, towards her own house. 'Shhh.'

CHAPTER FORTY-THREE

'Mum, Mum…' The words leave my lips without me even thinking about them. Words I haven't said for years. She has been my mother, your mother, her and other words for a long time now. Ugly words from my father, from me.

I look down at what I've done, at her body, at the way she has fallen, at the way she is looking at me, her brown eyes wide, incomprehension in her stare. Perhaps she didn't think I would do it. But she came at me. She threw herself at me to save them. They were the ones she was worried about, the ones she cared about. 'Mum,' I whisper because I cannot stop the word.

I have broken her the same way I broke the love of my life. The same way I broke Maddy. Maddy with her dark hair and blue eyes and the slight gap between her front teeth. Maddy who hummed songs in the morning while she brushed her teeth and liked to watch home renovation programmes. I have broken my mum the same way I broke Maddy. As I look at her, their faces merge and they become one, the same.

The anger that I have been consumed by dissipates into the air, thins out and is gone. All that's left is confusion.

I stare down at the gun the way I stared down at my hands. They are still scratched from Maddy's nails as she fought me, still bruised from connecting with her cheekbone. They hurt. My hands hurt but the physical pain was nothing compared to the real pain.

How could I have done this? How could I have done that?

I remember running from the apartment, leaving Maddy on the floor, trying to erase the image of her broken doll body, running and crying, knowing that I had done the worst thing possible. But she had loved me and then she didn't. She just turned it off one day and that was wrong. It wasn't supposed to happen to me. Not again.

When I stopped running, I hid in a park, behind some trees, sweat drying on my skin in the cool breeze that blew up, and I tried to work out why I had hurt the woman I loved.

I couldn't stand the idea of her not loving me anymore and she wouldn't listen to what I had to say. I promised to change, to become who she wanted me to be even though my father said I should never do that. But I would have done it for her.

'You can't change, Patrick,' Maddy said. 'This is who you are.'

'You need to leave,' she said.

'I've tried my best, but this isn't going to work.'

But I was trying my best. I was trying to be who she wanted me to be but it was just too much, too hard.

Maddy said, 'Speak to your mother, she loves you.'

Maddy said, 'You should forgive your mother; she's never stopped trying. I've read the emails.'

Maddy said, 'My brother doesn't think we're good for each other.'

Maddy said, 'You need to stop treating me like this.'

Maddy said, 'If you hit me again, my brother will be on the first plane from Sydney to break your hands.'

Maddy said, 'Why are you like this?'

Maddy said, 'I can't do this anymore.'

Maddy said, 'I'm leaving you – or at least you're leaving my flat. Pack your stuff and get out.'

Maddy said, 'I don't want to hear you're sorry again. Just get out.'

And in that moment, as her eyes darkened and a scowl took over her whole face, I understood that I had become my father, that I would end up drinking and taking pills to forget, and that I would one day give in to the despair of losing someone who was supposed to love me. I would be as pathetic as he was.

I got angrier than I have ever been before and I lashed out and I kept going, even when her hands were up over her head and she was cowering on the floor.

And then I washed my hands, her blood running in the bathroom sink, dribbling away, and I left, taking money and a credit card from her purse. The tears arrived as the anger disappeared.

In the park, my heart slowed and the anger rose again. I started walking because I needed to walk, and I kept going for hours. She shouldn't have pushed me, shouldn't have hurt me. She got what she deserved. I wasn't going to be the only one suffering like my father. I expected the guilt to come but it didn't. The only thought that kept circulating was, At least I'm not pathetic like him.

But it wasn't enough because I knew that if I'd been a different man, Maddy would have still loved me. If not for the divorce and my mother's callous disregard for my father, my whole life would have been something else.

And the need to make the one person who was responsible for every terrible thing pay for it all, gnawed at me.

I found a cab and got myself to the airport and to Sydney.

I needed to come up here and make sure she understood. I am the way I am because of her, because of what she did, and she needed to know that and to pay for it.

But now as I watch her eyes blink, I am unsure. She's my mum. She never gave up on me – even when she really should have.

She never stopped emailing me, trying to contact me, trying to reconnect. I kept the messages, reread them sometimes. News of a new husband was a punch in the gut. 'You would like him,' she wrote, and I laughed at that. How could she ever have expected anything except dislike from me? She had replaced my father, clicked her fingers and erased her history with him.

She moved on, and I never believed her entreaties for me to come and live with her, to reconnect. I knew she didn't really want me there. How could she?

And then she told me about her new children, not just one but two, a perfect pair. My father was replaceable and so was I. And I believed my hatred for her would burn brighter in my soul than anything else until I met Maddy and her love cooled the hate. I don't know why Maddy had to be just like her, just like all women.

I came to find her to make her pay.

I wanted… I don't know now what I wanted. I'm not sure. I don't think I meant for this to happen. It's all wrong now. My head is spinning and the light in this room is strange and I can smell the burning scent of a fired gun.

I put my head in my hands, the hard metal of the gun scratching my cheek, burning it a little. The barrel is hot. Then I hear a sound, and I look up.

CHAPTER FORTY-FOUR
Katherine

It's a shocking thud to her body, more than it is pain. She takes two steps backwards and then her knees give out and she falls, expecting the floor but landing on the sofa. She looks down at her white T-shirt where the blood is growing and spreading, the red paint of her blood turning the white of her shirt dark pink. A firecracker smell is in the air. 'Oh Patrick,' she murmurs, 'oh baby, what have you done?'

'Mum,' he says, a word she hasn't heard from him in years. 'Mum, Mum…' and as she struggles to breathe, despite everything she is overcome with an overwhelming need to comfort him, to comfort her son. She starts trying to get up but her body won't obey her.

She has always loved him, has been unable to contemplate not loving him. *Where did all that love go?* She held him to her breast, she kissed a scraped knee, she taught him how to sing the alphabet song. She bought him his favourite toys and cooked his favourite meals. She helped with homework and held him tightly in her arms when he was sad – but it wasn't enough. It couldn't combat what his father did, what he said. 'What kind of a man teaches his son to hate his mother?' was a question she asked of therapists and teachers and friends. When she married him, stars in her eyes and a silver ring on her finger, she had never imagined he would one day hate her enough to turn her own child against her. She could never have imagined this.

John's face comes to her, a man on an elevator who became a friend and then a lover and then a husband. It was not expected, because second chances don't come along very often. But there he was, willing to take on her baggage, to listen when she spoke of her first husband and lost son.

The perfection she had hoped for with her second chance was not possible because perfection doesn't exist. She wonders if he's tried to call her today, or if he is still angry. The argument from last night would have weighed heavily on his mind as it had on hers, before her son arrived to upend her life. It was another whispered, tense conversation, but it was one that could have meant the end for them. She had threatened and he had cajoled but she was tired of fighting, of fighting with him and for him.

'Who is she, John?' Her hands on her hips. She believed she already knew the answer. She had done this before.

'Just someone from work.' He looked down, not wanting to meet her gaze.

'Why is she texting you with heart emojis like some ridiculous teenage girl? Why are you allowing her to text you?' His phone was in her hand, the evidence on the screen. She had read and reread the messages, trying to discern their true meaning.

'She's just… that's the way she is. She's friendly. She knows I'm married. I talk about you and the kids all the time. She's just like that.' He threw up his hands and then reached for his phone but she pulled it back.

'She's like that because you haven't made it clear that you have a wife that you love. Being married doesn't mean anything to her obviously.'

He sighed sadly, shaking his head. 'Kate, you're not thinking straight. You're blowing everything out of proportion these days. You can see that I don't reply the same way. You can see that I keep my texts short and to the point.'

'Maybe you knew I'd look at your phone.'

'Why did you look at my phone?' It was a genuine question. He didn't understand the fear of finding herself in the same situation once more.

'I told you, I wanted to find mine. I put it down somewhere!'

'Kate, if I had something to hide, why do you have my password?' He smiled as though he had bested her, proved her wrong.

'What I'm worried about, John, is that there are things you're saying and doing when you're together at the office, and instead of reassuring me, you're making me more worried. Are you having an affair with her or not?' Some part of her wanted to let it go, to believe him, but she kept pushing, asking, almost needing him to confess so that she would know that she had been right all along.

'Oh Kate, you make me sad.'

They went to bed separately, in different parts of the house. She curled up alone in their bed, fear over the future replacing anger, exhausting her to sleep. At some point, in the middle of the night, she woke to feel the bed dip and then a hand on her back. When she lay still, he climbed into the bed and pushed up against her and, knowing that she was awake, whispered, 'Why would I cheat, when I have you? You and the children are everything I have ever wanted. I'm not cheating, Kate, I promise.'

She didn't reply but she didn't move away from him either, lying still until he returned to his sofa bed.

This morning he was having breakfast when she woke up. 'We need to talk,' she told him, when she walked into the kitchen. Maybe it was the end of their marriage, maybe it wasn't, but she knew that it couldn't continue. He didn't want her to leave but he didn't want to change, to reassure her as she needed to be reassured even when he knew her history with cheating husbands. And she wasn't going to live that way. She had done that for years once before. Her marriage to John was a second chance, but she wouldn't sacrifice the happiness of her children by staying in a bad marriage.

She thought about her lost son, the one who would not speak to her, the one who had been estranged for years, and she knew that she couldn't let that happen again. Better to divorce early and remain amicable than to let a situation descend into enmity and blame.

'I can't live like this, John, I mean it. Either we sort it out or we part.'

'I agree,' he said. He took a bite of his toast and chewed. A small dab of butter was on his lip and she watched him, remembering that at one time she would have kissed it off or wiped it off for him. The twins had been her full focus for a long time. They only had sex occasionally, laughed very little together. There was some distance between them that they needed to bridge, she thought. And it was getting bigger every day. And then he looked at his watch. 'Oh shit, shit, the mechanic, I forgot about the mechanic. I thought I had more time… We'll talk, I'll call you from work. Wait, I have that conference today,' he rubbed at his hair, messing it up and then smoothing it down again. He sighed. 'It may end early… We can go for a walk later, or get a babysitter…' He looked at his watch again. 'Shit I'm so late.'

'You're not allowed to swear, Dad,' said George, coming into the kitchen, his yellow shirt tucked neatly into his khaki-coloured shorts, his curly hair slicked down with water. He liked to look smart for school and her heart melted at the sight of her little man.

'You're right, George,' she said, 'Daddy shouldn't swear,' and he rewarded her with a smile.

John dashed out. She picked up his plate and took out a bowl for George to pour his cereal as she heard John's car screeching off. And then she looked at the kitchen table and felt laughter bubble up inside her.

'What's funny?' asked George.

'He forgot his briefcase and his phone,' she said. 'He'll be back soon enough.'

And he was. A few minutes later, he walked back in and said, 'I—'

'Here you go,' she laughed and handed them to him, but she didn't kiss him goodbye, stepping back just a fraction so he couldn't kiss her either. And she saw the hurt that caused in the way his green eyes darkened. Green eyes like her ex-husband's eyes but a different green. Anthony's eyes were a pale green, light and touched with brown, but John's eyes are deep and intense, almost emerald in colour, just like her children's eyes.

Dismissing the hurt on his face because she needed to get on with her day, she went to the laundry to start the washing machine.

'Mum… Mum… Mum, come here,' George called.

'What's wrong, sweetheart?' she said, following his tentative call. He was standing at the open front door.

At first, she hadn't recognised him. His hair was longer and he was thinner than she remembered. But then he took off his red cap and smiled and she experienced a moment of delirious happiness, because she thought he was back, in her life, in her family – that he had come back. But then she saw the gun and her body felt cold in the morning heat, and fear made her silent.

She has never stopped contacting him. Pregnant at twenty, she had imagined that her hastily arranged marriage to Anthony would survive. They had both loved their only child, adored him and each other until marriage and a child began to stifle Anthony and he became secretive and sly. She hadn't trusted her intuition about other women until money disappeared from the bank account and he couldn't hide what he'd been doing.

Patrick was her only concern and she was willing to give everything to their relationship. But she hadn't understood the level of manipulation her husband was employing against her as he worked to sever her relationship with her son.

Patrick has an email address that he has never changed, and all these years, every once in a while, so that it wouldn't be too much, she has sent him a message.

Dear Patrick,
I miss you every day.

Each email is begun the same way, the same way for seven years now. And each time she has typed it, she has known it to be true. He rejected her. He moved in with his father and then cursed her for the man his father was. After Anthony died, after he killed himself with two packets of sleeping pills and a bottle of whisky, she had begged him to come home. But he wouldn't. He blamed her and didn't want to be anywhere near her.

The boarding school she sent him to was on a large piece of land where students were part of a working farm and completed their studies. She had thought he would love it. She had gone without to pay for it, taking on a second job doing cold-calling at the weekends just to keep him there, in addition to being a saleswoman in a department store. She hoped he would find friends and a purpose in life, but he had only grown angrier with each passing year.

Please don't come to my graduation. I don't want to see you there.

He had emailed the words as she got ready to get into her car to drive out to the rural property, imagining a reunion where they would be able to talk things through. She had gone anyway. And he had refused to get on stage or to see her.

'I would give him some time,' the headmaster of the school comforted her as she sat weeping in his office. 'He's struggled with discipline and he needs some time away from everything. He's an adult now. Sometimes it's best to set our children free so that they can return to us when they're ready.'

But what if they never return? she wanted to ask the man whose glasses had slid down his nose as he tried to look capable of dealing with her tears.

But she had done that, as much as she could. She had pulled back, let go and tried to move on with her life. She kept emailing him and occasionally, rarely, sometimes not for months, he would reply. Terse missives that broke her heart.

I'm getting on with my life, you get on with yours.

When she married, she contacted him because she never wanted him to find out from anyone else but her. When she got pregnant, she did the same and she sent him pictures of the twins when they arrived. And she kept hoping that something, anything, would get through his anger at her. She always sent him a birthday message, and as he entered his twenties, she thought that there might be a shift in how he felt – that along with age-maturity, an ability to see her as a person would come.

She was wrong. She can see that now.

His anger has grown, thrived. He has kept it fed as his father wanted him to do. Anthony never thought about the cruelty of turning a child against his mother, only of finding a way to cause pain. The idea of her child as a pawn between them has eaten away at her but she could never fight Anthony's skill at manipulation.

But something has happened to bring him here today, to do this. She has known this all day as she has watched him, and it seemed to her that something was missing in the way he looked at her and at George and Sophie, some spark of compassion that all human beings should feel for each other. And she knew that she and her children were in danger. The man Patrick had no shred of the boy Patrick.

He was an angry, hate-filled stranger. And that meant he was capable of anything.

She should never have given him her address, never have let him know where she was and what was happening in her life – but how could she have known what he would one day do?

Blinking slowly, she watches him as he rubs his head in distress, remembering him as a toddler doing the same thing. *I can't do it, Mum, help me, help me.*

And then he lifts the gun to his own temple and she wants to shout no, to scream it and grab the gun, but she can't move.

Her body is heavy and she is no longer hot but growing cold.

A sound makes her try to turn her head and she manages a slight movement. Everything is hard, impossible.

Someone else is in the room. A giant of a man, tattoos everywhere.

Katherine thinks she may be hallucinating.

'What are you doing here?' Patrick asks him, and she has a moment of feeling grateful that the man is indeed there. Perhaps he has come to help, but she finds that she doesn't care if he has or not. The children aren't here. She cannot hear them in the house and she prays they are with Gladys or another neighbour. George will tell someone to call the police.

And then… her eyes blink slowly. She is very tired. She wants to sleep. She cannot feel any pain in her wrist and she's happy that her children are not here to see this. Only one child is here, only her first-born, and it seems to her now that this is always how it was supposed to go. She used to worry about him so much when he lived with his father and when he was at boarding school and when he became an adult and moved away. *What will become of him? What kind of a man can he be after everything that has happened to him?* He never wanted to meet John, never wanted to know his half-brother and sister. George and Sophie were her second chance at motherhood and she is grateful that they are here in the world.

They will miss her but they will be alive to miss her and that's the most important thing.

I can let go now, she thinks. *I can close my eyes and rest.* Patrick and the man are talking, arguing, she's not sure but it goes on and on. Her eyes open and close, open and close. She needs to rest, but as her eyes begin to close again, she hears shouting, running. Her second son, her little boy, bursts into the room, arms whirling, and launches himself at Patrick, fury in his words.

'You leave my mum alone!' Such strength, such determination.

No! she wants to tell him, to shout to make him stop. He's not supposed to be here but she cannot speak.

'Wait!' shouts the man, and he moves as her body gives up the fight to stay conscious.

She doesn't hear the next gunshots. She doesn't hear anything else.

CHAPTER FORTY-FIVE

Logan

It's him. He's been worrying that the man who hurt his sister, that Patrick, would come looking for him, and all day he's been here, terrorising this woman and her children. Why? What on earth does he have to do with them?

Logan stares at the man holding the gun and then he glances at the woman lying across the sofa, her blood soaking into the blue material.

'Patrick,' says Logan. He feels stupid, lost. He has no idea where to begin. Patrick is holding the gun at an angle so he could easily shoot the woman again, or just as easily shoot Logan. He is sweating, his hand shaking, and he keeps looking at the woman and looking away as though he cannot witness what he's done.

'How did you find me?' asks Patrick. 'How did you find me before I found you?' He is as confused as Logan is. 'Did you get my text? Is that how you…' He stops speaking, his eyes darting around the room.

Patrick was coming for him. Why is he here?

'I wasn't looking for you,' says Logan.

'I hurt Maddy,' whines Patrick, and he lifts his arms above his head, the gun still clasped tightly with one finger resting on the trigger. He takes a ragged, anguished breath. 'I hurt Maddy,' he repeats.

'I know,' says Logan, and although he wants to be angry, furious, to step forward and wrench the gun out of Patrick's hand and shoot him with it, he doesn't move. There is a chance that no one else will get hurt. He can see regret on Patrick's face, and if he handles this correctly, it can end right now.

'Maybe it's time to put that down,' says Logan.

'I don't think so, I don't… I didn't mean to hurt her… I just…' He looks at the woman again.

Logan raises his hands, hoping to calm Patrick, who is pale and jittery. 'If you just put the gun down, we can talk and then it will be fine. I need to call an ambulance for her, I need to get her some help. Can I do that?' He bends his knees a little, gets ready to dive towards Patrick, knock him over.

'It's too late,' says Patrick, shaking his head, and he lowers his arms, holds the gun out in front of him, moves it between Logan and the woman on the sofa, as if deciding who to shoot first.

'It's not,' says Logan. 'It's never too late. She seems to be breathing, so just put the gun down and I'll call for help. I'm going to slide my hand into my pocket now to just get my phone, okay?' Logan speaks slowly, his voice calm and even. He's talking someone off a ledge here.

'No, not okay, don't do that.' His voice is a warning.

'Patrick, if we don't get her help, she will die. Do you want her to die? That's not what you want, is it?'

'Is Maddy dead?' he asks.

'No, no, and if you give me the gun, we can talk about that.'

Patrick shakes his head. 'She doesn't look old enough to have a twenty-three-year-old son, does she?' he says as though they are chatting over a beer.

Logan looks from the woman to Patrick and back again as pieces click into place.

'She's your mother?'

Patrick nods. 'Maddy, Maddy wanted me to see her again. Maddy thought I should forgive her. She read all her emails on my computer and then she nagged and nagged, and then she just dumped me, dumped me and wanted to move on with her life the same way my mother did after she divorced my father. Why do women do that, Logan?' It's a genuine question. He wants an answer.

'I don't know, mate,' says Logan softly. He can feel a chink in Patrick's armour, sees the possibility that he can talk him down. The minutes are ticking by and he can tell that the woman on the sofa is slipping in and out of consciousness. Her chest rises and falls but slowly, and underneath closed eyelids there is the occasional flutter of movement.

'I want you to put that gun down now, Patrick,' Logan says, raising his voice a little, taking a step towards him as he stares at the woman on the sofa.

'I was so happy with Maddy,' says Patrick, muttering the words, speaking to himself, 'so happy with her and then she just…' He looks at Logan, his eyes narrow. 'You didn't want us to be together. She told me. You were the reason we broke up. It was you.' He points the gun directly at Logan's chest, away from the woman, and Logan lets the relief of that seep through him. He could probably survive one bullet but this woman won't survive another one.

'Maddy is in hospital,' he says, raising his voice to keep Patrick looking at him, 'and you've hurt your mother. The police are on their way and there will be nowhere to run, mate. I promise you there will be nowhere to run. You need to give me that gun. You need to give it to me now.'

Patrick swings the gun back to the woman and then he starts laughing. 'Kill two birds with one stone,' he giggles. 'That's what I'm going to do, Logan, kill two birds with one stone. How lucky am I? The woman who ruined the start of my life and the man who helped ruin the end of my life in the same room. And you're both going to die. She's still alive, you can see that, can't you? But not for long.' He angles the gun to her chest. 'Bye, Mum,' he says.

As Logan takes a step there is a blur of movement beside him and the little boy launches himself at Patrick, shouting, 'You leave my mum alone!'

'Wait!' shouts Logan. 'Stop, no!'

Patrick is pushed back into the chair behind him and he kicks out his legs, and then, still holding the gun, he pushes the kid off him and points the gun directly at his little face.

'No!' shouts Logan, and he grabs the hand that has the gun, moving it away from the boy, who falls to the floor and crawls over to the sofa. Patrick pulls against Logan's grip but Logan holds on tighter as the gun is turned to face his chest.

And Patrick fires. He fires twice. Logan watches it happen, time slowing down, sees the fear and confusion on Patrick's face. The gun seems to have fired itself.

He feels the bullets thud into his chest. He staggers a little, steps backwards, lets go of Patrick's hand but doesn't go down. He needs to stay on his feet. He needs to get the gun. He needs to stop Patrick from shooting again because a gun has six bullets and he's only used three.

'Oh God, oh God,' Patrick moans.

'Give me… the gun,' pants Logan.

Patrick lifts his hands over his head again, his eyes darting all over the room, and says, 'Oh God.'

'Give me… the gun,' says Logan because he can't seem to breathe. His body sags, unable to hold its weight with the hot air in the room pressing down on it. Logan drops to his knees.

'I'm sorry, Logan,' says Patrick and he lifts the gun to his own head.

And then there is the sound of footsteps in the house, moving quickly.

'Police,' hears Logan, as his body hits the floor. His head is next to a blue rug with a border of yellow camels.

He struggles to get some air into his lungs.

He glances sideways and up, seeing Patrick with his face scrunched up, his hand shaking as he holds the gun to his head. 'Don't come near me,' he says and Logan can hear he is crying. He sounds younger than he is. There is no trace of a man left in his tears.

'Put the gun down now!' One voice, a woman, loud and strong.

'Put the gun down.' Another voice. 'Down on the ground.'

'You don't understand,' says Patrick as Logan gives in to the need to close his eyes.

The sound of a single gunshot pierces the air.

Logan feels his body floating.

He hopes Debbie is feeling better.

He hopes the promised cool change arrives.

He hopes he gets to live.

CHAPTER FORTY-SIX
Gladys

She took the children into her house and made them sit on the floor in front of the television set. But she wasn't able to stay with them. She needed to see what was happening.

'Watch them, Lou,' she commanded. He nodded, his face pale with shock. The gunshot had echoed through the air, terrifyingly and certainly confirming that something had been wrong all day.

'My mum,' wailed George, 'he'll hurt my mum.'

Lou reached out for the boy who instead cuddled his sister, holding on to her tightly.

'Stay here, George, I'll see, I'll go and see, just stay here.' She dashed out of the room and her house, her heart pounding.

Now she is looking down the road, waiting for the police. Doors have begun to open, people emerging from air-conditioned homes into the street, drawn by the sound, curiosity dragging them from the safety of their own walls.

Go away, Gladys wants to shout at those she can see, but will they listen? Will they believe her?

The police finally arrive, parking slowly, without a care in the world. A woman constable gets out of the car with a smile on her face, angering Gladys. A man climbs out as well, his hat in his hands, a sheen of sweat instantly appearing on his face. Neither of them looks terribly concerned. Gladys explained what was happening on the phone and she had expected, had wanted, lights and sirens and urgency from the police.

'Quickly, quickly!' Gladys shouts, hurrying them up. 'He has a gun. I heard a shot.'

'Why don't you explain…' begins the constable, holding up her hands to calm a hysterical woman. Gladys wants to grab the woman and shake her. *Don't you understand? Why don't you understand?*

'Gladys, Gladys,' Lou shouts, frantic panic in his voice, 'the boy has run away, he's run away.'

Gladys darts away from the police, back to her own house, to see what Lou is doing.

'What?' she says.

'He's run away, the boy, he left.' Lou has gotten himself into his wheelchair and wheeled himself to the front door of their house and is struggling to get up.

'But you were supposed to watch them, oh Lou,' she cries, knowing that he did what he could.

Gladys turns back, runs down her front path, her lungs burning with the unwelcome activity. The policewoman is still standing there, just waiting. 'There's a child… a child,' she stutters, unable to get the words out. She didn't see George come past her but he must have gone back into the house, he must have.

'Okay wait, just…' begins the policewoman.

And then there are two more shots.

Two more shots.

The two constables run towards the house, down the side, disappearing from view. They know what they've heard.

'Oh no,' moans Gladys as they disappear from sight, her knees sagging.

'What's happening, Gladys?' she hears, and she looks across the street to see Margo, holding Joseph. She is right across the road, standing at her open front door looking directly into

Katherine's front garden over her low white fence. The baby smiles widely.

'Oh Margo,' she says, standing up straight again, looking at the baby, the precious baby in Margo's arms, 'go back inside, go back. He has a gun. Go inside.'

'What?' Margo sounds confused, disbelieving. Gladys desperately tries to make her understand, waving her arms.

'Get back inside, Margo. It's Katherine, it was… Didn't you hear? It was gunshots… Please go back, take the baby away.'

She looks down the street at other residents who are making their way onto the road. 'Go back into your houses,' she shouts, hurting her throat.

Margo opens her mouth to say something else but then Joseph says, 'Gaah,' and she nods her head and scurries back inside her house, behind the safety of her walls.

Gladys cannot believe what's happening, what she's heard. How can such a thing be possible on this quiet street on a broiling afternoon when even dogs cannot be bothered to bark?

Three gunshots. That's what she heard and she knows it's the truth. She has been right all along. Something has been going on in that house all day and instead of calling the police earlier, she has allowed Lou and her own need not to be seen as the interfering neighbour to stop her from doing so. She is so grateful the police are in the house now. She can hear them shouting. She imagines John with his wide smile and quick laugh holding a gun, pointing a gun at his wife and children. It's a horrifying image. Where is George? Where is Sophie? She darts back up her front path, her panting breath burning her lungs. 'Sophie?' she asks Lou, who is still trying to get out of his chair.

'She's in there. George told her to stay. She's watching the television but don't worry, I'm coming, Glad, I'm coming.'

'No, no,' she says, moving down her front path again. *What is going on? What has John done?*

She has always liked him but at the same time she has not liked him. He was nice enough but also a little too nice. No, that's not fair. She's trying to pretend she had an inkling about John but she didn't have one – not at all. Gladys shakes her head. She's going around in circles.

She knows that sometimes when you find out the truth about a person, you are able to point to something, some small thing about them that always made you just a little suspicious. But that's not the case here. That's not the truth. John is a lovely man. Last year when the big storm blew through the suburb, ripping roof tiles off and allowing the rain to come pouring in, she called the State Emergency Service but they were so busy they told her they'd be hours. She pulled the ladder out of the garage and leaned it up against the wall, a plastic sheet in her hand. She meant to try and get the sheet on the roof. She had some bricks in a bucket to hold it down.

But before she even set a foot on the ladder, John was there. 'Gladys, what are you doing? Let me. Why didn't you just call?'

He climbed up, a tool belt on his hips, and secured a tarpaulin. He had been soaked to the bone but still grinned when she offered him a cup of tea.

Gladys had been almost tearful after he left. He was a good man, a nice man, and he loved his children. She's seen that he loved them. He took them to the beach and the park and he built them a treehouse in the large fig tree in their backyard. How could he want to hurt them now?

She wants to run in after George, but the police are there.

She hears a crash and she knows that Lou has fallen down. She turns and speeds for her house but stops to look when she hears a car pull up, the crunch of tyres on gravel. It's a blue sedan, not one she's seen before in this street.

John climbs out. He is dressed in a suit, rumpled from the long hot day, his tie askew. His hair is blonde but filled with the same kinks and curls that George has, and his green eyes are bright in his tanned face.

'Oh,' says Gladys, shock stealing her words. She stops.

'Gladys,' he replies. 'What's going on? Why are the police here? Is Lou okay?'

'No, he fell down… oh Lou, I'm coming…' she yells and she runs up her front path.

John follows her, dropping the briefcase he is holding, and together they lift Lou back into his chair. 'You're home early and you weren't… you weren't at work,' says Gladys as she helps Lou sit up straight.

'I'm… Yes, it was a conference and then the mechanic needed the car overnight… How do you know I wasn't at work? What's going on, Gladys?' John stands up straight, his face damp from the effort of lifting Lou.

And another shot rings out.

John looks at his house, his mouth opening and closing again as he tries to process what he has just heard.

'I thought you were in there,' says Gladys. 'I thought you were home.' In the heat she feels her face flush red at all the assumptions she has made. All the things she has gotten wrong today. She opens her mouth to try and explain but it is too much to describe, she has no idea where to start.

'But what?' says John and then as the sound of more sirens fills the air, he runs for the house. 'Oh God, oh God, Katherine, Katherine, Sophie, George…' he shouts as he sprints for his front door.

'John, don't,' calls Gladys, racing after him, but he is already gone, and as he gets there the door opens and a policewoman holds up her hands.

He pushes past her, screaming, 'Katherine, George, Sophie!'

Gladys sinks to her knees by her front gate. Sophie is in her house but not George. The little boy ran to his mother. Did he run to his mother? Where is George?

She feels like she might pass out. This cannot be happening.

'Gladys, old girl, are you okay? Are you okay, old girl?' says Lou, fright making his voice tremble.

Gladys drops her head into her hands. 'Oh Lou,' she says and then she begins to cry.

CHAPTER FORTY-SEVEN

Physical pain is a strange thing. It concentrates the mind. It sharpens your senses. I can smell the honeysuckle from outside, overripe in the heat. I can feel the heavy hot air in the room. I can hear sirens. I drop the gun because my hand doesn't seem able to hold it anymore. It falls onto the floor with a clunk. And my body slowly folds, sinking onto the carpet.

I was going to shoot myself in the head, straight into my tortured brain. She could have just done it for me. I don't know why she aimed for my stomach instead of my head.

'Get down on the ground,' says the policewoman. I am already down on the ground. Her voice is trembling a little and I wonder if I'm the first person she's ever shot.

I came to punish her, and then I was going to punish him. It's her fault Maddy didn't love the man I was. And it's Logan's fault that she broke up with me. But I don't know if I meant to… kill anyone.

I turn my head to the side and I see yellow camels. Why are there yellow camels? There was a rug in our house, and later in the flat my mother and I lived in, that had yellow camels. I used to count them sometimes, imagine them all walking across the desert in a slow bumping row. I look up and blink slowly, watching a small fly walk across the white ceiling. I turn my head and I can see my mother's legs sprawled over the sofa.

She used to sing to me when she woke me up in the morning, and the song goes round my head now. 'Good morning, good morning, it's early morning light, so I want to say good morning to you.' She put notes in my lunchbox when I was little: 'Have a good day, I love you' with a smiley face. She made me macaroni and cheese when I asked for it, even if she needed to go out and get the ingredients. She read me stories at night in bed, books about places that didn't exist where animals could speak. She held me when I woke from a bad dream, telling me that the monsters had no chance against her. She wanted me to grow up to be a good person, a good man, but she didn't have a chance against everything he said to me, everything he told me. She would have forgiven me anything. As I struggle to breathe, I acknowledge that truth. She would have forgiven me anything and welcomed me back into her life. I was going to break in through the back door but then I decided to ring the bell in the front, just stood there and waited. I saw some of my own features in her little boy's face but that just made me angrier.

Her expression as she saw me at her front door only hours ago is imprinted on my mind. She was filled with delight and she even opened her arms, ready and waiting for a hug. She opened her arms and I showed her the gun. I could have made a different choice. I could have stepped into those arms and changed my life.

There is a burnt metal smell in this room. A thick, dark smell of blood and fire. There is a scent of sweat and honeysuckle. My eyes are heavy and I can't quite breathe in enough air. I try to take a breath and hear a gurgle in my throat, taste something hot and salty. Am I dying?

I think she was a good mother. Maybe I was just a bad kid with a bad father. I don't hate her. I love her, and now she's gone.

I don't know why I was so angry.

I don't know why I came here.

I don't know anything.

EPILOGUE

Three weeks later

Logan

'Don't you have to go back to work?' asks Logan.

'No, Maya told me to take an extra-long lunch break. We've no women in labour up there at the moment. I know that's going to change soon, so I'll just be here with you, unless you have someplace else to be.' She is darting around the room, quick and light on her feet, straightening his linen, filling his water jug and making sure the flowers in the vase next to his bed are arranged neatly, all in one whirling movement. Her hair is held back in a tight bun with bobby pins keeping everything smooth, but there are still stray escaping curls. He can see bluish-grey shadows under her eyes that he would like to smooth away but knows not to mention.

'Not leaving, are you?' she asks.

'Ha, ha, very funny,' says Logan and he chuckles and then raises his hand to his chest as the pain rattles through his body. 'Don't make me laugh.'

'Sorry, babes.' She grimaces as though she has felt the pain in her own body.

'You should sit down instead of doing that,' he says as Debbie keeps moving, fixing the blinds so that the sun doesn't hit his face and make him squint in the bright light. He wishes she would sit still so he could touch her. He loves her in her uniform, loves it when she transforms herself from home Debbie to work Debbie, ties up her hair and becomes someone completely capable and efficient.

'I'm pregnant, babes, not sick.' She stops in front of the window, a secretive smile touching her face.

Logan smiles at the words. When he woke up from surgery, she told him the news before he'd even said anything, before he'd even remembered fully what had happened and thought to ask about Katherine and the kids. He had opened his eyes, somewhat surprised to see a blurry white ceiling above him. He had blinked twice to clear his vision and then Debbie's face had appeared above him. She was pale, her hazel eyes rimmed in red, a new line just above her nose as she creased her forehead. He'd never seen anything so beautiful in his life.

'You make sure you get through this, big man. I'm not raising a kid on my own,' she whispered.

'What kid?' he managed to ask, his throat cracked and dry.

She moved his bed a little, tilting him up. He didn't feel any pain, which he assumed meant he was loaded up with drugs.

Debbie took a cup off the table next to his bed and let him take a few sips. 'Not too much,' she warned in her most competent nurse voice.

'What kid?' he asked again, his brain struggling to understand.

'Our kid. Turns out that I get a runny nose along with everything else when I'm pregnant.'

'You're pregnant?'

'I am and…' She grabbed his hand then, tears appearing in her eyes and spilling onto her cheeks. 'I was so scared, Logan. They called me to come in to emergency and I explained I was sick but then they told me… you were here and I'd been waiting for you to call…'

'But I'm okay?'

'You're okay. The bullets missed all the important bits.' Her light tone made it sound like a joke even as her face told him how worried she was.

'A dad needs his important bits,' he rumbled.

'He does,' she laughed, swiping away stray tears.

There have been a few rough nights, nights when he has wrestled with raging anger at Patrick for what he did to Maddy, and at himself for allowing the man to be in his sister's life, even though he knows that he couldn't have stopped her.

'It's not like I would have listened, even if you told me I couldn't see him,' his sister has since said. 'You did your best – and I'm an adult. I'm going to make mistakes and you can't save me from them.'

'Maddy, growing up and making your own mistakes usually involves buying a lemon of a car, not getting involved with a psychopath.'

'Yeah, well, big lesson learned there.'

Maddy has just been released from hospital in Melbourne. Logan was so relieved to hear that she has a friend to stay with until she heals. She told him they'd met at university. 'He's also training to be a primary school teacher and he's been to visit every day. He says I can stay with him when I get out of hospital. He lives with his grandmother so I'm not sure how that's going to go, but he says she's knitting me a scarf for winter so maybe we'll get along.'

They FaceTime every day, and Logan is used to the way her face looks now, has watched the bruises lose their purple colour and fade to a sickly yellow. She will need dental work and her arm is still in plaster with pins to help it heal. He's not sure how she survived.

'He just kept saying, "I won't be him; you won't make me him,"' Maddy said. 'He hated his mother so much and he was so angry when I read the emails from her and started asking questions. He had one version of reality and he didn't want another.'

'He wouldn't be the first person to view the world that way.'

'I felt sorry for him,' Maddy told him.

'I worry that your good heart leaves you open to men like him, Mads, I really do.'

'Okay, more time for another lecture tomorrow. Give Debs my love, and hopefully I'll see you guys soon.'

'I'll send you a ticket.'

'I'm counting on it. I will be the best aunt the kid has ever met.'

Logan had been fearful when the detectives first visited, worried that they had somehow found out about that one desperate night, the night of his last break-in. He didn't take anything, that's what he keeps reminding himself – he didn't take anything. The broken lock was probably easily fixed the next day. Some secrets are okay to keep.

He told the police everything he could remember about the day he knocked on Katherine West's door, parcel in hand.

'What made you suspicious?' the detective asked at least ten different ways.

Logan described Katherine's voice, the strangeness of the whole experience, and finally he said, 'Honestly? Instinct. I've been on the wrong side of a situation enough times to know when something is not right.'

The detective nodded that he understood. 'You're a bit of a hero, mate. Sure you've seen the press – enjoy it,' were his parting words.

Logan doesn't feel like a hero, despite what they were saying on television. There were kids and a woman who had to be protected, that was it. George is only five years old and his life very nearly ended that day. Logan knows that if he had died saving the child, he would have been okay with that. It seemed a fair trade: his messed-up life for the life of a child who had not yet begun to make mistakes.

He will always marvel at the fact that the universe chose him to turn up at that house that morning. Someone else could easily have been given the package to deliver. Someone else could have shrugged their shoulders and just gone on with their day. Someone who had not been in prison, had not learned to read people and voices and the atmosphere the way he had. And he still doesn't know why he stopped that last time but the nearest he can get is that he felt a pull to the house – something wanted him there.

Maybe that was Karma. Maybe the bill has been fully paid?

'What are you thinking, babes?' asks Debbie now.

'I'm thinking that I hope the kid looks like you. I'm a bit of an ugly bugger.'

'Yeah, well,' she says, planting a soft kiss on his forehead. 'I hope he or she has your heart. It's pretty spectacular.'

Logan smiles and closes his eyes as she kisses him, enveloping him in her soap and flower scent.

There's a light knock at the door and Debbie goes to open it, smiling when she sees who it is.

'Oh, I'm not interrupting, am I?' asks Gladys. She peers into the room, clutching her large striped bag that she always has with her. Today she is dressed in black pants and a top with a sequined cockatoo embroidered on the front. Logan smiles and bites down on his lip.

'I have to get back to work anyway. You keep him amused for a bit.'

'How are you feeling, Debbie?' Gladys asks, concern in her voice.

'Excellent. Lou okay?'

'He… well, you know.' She shrugs her shoulders.

'I do. I'll pop by this weekend again.' Debbie doesn't ask if she can visit, but then she never does. She never says to those in her family, 'Can I do anything?' She just does it and she knows that her visits to Lou are appreciated, if only because she plays a good game of chess. 'He's weaker on some days and I can see how Gladys watches him, wanting to do things for him. It's heartbreaking but you can see how much she loves him,' Debbie has explained to Logan.

'That would be lovely,' smiles Gladys and she touches Debbie on the arm, giving her a quick pat.

Debbie leaves and Gladys sits down. 'I thought we could play a game of rummy,' she says, extracting her cards from her bag. Logan nods. Gladys has already signed herself up for babysitting duty. She's got her niece's new boyfriend looking for an affordable house for them since he's in real estate. A few days ago, she showed him and Debbie a picture of a clapboard house with some scraggly rosebushes in the front. It's quite far from the city but it has a yard big enough for a dog and a kid. And if Logan works every hour possible, they could probably afford it.

'My dad said he would help,' said Debbie as she and Logan talked about the house, clicking through pictures on the internet of the large open rooms and the brown kitchen that Debbie called 'retro' instead of 'ugly'. What Logan likes most about the house is the wraparound balcony with wrought-iron railings; it still has two wooden rocking chairs from the previous occupants. He can imagine sitting there with Debbie after a day at work, watching the sun go down as a little boy or girl chases after a Labrador that looks a lot like Betty.

Logan's not sure about borrowing money from Paul, but he knows that he will work the rest of his life to pay the man back.

Lou has a lot of old contacts who are mechanics, having been in the car game for so long. 'I'll get you a job, don't you worry,' he said when he called Logan to speak to him. 'You may have to start off with a small salary but trust me when I tell you I'll get you one.'

'You don't have to do that,' Logan said.

'I don't have to do anything, but I want to. If not for you, my old girl might have gone into that house herself and she would have been no match for that boy, no match at all.'

Logan likes Lou. He's someone who should have gotten the chance to be a father and it feels as though he's lavishing some of that missed fatherly attention on him.

'I'm grateful, Lou, but if you can't find anyone willing to give me a go, that's okay. I understand.'

'Just you wait,' said Lou. 'I can't get around but I can make a call, with Peter's help. And I've seen a lot of men start their lives over and become the people they want to be, believe me.'

Logan already has three interviews set up for when he is ready to work again. 'I've been to prison,' he has said each time he's got the call from a garage. None of them seemed fazed. 'I reckon we all have a past,' one man said. 'You should look into some TAFE courses so you can brush up on your skills. We're not exactly a bunch of accountants here, we can deal with a man with a past.' Logan thanked the man, whose name was Bill, keeping his voice strong so he wouldn't betray the emotion he felt.

Gladys is knitting and sewing. She's kind of adopted him as well and he doesn't mind. He never had much of a family to speak of, just him and Maddy. His mother has yet to visit Maddy down in Melbourne or him, but she has called them both to let them know that she's thinking of them. He supposes it's the best they're going to get from her.

He's less bothered now that he has other people to bring into a baby's life, other people who feel like family. Gladys and the Wests. He has something more to offer a child than just himself and a murky past. And, of course, the kid will have a very attentive Auntie Maddy.

He hates card games, remembering long hours in prison when they were the only thing to do, but he sits up a little and gets ready to play. Gladys talks and talks, about Lou and about the Wests and about how John is coping. She hardly stops to even draw breath and there are brief moments when Logan wishes he was alone, but he never lets that thought stick around for too long. He used to be alone, completely alone, except for the responsibility of a little sister he felt he couldn't help enough… So, he smiles and nods and listens, because that's what you do with family.

Gladys

Gladys gathers up her things and tiptoes quietly out of Logan's room. He's fallen asleep in the middle of the game. The poor man really needs his rest. Patrick shot him twice, Katherine only once. That idea of someone she knows being shot is so shocking that Gladys has trouble wrapping her head around it. The idea that Patrick was Katherine's son is almost as shocking. She feels as though she has been in the middle of some television crime series instead of just a neighbourhood drama.

It's a long, complicated and very sad story, but Gladys hopes that everyone will find a way forward now. She's been babysitting the twins a lot as it's the summer holidays now and poor John needs all the help he can get. Gladys is loving every moment with the siblings, even though there are times when she looks at them and wants to cry. Lou is teaching George to play chess. Sophie is a real chatterbox but Gladys has noticed that her twin brother is more circumspect, quieter, after what happened. His little life was turned upside down in a day. Nothing will ever be the same and she can see that both children are carrying a heavy sadness. Things could so easily have been worse. George could easily have lost his life, Sophie too.

She doesn't like to think of Patrick and of the idea that he was in her garden the day before he did what he did to Katherine and her children. She couldn't have known what would happen, but sometimes she feels guilty for not saying anything.

'It wouldn't have changed anything,' John says all the time. 'He came to the house to hurt Katherine and he meant to hurt her no matter what.'

Patrick sounds like a very damaged young man. She understands why, losing his father like that. But at some point, people have to grow up and make a choice to leave certain aspects of their past behind. Logan has done just that.

He's really challenged some ideas that she's held for a long time. Everyone deserves a second chance. Gladys feels like she's also been given a second chance – a new start in her own neighbourhood, where everyone knows everyone and where her interest and concern are actually appreciated. People are chatting out on the street more than ever now and the Patels have asked her to look after Charlie while they're away – and even though she's a bit wary of their large dog, he's perfectly friendly once he gets used to you.

Margo pops in a lot now as well. She's a bit lonely at home with the baby all day long and she finds it relaxing to sit in Gladys's kitchen and watch her bake – or that's what she says at least. Gladys is delighted to have the baby to fuss over and of course she will also get to fuss over Debbie and Logan's baby once it's born. She feels like a real grandmother now, even though none of the children are really related to her. It's strange how a crisis can bring a neighbourhood together. Life seems very full these days at any rate.

She makes her way to the parking lot of the hospital. Logan will be going home next week and she wants to make a few meals for Debbie to put in the freezer. Lou is with Peter for another couple of hours so she can go shopping.

'You were a hero as well,' Lou keeps telling her as he holds her hand, softly stroking her skin. She can feel his worry in his touch and knows that his fear of losing her is as great as her fear of losing him. In her reflective moments she is grateful that she has had the chance to love and be loved this way.

'If you hadn't insisted on the police coming,' he's said more than once, shaking his head, 'they may have all died. If you hadn't had that inkling that something was wrong… well, who knows what might have happened.'

'All I did was what I usually do,' she replies when he talks this way.

'And what's that, old girl?'

'I interfered,' says Gladys, proud of her busybody status now. 'I interfered.'

Katherine

'Mum, Mum, Mum,' shouts Sophie, flinging open the bedroom door, 'we got you so, so many flowers on our walk. I got red and pink and white and George found some purple ones!'

'Sophie, wait,' she hears John call from downstairs, 'I told you Mum might be sleeping.'

'She's not,' says the little girl.

'You're right, I'm not,' agrees Katherine, even though she had been. She struggles slightly to raise herself in her bed.

'Wait,' says George, coming into the room. 'You need to let Dad help you sit up.'

'I'm fine. I can do it myself,' she says, giving him a smile.

He watches her, biting down on his lip while she gets comfortable. He watches her closely every time she moves. If he's in the bedroom and she gets out of bed, he insists on holding her hand and walking her to the bathroom. He is waiting for her to get better, waiting for her to go back to being the mother she was three weeks ago, believing that her physical healing will return their lives to the safe routine he was used to.

Both he and Sophie have had their first appointment with a child psychologist who specialises in trauma. 'He's pushing a lot of his feelings away,' the psychologist explained in a phone call. 'He is still trying to be brave for you and Sophie, even though the threat is no longer there. It will take a little time for him to open up.'

Katherine worries about him more than she worries about Sophie. Her daughter has nightmares about what happened, waking and shouting about a gun and her stuffed monkey, but she will talk to whomever will listen, describing her older brother as 'mean'. She feels no connection to him and is able to dismiss him as a bad man, as she would a character on television, but George asked once, just whispering in her ear, 'If he's my brother, will I also try to hurt people when I'm big?'

'You would never do that, my darling,' she told him, even though the words hurt. She hates the idea that her older son is something that George fears he could become.

'Right, kids, you need to take the flowers down to the kitchen so I can put them in a vase for Mum,' says John, and the children trail him out of the bedroom as Katherine moves to get herself more comfortable.

Today is John's last day at home full-time before returning to work. From tomorrow morning, Gladys will have the children for a couple of hours in the morning and the new nanny, Abigail, will fetch them for afternoon playdates and summer holiday adventures. Katherine is itching to get out of her bed, but the doctors had to be persuaded to send her home as early as they did.

'My children need me at home,' she kept saying, knowing that John was struggling with two sleepless children sharing his bed. Sophie would wake from her nightmares and George would sit up for hours, listening for noises in the house. He checks all the doors now before he goes to bed, insists on making sure everything is locked, and John says he freezes when the doorbell rings, just stands completely still and waits. Katherine's heart breaks for him. He is struggling with so much right now and every night she prays that he can find a way forward and that, eventually, the idea that he is safe at home will return.

Once Katherine came home, things slowly got back to a certain amount of normality. Gladys has been a godsend and the whole school community has rallied around the children. Things will never be the same, and the twins will carry that hot summer's day with them forever, but Katherine hopes that one day the memory will feel manageable. She cannot allow her two young children to be haunted by her older child – and by her failure to realise just how damaged he was.

'You did everything you could for him,' John keeps saying, but Katherine wishes she had done more. She could have insisted he stay with her after his father's death, could have worked harder to make sure he had the right therapy. She should never have limited her contact as he asked her to, and at night, when she wakes from dreams of her older son as a boy that change into nightmares of him, his face changing into his father's face and a gun in his hand, she knows that she should never have said yes to him living with Anthony. The guilt over not saving him when he was younger catches her in moments when she is not concentrating and then she will see only the little boy who liked to be sung to and loved adventure stories. When she thinks of him, she sees him at two and five and ten years old, his face bright with laughter. He used to sit next to her and stroke her hair as she read to him. Her heartbreak over the loss of her child is a physical thing that steals her breath and hurts her soul.

Maybe if she had never remarried and had more children, Patrick would have been more likely to come back into her life, but she cannot be sure of this. Anthony did a lot of terrible damage. He turned a surly adolescent into a young man who was capable of hurting others, who wanted to hurt those he felt had hurt him.

She has not spoken to Maddy, to Logan's sister, but she is writing and rewriting an email to her. She is struggling to get the words right, trying to find a way to apologise for the man her little boy became. She will send it soon but she keeps rereading it, worried that the words will be all wrong.

Katherine is also talking to a counsellor, but she is aware that no matter what she hears the truth will always be that her son is gone, and she believes that if she had tried harder, she could have saved him.

On terrible nights when she cannot close her eyes to rest, she will take out a notebook and write a list of questions for her son.

Did you really want to hurt me? Had you really stopped loving me? What could I have done better? How could I have helped you? What did you need that I didn't give you? Were you ever happy? Who did you want to be? What did you want to do with your life?

The notebook's pages are filling up but she will never be able to ask Patrick everything she so wants to ask him.

When she cries over her lost son, she tries to do it so the children and John don't see. It's hard for them to fathom the love she still holds for him after everything he did.

Patrick couldn't be saved. She was on an operating table herself when he died during surgery. That thought makes her touch her heart and have to cover her eyes with her hands, hoping the image of him alone in an operating room will go away. She never got to say goodbye, to tell him that she loved him no matter what, and if she had been given the choice, she would have thought the same thing she thought about her twins. *My life for theirs. My life for his.*

John organised everything for the funeral, knowing that there was no one else to do it. It was an act of kindness, of generosity, on his part and it has changed the way she sees her husband. What has happened, the terrible shock of how easily Katherine and the children could have died, has helped them find their way back to each other step by step.

'I thought you were dead,' John repeats. 'I saw you on that sofa and I thought you were gone and I understood that I had let so much petty bullshit stop me from being the husband and father I wanted to be. I prayed when they were operating on you, begged for another chance.'

'I thought of you just before I closed my eyes,' she has admitted to him, 'and I think I was at peace because I knew you would love our children the way they needed to be loved. And I knew that you loved me. Nothing else mattered.'

She feels they have both been gifted a second chance and not everyone gets a second chance.

'Right, here you go,' says John, returning to the bedroom, followed by the children, with a haphazard arrangement of the flowers they collected on their walk: purples and yellows, pinks and oranges.

'Lovely,' she says.

'It's time for you to read to us,' says George.

Every afternoon she reads for as long as her strength allows. They are reading *Harry Potter* and the children are enthralled. She hopes that one day they will remember these afternoons of comfort in the big bed as she recovered, rather than what put her there in the first place.

'I spoke to Logan – he's doing well and should be home soon,' says John.

Katherine feels a pang whenever she thinks of Logan. She is overwhelmingly grateful to him, for his instincts and for him being the kind of man who, while worrying about his own sister, still took the time to be concerned for a complete stranger. George writes letters to him, filling up the pages with pictures of superheroes, Captain America featuring more than most. George and John have been to visit him in the hospital and John says their son has decided that Logan's new baby will be his cousin, even though they are not related. Katherine has a feeling that Logan and Debbie will become part of their lives and she's happy about that, but whenever she looks at Logan, she wonders how it is that he went a different way. They have spoken on the phone, discussed Patrick and how he came to be who he was, and Logan has shared his own childhood stories. Whoever he was as a younger man he is not that man anymore, and Katherine mourns that Patrick never got a chance to change, to become someone like Logan. A man with a past but able to put it behind him.

Patrick will forever be twenty-three and angry. Her tears are for the child he was and the man he will never be. She cannot hate him for what happened. It's not possible. He was her son and now he's gone and she wishes that at least she'd been able to comfort him at the end, to hold him as she had when he was a baby, to wrap him in her arms and keep him safe.

'Come on, Mum,' says George, 'page thirty-two.'

Katherine wipes at her eyes quickly and begins.

A LETTER FROM NICOLE

I would like to thank you for taking the time to read *The Family Across the Street*. If you did enjoy it, and want to keep up to date with all my latest releases, just sign up at the following link. Your email address will never be shared and you can unsubscribe at any time.

www.bookouture.com/nicole-trope

One of the reasons I became a writer was because I was always fascinated by what was actually happening behind closed doors. It's human nature to want to hide the parts of your life that you consider problematic. People do reveal themselves on the internet but anonymous threads are more popular than those where the person can be identified. I often look at my neighbours and wonder if the little I see and know of them is a true reflection of who they are. I have met people whose lives seemed perfect and found myself shocked when the truth was revealed.

I've met a few people like Gladys, who long for days when neighbours really connected with each other. It feels harder to do that in a time when the internet rules our lives.

The character of Logan was inspired by a short clip I saw on Facebook about a photographer who photoshopped the tattoos off the faces of ex-gang members to show them what they would have looked like if they had not covered their faces in ink. One man who tearfully said that he could have had a normal life has always stuck with me, reminding me that judging people by their appearance is always a mistake. I was so pleased to give Logan a second chance, to give everyone in that quiet street a second chance. Logan is going to be a wonderful father and Gladys is an excellent surrogate grandmother.

If you have enjoyed this novel, it would be lovely if you could take the time to leave a review. I read them all and find it inspiring when readers connect with the characters I write about.

I would also love to hear from you. You can find me on Facebook and Twitter and I'm always happy to connect with readers.

Thanks again for reading.
Nicole x

NicoleTrope

@nicoletrope

ACKNOWLEDGEMENTS

Thank you to Christina Demosthenous, who remains the most supportive, encouraging editor I have ever known. I look forward to her notes on every novel and I hear her voice in my head with each new book. Thanks to Victoria Blunden for the first edit that pushed this novel in the right direction and to DeAndra Lupu for her precise copyedit.

Also to Liz Hatherell for the proofread, Lauren Finger for editorial management and Lisa Brewster for the perfect cover.

To Sarah Hardy for all her work in publicity and the rest of the team at Bookouture, thank you for being such lovely, approachable people. I never have to worry about asking questions or sending an email. You really know how to make a writer feel supported.

I always have to thank my mother Hilary for being my first and last reader. I'll always trust your judgement on whether or not a story works.

I have to mention my family, who celebrate each new novel and understand that the week before publication is always fraught. It will always be so – thanks for accepting that.

And once again thank you to those who read, review and blog about my work. Every review is appreciated.